AMERICA[illegible]RISIS TASK FORCE— CODENAME: TRIAD.

Drexell, William The man in command. Tough. Exacting. And with a love of action still great enough to propel him into the heart of the most dangerous Triad maneuver. Now he heads the most covert operations of the U.S. in every part of the globe—and in many ways, holds its future in his hand.

Lisker, James As tense as a cobra and as deadly. A martial arts expert, was all too well known for his guerrilla capabilities during the Vietnam War. The group's master of communications, he is equally at home decoding a piece of Russian intelligence and "coaxing" information out of reluctant enemy agents.

Hahn, Jerry His two years in Navy intelligence barely prepared him for the grueling physical demands of Triad. A leading political analyst, he now can—and must—fight and survive the bloodiest guerrilla operations in the world.

Zoccola, John Lithe, dangerous, and good-looking. A street fighter from New York as proficient on the battlefield as he is in the world of international finance. Able to play any part and assume any role, he can be found in the thick of any Triad maneuver—often with a beautiful woman at his side.

The COUNTDOWN WW III series from Berkley

#1: OPERATION NORTH AFRICA
#2: OPERATION BLACK SEA
#3: OPERATION CHOKE POINT
#4: OPERATION PERSIAN GULF

COUNTDOWN WW III: OPERATION PERSIAN GULF

A novel by W. X. Davies with the Strategic Operations Group

BERKLEY BOOKS, NEW YORK

This is a work of fiction. The characters, incidents, places and dialogues are products of the author's imagination and are not to be construed as real. The author's use of names of actual persons, living or dead, is incidental to the purposes of the plot and is not intended to change the entirely fictional character of the work.

COUNTDOWN WW III: OPERATION PERSIAN GULF

A Berkley Book/published by arrangement with the author

PRINTING HISTORY
Berkley edition/December 1984

For information address: The Berkley Publishing Group, 200 Madison Avenue, New York, New York 10016.

ISBN: 0-425-07388-2

A BERKLEY BOOK® TM 757,375
The name "BERKLEY" and the stylized "B" with design are trademarks belonging to Berkley Publishing Corporation.
PRINTED IN THE UNITED STATES OF AMERICA

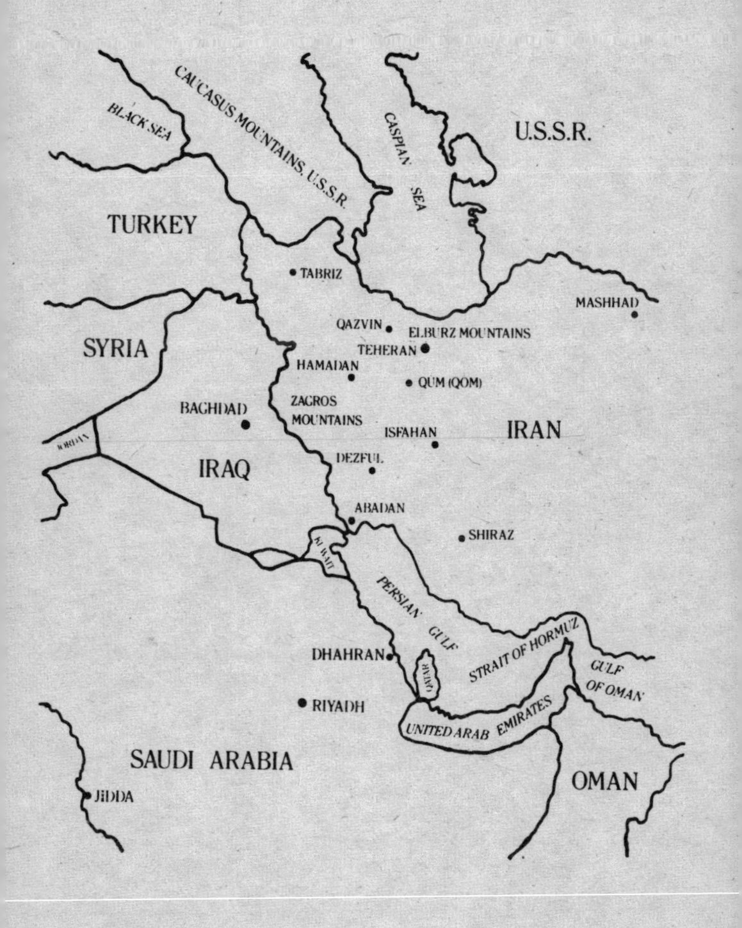
BLACK SEA
CAUCASUS MOUNTAINS, U.S.S.R.
CASPIAN SEA
U.S.S.R.
TURKEY
TABRIZ
MASHHAD
QAZVIN
ELBURZ MOUNTAINS
SYRIA
TEHERAN
HAMADAN
QUM (QOM)
BAGHDAD
ZAGROS
MOUNTAINS
ISFAHAN
IRAN
DEZFUL
IRAQ
ABADAN
SHIRAZ
PERSIAN GULF
DHAHRAN
STRAIT OF HORMUZ
GULF
OF OMAN
RIYADH
UNITED ARAB EMIRATES
SAUDI ARABIA
OMAN
JIDDA

PROLOGUE

In the late 1980s the rivalry between the two superpowers had developed to the point where it was no longer possible to distinguish between a cold and a hot war. Despite repeated attempts on the part of both the United States and the Soviet Union to negotiate settlements to the conflicts that divided them, the only prediction that anyone could make with certainty was that things would get worse.

The current tensions began with what is known now as the North African crisis. This crisis was triggered off when Libya's Colonel Muammar al-Qaddafi attempted to overthrow pro-Western regimes in Morocco and Tunisia. And while Moscow claimed to have no responsibility in the affair, Western intelligence analysts were convinced that he was acting with the knowledge and connivance of the Kremlin. The effort to destabilize the two governments did not entirely succeed, but it nonetheless did much to undermine Western interests in the Mediterranean area.

About half a year later, a clash occurred between two of NATO's southern members, Greece and Turkey. The conflict hinged on air and sea rights in the Aegean Sea, and the Soviet Union again intervened, hoping to expand its influence in the Mediterranean. This time the Russians threw their weight behind Greece, forcing Turkey to resort to drastic measures to shore up its own position—measures that represented a direct threat to Soviet shipping through the Bosporus. After Russia broke the blockade, the war ended in stalemate between Greece and Turkey, but NATO was left in serious disarray. It was not at all clear to the President's top advisers how the West was going to recover so much lost ground.

Several months later Soviet and American soldiers exchanged fire for the first time in postwar history in a bizarre nighttime incident in the Venezuelan jungles that was hushed up by both sides. A long-simmering territorial dispute between pro-Western Venezuela and pro-Soviet Guyana had begun to engulf both superpowers. And while the main brunt of the fighting was done by Venezuelan, Guyanese, and Cuban troops, it was the fact that Soviets and Americans had fought each other that made this Caribbean crisis so ominous.

And now, in early spring of 1988, the United States and the Soviet Union again found themselves at loggerheads. This time the country they both coveted was of even greater strategic importance than before: the oil-rich Islamic Republic of Iran.

Since the exile of the Shah, Iran had been ruled by Shiite Moslem fundamentalist leaders. In spite of a war with Iraq, factional squabbles, thousands of executions, a spate of political assassinations, and a faltering economy, the mullahs, as these fundamentalist leaders were called, managed to retain power. But that was only because of one man who held everything together with his charisma and his iron will, the Ayatollah Ruhollah Khomeini.

What most political and military analysts wondered was what would happen when Khomeini died. Very few thought that the mullahs would be able to keep Iran from falling apart; several believed that the chaos that might result would prove fertile ground for Soviet intervention.

On March 10, the Voice of the Islamic Republic, broadcasting from Teheran, announced that the Ayatollah Khomeini had succumbed to a heart attack and would be interred in the holy city of Qum, to the south of the capital.

Now the world would have a chance to find out the answer to the questions the political and military analysts had been asking...

METRIC TOP SECRET OP OP OP
PRESIDENTIAL DIRECTIVE 1414
From: President
To: Secretary of State/Secretary of Defense/
National Security Advisor
02118B February 14, 1986

TOTALITY. All ack. personally.

1. In light of the aggravated tensions around the world, instigated and inflamed by the Soviet Union and its client states, the need for a new intelligence unit, answerable directly to the President of the United States, has become an urgent necessity.

2. This unit shall function as a small, close-knit group composed of individuals expert in political, economic, communications, and intelligence affairs.

3. Its purpose shall be to pinpoint those regions of the world where an international crisis is most likely to arise; to formulate contingency plans to prevent the crisis from occurring; and to arrest the crisis if it does occur.

4. In the event that direct intervention, requiring clandestine action on the part of the unit, is deemed necessary, the President shall have the power to mandate such intervention.

5. The name of this intelligence unit shall be the Global Crisis Task Force. In view of the three-pronged nature of the Global Crisis Task Force's mission, its code name shall be Triad.

Signed *Creighton Turner*,
President of the United States

1

APRIL 3
TEHERAN, IRAN

On the thirteenth day of the holiday Now Ruz—a day called Sizdah—virtually the entire population of Teheran flees to the countryside. For Sizdah is regarded as an unlucky day and the most prudent thing for anyone to do is to get out of the house. Consequently, all those who can do so, regardless of social rank, escape to the countryside, there to spend the day picnicking.

Early on the morning of Sizdah, the roads leading out of the capital are clogged with buses, trucks, cars, bicycles, and caravans of mule-drawn carts. By the time the sun has risen above the tips of the minarets, Teheran has taken on the look of a deserted city. The air has an eerie stillness about it; cocks crow almost as if in protest against the unaccustomed silence.

Although it is believed that you invite catastrophe by remaining in the city on Sizdah, today one man by the name of Osman Khalif could be found at his office desk just as he was every other day. Osman Khalif, a prematurely balding bureaucrat of forty-three, worked as a senior adviser to the President of the Islamic Republic. From his office window you could see nothing but a blank wall.

There were, in fact, walls surrounding the entire Presidential complex, fifteen-foot walls of reinforced concrete topped with steel sheets, barbed wire, and a pillbox manned by a Revolutionary Guard with a machine gun. For security reasons all the nearby houses had been evacuated, and visitors to the compound were obliged to surrender keys, money, combs, wedding rings, notebooks, and pens. Despite his position, Khalif each day had to endure a rigorous body search; even his shoes were inspected to make certain that he wasn't trying to smuggle in a concealed weapon.

Throughout the short history of the Islamic Republic, from the Ayatollah Ruhollah Khomeini's ascension to power in 1979 following the fall of the Shah, times had been difficult in Iran, fraught with tension and sudden eruptions of violence. The protracted war with Iraq over rights to the Shatt al Arab, the waterway spilling out into the Persian Gulf, had subsided into an uneasy peace, but there was every likelihood that it might break out again. Even with the cessation of hostilities, there were sporadic exchanges of artillery fire across the border.

But now the situation was graver than ever. Three and a half weeks previously, it had been announced that the Ayatollah had been stricken by a fatal heart attack in the holy city of Qum. News of his death had been kept from the public for four days by the mullahs who collectively shared power in the Khomeini regime. When they could no longer keep it a secret, they announced that everything would continue on as before. The religious leaders would remain faithful to the fundamentalist policies laid down by the Ayatollah from the moment he came to power. It was no surprise when even more suspected dissidents than usual were rounded up and placed in the notorious Evin Prison: businessmen with suspected ties to the West, Bahais, members of the Tudeh, the outlawed Communist Party, and a variety of students and intellectuals who'd dared criticize the government or its prosecution of the war with Iraq.

But the authorities were not reassured; there were constant rumors of conspiracies and coups. Every hour Osman Khalif was told of another attempt that would be made against the life of the President or one of the leading mullahs whose instructions the President was expected to take to heart. He paid scarce heed to most of these reports; the more serious ones he relayed to the interior ministry. One conspiracy, however, he breathed not a word of. Not because he did not believe it was not going to take place or because it didn't pose a threat to the security of the state. The reason he didn't pass on information about this particular conspiracy was because he himself was a part of it.

At precisely 11:00 on the morning of Sizdah, Khalif reached over to his phone and dialed four digits. The phone was picked up on the fourth ring.

"This is the hour of waking," Khalif said, reciting the previously agreed upon code.

"It is indeed," came the answer. *"Insha'allah,* we shall begin."

The call was then terminated.

Khalif's secretaries were away in the countryside, so there was no one else to hear when the phone rang five minutes later.

He waited until the fourth ring before answering.

He recognized the voice at once.

"Khalif," the man said. "I understand that you are not feeling so very well."

"A sudden fever," Khalif agreed. "It will pass quickly."

"I suggest that you go home and spend the remainder of the day in bed. Only with rest will you fight off your fever."

"I value your advice and I think that I will do just that, my friend."

"I look forward to your recovery," the man said, concluding the exchange.

Khalif rose from his desk, slipped on his jacket, and gathered whatever private documents he wished to take home with him. According to the schedule, updated just twenty-six hours before, he had eight minutes to leave the presidential compound before the attack on it began.

Security at the compound was more relaxed today since there were so few ministers at work to protect; even President Rashid Nasreddin was in the country and was not expected back until tomorrow morning. Unlike the procedures required for entering the compound, there was little problem in leaving it. Khalif was on the street within four minutes. His driver was waiting there to transport him home.

But he wasn't going home. Instead, he surprised his driver by instructing him to take him to a town thirty-five miles outside the capital, reached by a rocky road that proceeded through barren hills. The town was called Barquijan and only 1,500 people lived there. It was an obscure place, a refuge, and there Khalif intended to wait by the radio. If the conspiracy succeeded, he would return to the capital by nightfall; if not, then Barquijan was as good a place as any to begin one's exile.

Led by Colonel Ibrahim Shastri, a decorated hero of the Iraqi-Iranian war, two battalions of Iranian soldiers moved on Mehrabad Airport at quarter past eleven. The airport, guarded by a brigade of Revolutionary Guards, was one of the key targets of the insurgents. With light arms, supplemented by 180mm S-23 guns and two B-4M howitzers, the rebel forces launched their attack to the west and south of the airport.

At seventeen minutes past the hour, six shells fired by the howitzers tore into the conning tower, smashing the radar and killing four of the air controllers there. An Air France 747 was in the process of landing when the fighting began. It touched ground moments after the conning tower was hit. The morning sun was soon obscured by the smoke from the detonation, and, to those few residents of Teheran who hadn't left for the countryside, it looked as if a surprise storm had come up.

Machine gun fire broke out all along the tarmac as rebel soldiers moved out to seize control of the runways. The unfortunate Air France jet was caught in the middle of the fire, and bullets riddled the fuselage, puncturing the tail.

Captain Marcel Langois, in command of the Air France jet, realized that his only recourse was to try to take off again. His instruments registered a problem in the third engine, presumably from the damage sustained by automatic fire, but otherwise the jumbo appeared reasonably intact.

With no one to give him clearance to take off, he had only his instruments and instincts to guide him. He immediately set about turning the craft around; from his cockpit window he had a view of armed men just a couple of hundred meters in front of him. They were racing in the direction of the terminal buildings. He had no idea who these men were nor did he much care. His only concern was with the safety of the 118 passengers on board.

As the jet increased its acceleration, there was another round of firing, more intense this time and directed at the 747 itself. Both the rebels and the Revolutionary Guards defending the airport believed that the jet was somehow involved in a military mission for the other side.

Even so, the 747 managed to get into the air right before the very end of the runway; as it rose, gray smoke trailed out from under the right wing. Twenty-two seconds after takeoff, it abruptly dipped, then spun rapidly out of control, plummeting back to earth, where it was instantly obliterated in a ball of fire that, for a moment, could have been mistaken as the sun's twin. All passengers and crew were killed.

Ambulances and fire trucks, their passage accompanied by the din of sirens, were shot at by rebels as they sped across the tarmac.

Already the defenders were withdrawing back into the terminal, routed by the superior firepower employed by Shastri's forces. The army and the Revolutionary Guards had always been at odds; where the one was professional and had been built up by the Shah, the other was made up of youthful fanatics, many of them barely in their teens, who substituted loyalty to the Ayatollah for combat training. In the war with Iraq, it had been the Revolutionary Guards who'd spearheaded the assaults, throwing the Iraqis back at the cost of hundreds of thousands of dead and injured. The generals of the army, however, had proven more reluctant to sacrifice their troops for the sake of a few square miles of disputed territory.

Now, for the first time, the two rival forces were pitted against one another in combat. The element of surprise was vital to the success of Shastri's effort. The Revolutionary guards were no match for the veteran soldiers challenging them.

Howitzers were now deployed in front of the terminal

building where the Revolutionary Guards had taken cover. The first shells ripped jagged holes in the structure; fire leaped from the shattered windows and debris rained down on the defenders.

Five T-72 tanks were brought into action, arriving somewhat behind schedule from the army base at Qizil Hissar, sixty miles from the capital. Their presence at Mehrabad was decisive in determining the course of the battle.

Drawn up by the terminal building, the Russian-built tanks arrayed themselves in a row. It was then that Colonel Shastri dispatched a soldier with a white flag to the terminal building with a demand for unconditional surrender.

The demand was refused.

At ten minutes to twelve, as F-5 Freedom Fighter jets and Mirage 2000's made a flyover of Mehrabad in support of the rebel detachment, Shastri gave the order to fire on the terminal.

Together, the tanks and the batteries demolished the terminal building within half a minute. Flames spilled from the destroyed observation tower as a substantial portion of the structure's upper level came tumbling down. Those few defenders who succeeded in escaping the conflagration were cut down mercilessly by Shastri's soldiers.

The seizure of the airport was only one part of the military operation that went into effect on April 3. In Teheran proper tanks and armored personnel carriers had begun to fill the empty streets. Earlier in the morning Shastri had instructed the government that he planned to use the holiday for some routine maneuvers to maintain the necessary level of preparedness. In view of the many threats to the security of the state, the mullahs agreed that even the occasion of Sizdah was no time to relax one's vigilance. Enemies were everywhere and they did not take holidays off.

Little did they realize that the fifty-year-old colonel who'd displayed such valor against the Iraqis on the battlefields of Fakah and Mandali was also one of their enemies.

In the capital one of the first targets to fall to the rebel forces was Teheran radio.

Shortly after noon, a spokesman for Colonel Shastri stepped over the body of a spokesman for the mullahs, took hold of the microphone, and declared: "This is the Voice of the Democratic Iranian Republic. Acting at the behest of the people of our country, the armed forces have agreed to assume power and remove the dark hand of the fanatics who have so long bled and crippled and murdered us. To those patriots, to the true God-fearing people of our country, we say: You have nothing to fear from us. To the blood-thirsty butchers who hatch plots against our people and imprison and torture the innocent, we say: Your days are numbered. There is nowhere to flee. To those who have betrayed the revolution, who saved us from one tyrant only to give us another, we say: The day of revenge has come."

In spite of the confident words voiced by the announcer, there was more fighting yet to come. Teheran by no means could be said to have fallen to the military. Battles broke out throughout the city: by the old American Embassy, in front of the fortified archeological museum, on the grounds of the former palace of the Shah, and among the shuttered bazaars where revolutionary fervor was as much of a tradition as commerce and trade. But the most severe fighting occurred at the presidential compound.

No longer the quiet, half-empty establishment of an hour ago when Osman Khalif had left it for Barquijan, the presidential compound had been transformed into a scene of carnage. Revolutionary Guards, sheltered in the evacuated buildings nearby, laid down a withering fire on the attackers as the latter's tanks and personnel carriers pulled into the street that fronted the compound.

Rather than engage in house-to-house combat, Shastri's tanks went into operation, opening fire on any building sending out opposing fire.

In a matter of minutes three of these buildings lay gutted, their smoldering ruins exuding the stench of charred flesh. The pillbox atop the wall of the compound was immediately taken out, but penetrating the wall itself was a task of far greater difficulty. The Revolutionary Guards acquitted themselves well, staying the attackers for over an hour until Shastri, directing operations from the airport, ordered in a pair of Mirage V clear-weather fighters to attack the compound.

Antiaircraft fire from the compound was wholly incapable of stopping the planes as they swooped low over the compound and dropped antipersonnel bombs and napalm. While damage to the buildings was relatively light, considerable injury was done to the defenders. After their bodies were hit by napalm, men ran crazily, their limbs twitching, as their skin burned away. Their screams died in the uproar of artillery and automatic fire.

With the government positions softened by air bombardment, the attackers, composed mainly of the Eighth and Thirteenth Brigades of the Iranian Army, managed to break through the walls and advance to within forty yards of the office of President Nasreddin. Here the artillery duel became especially fierce, continuing for fifty minutes before the Revolutionary Guards, their ranks drastically reduced, bowed to rebel demands and capitulated. With the capture of the presidential compound, the last strategic installation of Teheran had fallen. Other places of importance, including several of the ministries, had easily been captured, their skeletal security forces overrun in a matter of minutes.

Simultaneous with the events in Teheran, other units of the army and air force were striking at centers of the mullah's power across the country. Reports of clashes began coming into the capital from Isfahan, from Shiraz, from Kashan, from Hamadan, and from the oil city of Abadan in the south. Members of Nasreddin's government were arrested where they were found; some were hauled away from their picnics in the countryside, unaware of the drama that was taking place all around them.

Resistance to the rebels was often quite frenzied—and effective. In the north and in the area around the holy city of Qum, where the followers of the Ayatollah held undisputed sway, the counterrevolution was halted in its tracks. Radio and television outlets still under the control of the mullahs announced that, far from succeeding, the rebellion was about to be crushed. They asserted, with some basis in fact, that much of the army was holding steadfast and had not defected to the ranks of Colonel Shastri. Popular uprisings anticipated by the rebels failed to materialize when Sizdah came to an end and the holiday throngs returned home.

On the contrary, as soon as night fell people refused to come outside, preferring the relative security of their homes. At eight o'clock Teheran television mysteriously went off the air. Teheran radio continued to pronounce the success of the revolution while offering no convincing details to back up its claim. Contradictory reports had President Nasreddin arrested, executed, or in hiding.

But shortly before midnight, Teheran time, Nasreddin—or someone who had an astonishing ability to mimic his voice—came on the air. Without identifying his whereabouts, he said that he was safe and declared that he was still the legitimate representative of the Iranian people. Repudiating the rebels under Colonel Shastri, he said, "They are all traitors, they are all in league with the Great Satan, the United States, and they are all liable to execution as enemies of God. In view of the grave threat to our nation posed by the imperialists and by the Zionists, in consultation with the Grand Ayatollahs, I may have no choice but to summon help from our friends and allies to save the Islamic Republic."

Monitoring this speech in Barquijan, Osman Khalif was shaken. Something must have gone wrong. Shastri had miscalculated. Nasreddin should never have slipped through their net. The Grand Ayatollahs, representing the supreme religious authority of the country, should have been put under house arrest at once even before the capital had been secured. In the planning of this operation, the conspirators had all agreed that it would have to proceed swiftly and be completed in twenty-four hours. Otherwise the result was likely to be disastrous—a protracted struggle that could lead to years of civil war and perhaps to the permanent partition of the country.

But this appeared to be what was happening. More than twelve hours after it had begun, the revolution had lost its momentum, and many of the units Shastri had counted on to support him, having waited to see the outcome, now decided to hold back. Khalif, who'd expected to be appointed Minister of the Interior in the event of victory, now had no idea whether he should stay where he was, return to the capital, or flee the country entirely.

While Nasreddin did not in his declaration say exactly

whom he'd meant by "friends and allies," Khalif knew that he could mean only the Soviets. If the Kremlin agreed to assist him, and there was no reason to believe it would not, then forces of the Red Army could be expected to enter Iranian territory at any time.

Khalif, who'd been jailed by the Shah and subjected to torture at the hands of SAVAK, his secret police, would never under ordinary circumstances call on the Americans for help, much less offer his services. But these were no ordinary circumstances.

He checked the telephone in the house he'd leased for the day and found, to his surprise, that the line was still functional. He placed a call to the capital.

A woman answered.

"This is Osman," he said in a hushed, urgent tone. "I would like you to do a favor for me." He could hear her breathing, but that was all. "There is an American who entered the country two days ago. He calls himself Bill Gerard and poses as an international arms dealer. His real name is John Zoccola. You should be able to find him at the Hilton. When you do, bring him here. It is very important."

"I'll look for him tonight," the woman said.

Khalif replaced the phone, took another sip from a tepid glass of mint tea, and settled back to wait. Teheran radio was still proclaiming the triumph of the revolution while in the barren hills beyond Barquijan, the sounds of gun battles could be heard all night through.

2

APRIL 4
TRIAD HQ: PRINCE WILLIAM COUNTY, VIRGINIA

"Where the hell is Zoccola?"

The question, delivered in William Drexell's familiar booming voice, went unanswered. His aide, Lieutenant Colonel Steven Cavanaugh, had been trying for the last two and a half hours to reach Zoccola in Teheran, but to no avail. "He's not picking up or else he's not answering, sir."

Drexell rose from behind his desk and regarded Cavanaugh stonily, as if he were to blame for the disappearing act perpetrated by one of Triad's most valuable operatives. Besides which, Drexell was in an unusually cantankerous mood this morning, having had no sleep for the last thirty-six hours. Trying to keep abreast of the fast-developing events in Iran was wearing enough; losing contact with the man he most depended on to let him know what was going on was outright disturbing.

Zoccola was always getting himself into trouble, even when the circumstances didn't warrant it; now that they did, there was no telling what had happened. He might very well have been arrested or killed in the street fighting which, from all accounts, was still continuing throughout the country, especially in the capital.

"Sir, Mr. Lisker and Mr. Hahn are in the briefing room," Cavanaugh announced.

Drexell grunted an acknowledgment and proceeded past his aide, out of his office, and down the long, windowless corridor that led to the briefing room. Triad headquarters, situated at the end of an unmarked road in the rolling countryside of northern Virginia, had been designed like a fortress. With its reinforced-concrete structure and deep underground capacity, equipped with its own generator and food and water supply, it was meant to withstand all but a direct hit by a nuclear bomb.

Drexell found the building's fluorescent-lighted atmosphere oppressive, claustrophobic. He was more at home in the field, for it was there that he preferred to wage his battles, not in the confines of an operations room where war became an abstract thing: a sequence of electronic lights across a board map, a computer printout of kill ratios, a televised broadcast of a city vanishing in flames...

A man in his early sixties, William Drexell gave the unmistakable impression of a military man and, indeed, his biographical profile read like a history of the cold war. In his time he'd fought against Magsaysay guerrillas in the Philippines, the Vietcong in Vietnam, Che Guevara in Bolivia, leftists in Athens and Salonika, Russians in Hungary and Afghanistan, Palestinian terrorists in Lebanon, and the Baader-Meinhof Gang in Hamburg and the Red Brigades in Milan, Rome, and Naples. Not all of these conflicts had been waged out in the open, of course; Drexell's was a calling that took him into army barracks and back streets, where the dead were left to rot since their relatives didn't dare collect the bodies for fear of being shot themselves.

He was not only used to crisis; he thrived on it. His weathered face, reddened from too much exposure to the sun, was lined and fleshy, with deep-set eyes which looked with vast skepticism on the world. It was said that no one had ever seen him asleep save for his wife, and she rarely, since he was hardly ever at home.

Striding into the briefing room with Cavanaugh trailing behind him and a sheaf of documents clutched in his hand, Drexell nodded to the two members of Triad who'd been awaiting his arrival with impatience.

Jerry Hahn, the political analyst in the group, was at the

moment studying the situation map which dominated almost the entirety of the front wall, while James Lisker, Triad's military and communications expert, sat quietly in the corner, his eyes fixed on a Sony television where a CBS news commentator was summarizing what little was known about the latest crisis in Iran.

No two men could have been less alike, Drexell considered. It was no wonder that while the two might respect each other, there was never any display of warmth between them. Hahn had emerged from academic circles, with interludes in the Navy and at CIA headquarters in Langley. His was a world of think tanks and research.

When Hahn was first introduced to Drexell, the former had the air of an intellectual: he was slightly halting in manner, his face was pale from lack of sun, and his eyes peered through glasses that might have been designed for a myopic watchmaker. Slight of build, he certainly would not have impressed an observer as a prospect for the role of clandestine agent. But Drexell had read his reports, had listened to recordings of briefings Hahn had given at Langley and at State, and had studied his psychological profile. He had the feeling that Hahn would make a valuable addition to Triad. And so he had; almost all hint of the professorial air that had been present that day two years before had vanished. The operations he'd participated in in Tunisia, in the Balkans, and in Central America had given him the confidence of a veteran soldier. He was physically stronger, the glasses were gone, and he no longer acted so hesitantly. He might still be a noncombatant, but he was no longer a stranger to the battlefield.

On the other hand, combat was really all that James Lisker knew. If Hahn had a tendency toward indifferent posture and conveyed in his expression the air of an intellectual, Lisker maintained his body like a fine weapon that might be called into service at any moment. He was tall and lean and spare. He was a man who never wasted a movement, whose eyes, a pale, glistening blue, registered everything but gave away nothing. Little inclined to discuss his past or his personal life, Lisker did not deliberately cultivate an image as a dangerous man, someone prepared to go off to a distant capital to engineer an assassination, but dangerous he surely was.

Drexell took his place by the situation map. Lisker looked up from the television screen and said, "They don't seem to know shit. What have you heard from the White House?"

"The White House has been calling me all morning, asking what the hell's going on," he answered. "We're getting conflicting reports from the Pentagon, the National Security Agency, and the CIA."

"Hell, there's no counting on the Company," Hahn said. "Once the Shah was out, all their assets were finished. They never knew what was going on during Khomeini's time. I doubt they've made an unexpected recovery since."

"What about you, Jerry? From what you've heard, can you make any sense out of it?"

Impatiently, Hahn shuffled through the papers in front of him. "I think what we're seeing in Iran is, in essence, a partition of the country into two, maybe three different sections. On the one hand, you have the army led by Shastri. If there's anyone we might want to have in power, he's it. He isn't exactly pro-U.S.—that would be suicide for him—but from all I've been able to find out about Shastri and his cohorts, they're open to the West and have no patience with the Islamic militants. Many of them have become disillusioned with the drain on manpower and the economy from the Iran-Iraqi war. They figured that after three years of fighting, there should've been a way out, but Khomeini's people kept prolonging the war despite the other options."

"How much control has Shastri gotten?" Lisker asked.

"It's hard to say at this point. Teheran might be his, along with Isfahan and a couple of other cities and a few other scattered areas that his troops have secured," Hahn said. "But almost every square inch his men have taken is being contested by troops loyal to the mullahs."

"All right," Drexell said. "You've covered Shastri. What about the mullahs? Do you think they've got as much hold on the people as they did with Khomeini?"

"It can't be underestimated. The Islamic revolution was no passing fad," Hahn went on. "There are people who'll fight like hell for the mullahs even if they can't stand the sight of them, simply because they feel their gains since the Shah might be threatened by America or any other satanic power they might have dreamed up in their heads."

"But the key element in this, as far as we're concerned, is what the Soviet involvement might become," Drexell pointed out. "Just an hour ago I was told that President Nasreddin, who's been the mullahs' man all along, made a statement over the radio claiming the need to send for outside assistance. The implication was that that outside assistance was going to come from the Russians. Now, when I spoke to President Turner this morning, he still hadn't heard this from any of his sources. Nor has the statement been repeated by Nasreddin or anyone else over there."

"I talked with somebody at the Soviet watch desk over at State," Lisker put in, "and there's practically nothing of substance coming out of Moscow. Tass released a statement accusing the U.S. of instigating the coup attempt, but it was comparatively mild in tone. I have the feeling that the Russians are lying low on this one, waiting to see how things turn out before they commit themselves to any decisive action. What does John think about all of this? He's been over there since the beginning of the week; he might have picked up on something."

"I wish I could tell you," Drexell said. "The fact is, since Shastri moved on the capital yesterday, I haven't been able to raise him. I don't know what the goddamn hell happened to him. We just have to hope that he makes himself known soon."

"The way it breaks down, then," Hahn said, concluding his tentative analysis, "is that we have the rebel army under Shastri in control of a few sectors of the country, including Teheran; we have the mullahs dominating a great deal of the army that didn't go over to Shastri, and holding substantial regions of the country as well; and we have any number of breakaway factions that are undoubtedly ready to exploit the chaos, like the Kurds and the leftist dissidents—the Mujahedeen—who used to murder off the mullahs as if every day were the St. Valentine's Massacre.

"It is, in short, a situation ripe for the Soviets to intervene."

"Do you think they will?" Drexell asked. "How we choose to act's going to depend on how accurate our crystal ball is."

While Hahn had pondered this question frequently in the past, he still lacked a clear answer. "The political climate between the U.S. and the Soviets is so bad that maybe they feel they've got nothing much to lose. But after what happened in the Guyanese-Venezuelan thing, perhaps they won't risk a direct intervention."

Hahn's reference to the Guyanese-Venezuelan conflict, which began as a territorial dispute and boiled over into an international confrontation between the two superpowers, recalled to mind the first instance since the Second World War when Soviet and American troops had clashed.

While the battle had been brief—it was really just a skirmish, a result of two rival advisory teams stumbling into one another at night in the Venezuelan jungle barely an hour before a cease-fire went into effect—its implications were far-reaching. Never before had troops of the two nations shot at one another and drawn blood.

This incident had occurred six months before the present crisis, and afterwards both the Russian and American leadership had pulled back from confrontation, fearful of the consequences. First Secretary Alexei Kadiyev had, in fact, been proposing a new round of arms negotiations in Geneva in the last several weeks. "We cannot subject the world to the possibility of nuclear catastrophe," he told a well-publicized gathering of the Supreme Soviet only five days previously.

So there was reason for Hahn to express some degree of skepticism regarding a Soviet march into Iran.

"Of course they might decide to move some troops, possibly from the Turkestan and Transcaucasian military districts, into northern Iran. They did that, if you remember, right after World War Two until we pressured them into withdrawing—something they did elsewhere only in Austria," Hahn noted. "They might go in to prop up the mullahs, but it would be more to keep their own Moslem population happy than because they care a good goddamn about Khomeini's disciples."

Lisker was shaking his head. "I totally disagree. I think that not only will they go in, but that they'll head for the oil fields as well. They won't be content with keeping to the north; they'll go south, straight to the Gulf if nobody stops them."

"That's always been a possibility," Hahn said, "but the Soviets are still relatively cautious. They don't want to risk an outright confrontation with us on the ground."

"But suppose they feel that we won't really pose any substantial resistance," Drexell interrupted him. "It could take up to a month to get our Rapid Deployment Force and supplies on the ground there. In that time they could be bathing in the Persian Gulf."

"We can seal up their borders, block the mountain passes," Lisker said, "bottle them the hell up before they can take a single step into Iran."

"True," Hahn said, "but we can't really commit ourselves to that unless we know for certain that they intend to come across. We'd be starting the war, in that case. Even if they mass troops along the border and hold maneuvers, it could just be a show of force, not necessarily an overture to an invasion."

"I think that the only way we can settle any of this," Drexell said, "is to find out what we can ourselves, then put something together for the President with a strong recommendation on what course of action he should choose. We have to get in there and use every damned asset we can find, even the most questionable cases, because if Nasreddin has in fact invited the Red Army to come and join the party, we don't have a whole lot of time to work with."

Addressing Lisker, he said, "Jim, what I'd like you to do is make a general on-site survey of the border between Iran and the U.S.S.R., see what you can discover about any expeditionary force they might be putting together, and then draw up a strategy for bottling them up, if it should come to that."

To Hahn he said, "I'd like you to go to Teheran as soon as you can and find Zoccola—if that's possible. I want you and John to determine who's in control in Teheran and see if you can devise a way to bolster Shastri and at the same time undercut the mullahs' power."

"How are you planning on getting me into the country?"

"We can't have you entering through any quasilegitimate route, the way John did. He went in as an arms dealer, and we set it up so that the mullahs thought he had access to spare parts they needed. So they were eager to let him in. But now the airport's closed and there's no telling what's happening at the border checkpoints. So I've arranged for our assets in Saudi Arabia to figure out a way to get you in either by sea or air, whichever route they judge best."

Arrangements had already been made for Hahn to board a commercial jetliner for Jidda that evening. Once in Saudi Arabia, he would be given false papers and as much cover as the Triad assets could put together in forty-eight hours.

"There should be people inside Iran to assist you once you're over the border," Drexell said. "They might know what happened to John. On the other hand, it's possible that they've disappeared too."

"And then what?"

"Then, Jerry, it looks like you'll be on your own."

3

APRIL 5
THE STATE DEPARTMENT, WASHINGTON, D.C.

Secretary of State Jeffrey Schelling entered his office on the sixth floor of State to discover that his newly appointed Soviet counterpart, Foreign Minister Orly Seminov, was already waiting for him. He was standing impatiently in the shadows, conferring with an aide whose doleful countenance hinted at a life of tribulation from serving in the legions of Soviet bureaucracy.

Seminov was a slender, bespectacled figure who might be mistaken for the head of a private boys' school. It was difficult to imagine that he'd masterminded the invasion of Czechoslovakia by Soviet troops in August, 1968. The tactical abilities that had made him so invaluable to the Soviet intelligence apparatus operating in Eastern Europe were now being put to use as he represented his country abroad. He was in the U.S. now to present a disarmament appeal at the UN, where he would presumably expand on the proposals already put forth by First Secretary Kadiyev some days previously.

He had received an urgent summons from Schelling just as he'd settled into his hotel suite at the Waldorf, and he had immediately come to Washington by air shuttle. He did not look happy to be here.

Schelling had many years before been a senatorial candidate, and for a while there had been speculation in the press that he would become another Kennedy. He had a youthful appeal that seemed to have only been enhanced with age and a manner that suggested careful breeding and a life of a country gentleman. But his bid for political power got no farther than a disastrous showing in a Virginia primary race. From then on he was obliged to rely on his connections with the White House to acquire any sort of power at all. After serving as ambassador to the Court of St. James's, he was posted to Tel Aviv. There he was successful in cementing a Middle East accord that, at least temporarily, brought peace to that troubled region. This achievement established him as a diplomat of international renown, and no one seemed to blame him when the accord fell apart, victim of a series of Israeli bombing raids, nor was his cabinet nomination jeopardized when the *Washington Post* revealed that he was linked to a computer company suspected of bilking its stockholders.

At any rate, his was a career as far removed from Orly Seminov's as it was possible to be.

The two men shook hands, and Schelling motioned the Soviet minister into his inner office. Bright spring morning light was pouring in through the window behind his desk.

"You must forgive me for calling you in like this, sir, but a situation has arisen that requires clarification on both our sides."

Seminov lit a cigarette—an American brand, Schelling noted—and leaned toward Schelling as though he were having difficulty comprehending him. He remained silent and expressionless.

"I speak, sir, of the events in Iran that have developed in the last two days."

Taking a nervous drag on the cigarette, Seminov said, "It is a most confusing situation."

"That it is. And while I recognize how hard it is to determine the facts at this time, we would like to make absolutely clear that the United States government would regard any Soviet attempt to interfere in Iran with the utmost gravity."

"Mr. Secretary, my government has no such plans."

"It pleases me to know that. But I wouldn't want you to take away the impression that the United States would stand by in the event that any Soviet troops moved across the international frontier. I might add that my government would be forced to consider its options should Soviet advisers enter the country in any substantial numbers."

Seminov allowed himself a slight frown. "Am I to understand that you would react even if we are invited by the legitimate authorities? It would seem to me, Mr. Secretary, that you are claiming sovereignty over a country that is not yours to claim. Iran is not another Grenada or Nicaragua you can invade at will."

"The strategic interests of the United States government are what concern me, sir," Schelling countered. "The question of Iranian sovereignty must be weighed against the security needs of the United States and her allies in the Persian Gulf. One is inseparable from the other. You might consider this as a friendly warning. We do not want to see anything happen in the area that would harm the chances of world peace."

"I share your concern, Mr. Secretary. And I can assure you that the Soviet Union has no intention of committing any action that would do so. We are actively seeking peace in any available forum open to us. That is why I am in your country now, as you know. However, we do view the situation in Iran with alarm, and should that situation pose a threat to the interests and security of the Soviet Union, we will of course be compelled to act."

Schelling realized that the Soviet Foreign Minister was, very politely, telling him to go to hell. He'd suspected as much from the start. But his purpose in meeting with Seminov was to underscore how gravely the United States viewed the developments in Iran and to emphasize that under no circumstances would the administration allow any Soviet military movements into that country to go unchallenged.

There was a long silence before Seminov said, "If you have nothing more to say to me, then I will be on my way. I would like to get back to New York before noon."

He rose, his taciturn aide rose with him, and once again

Schelling and the Russian shook hands.

Three minutes after Seminov had left, the Secretary's phone buzzed.

"Sir, I have the President on the line."

"Put him through."

The President sounded hoarse. "Jeffrey, we've just heard some terrible news."

Schelling scarcely had the courage to ask what it was.

"Our embassy in Paris was attacked half an hour ago. A bomb went off, killing at least eight people. I'm told another twenty are injured, some critically."

"What about Max?" He was referring to Max Storey, the envoy to the Élysée Palace.

"Fortunately, he was home at the time. But the military attaché and a couple of intelligence boys were among those killed."

"Do you have any idea who's responsible?"

"A call was received at the offices of *Le Monde* from some people who claimed responsibility. They called themselves the 'Martyrs of the Revolution,' whatever the hell that might mean, and said they'd blown up the embassy in retaliation for our support of the coup in Iran. I expect that this is only the first round in a series of attacks we might see in the next few days. We can keep denying we had anything to do with Shastri, but it's obviously not going to impress many people."

"I'll send word out to all diplomatic personnel to take increased precautions," Schelling said. "We'll beef up security at our most vulnerable posts, put sandbags and Marines where they can be seen."

"I'm going to issue a statement this afternoon warning any terrorist group seeking the deaths of our representatives to be on guard. I'll let them know that we're not about to stand idly by while they attack."

"What kind of retaliation do you have in mind, Mr. President? And who exactly are you going to retaliate against? I mean, who the hell are the Martyrs of the Revolution?"

"You let me worry about that, Jeffrey," said the President, concluding the exchange.

4

APRIL 6
BANDAR-E-RIG AND TEHERAN, IRAN

It was still dark when the four-seater Cessna put down on the southwestern coast of Iran, near the port of Bandar-e Rig. The plane, flying too low to be picked up by radar, had managed to cross the Persian Gulf from Daharan, Saudi Arabia, undetected. But the pilot, a taciturn Brit who free-lanced for Triad in the Kingdom, was clearly nervous about hazarding the journey, and he gave Hahn only a couple of minutes to debark before taking off again. Before he left, he told Hahn that he could expect to be welcomed by his Iranian contacts at any moment.

Hahn, seeing that he was in what looked like the middle of nowhere—a desolate terrain marked by craggy mountains off in the distance—failed to be reassured by the pilot's words. He seemed to be the only person for miles around.

The cover for status arranged for him by the assets in Jidda included Syrian identity papers listing him as a Syrian national of French extraction. Although he was well versed in French, his command of Arabic was rusty. This disadvantage was offset by the fact that in Iran most of the population spoke Farsi, and so he assumed that he could—at least for a short time—play the part of a Syrian businessman convincingly. And while the situation in the country was so chaotic that not even an Iranian could be assured of safety, a Syrian stood a better chance than most of escaping the suspicion of the authorities. During the long Iraqi-Iranian war, Syria had stood steadfastly on the side of Iran, if only because the Syrians and the Iraqis were bitter rivals. In the Middle East, the enemy of your enemy is your friend.

Because Hahn did not look in the least like the conventional image of an Arab, it was decided to give him a French father to account for his Caucasian features.

But now that he was alone, Hahn took little heart from the papers in his possession, nor did the .32 light automatic in his jacket pocket inspire him with much confidence. Like Zoccola before him, he was not allowed to take his Triad transceiver in with him for fear that, if he were ever searched, it would be discovered, marking him as a spy.

Gazing up at the sky, he could just make out the Piper plane that had transported him here; it was a speck so minute that it could easily be missed among the many stars. A wind had risen in the north and, sweeping through the mountainous landscape, produced a hollow, ghostly sound.

All at once he heard the sound of muffled voices and footsteps. He scanned the horizon but saw nothing. A moment later three men materialized, shadowy figures in the Iranian night, clad in djellabas and wearing scarfs pulled up over their mouths. Slung over their chests were AK-47's, the conventional Soviet rifle used so ubiquitously throughout the world that their mere possession could not identify someone as either friend or foe.

With nothing but his .32, there was little Hahn could do should these men turn out to be foes. This was perhaps the most dangerous point; what, after all, would a Syrian businessman be doing here in this obscure corner of Iran? It was conceivable that the people who were to meet him had been arrested and tortured and that they'd revealed that an American spy was supposed to land that night.

Not a word was spoken until the three were within ten yards of Hahn. Then one of the men allowed his scarf to fall, exposing a thin pair of lips with an unhealed slit running through them, surrounded by a beard that had gone altogether gray.

"Hafiz sends his greetings," he said.

This was the prearranged recognition code. Hahn responded: "Sadi is honored to be here."

The exchange completed, the man motioned Hahn forward and then the three turned and began back in the direction they had come. About half a mile later, just over the rise of a hill, a Ford pickup van was parked. In the rear, protected by a sheet of canvas, Hahn saw several fifty-gallon drums, which he supposed contained fuel.

"In the back, please," the man with the sliced lips said.

The only space available was behind the drums, a little corner where Hahn was obliged to contort his body in order to squeeze in. The van no sooner set in motion than he began to feel painfully cramped. But whatever he did to relieve the agony in his limbs failed to work; there was simply no room to stretch out. Making matters worse, the van bounced wildly, its tires scraping against stones and rocks, which clattered against the chassis. It went on like this for miles, and while Hahn felt that he was certainly better off in the pickup than he would be in the bowels of a jail, he was happy when the current torture ended after the van reached a road surfaced in gravel.

Through rips in the canvas a bit of sun penetrated, waking Hahn. He hadn't thought it possible to fall asleep in such an impossible position and yet he'd evidently done so. By propping himself up so that he could see above the tops of the drums, he managed to have a view out onto the road behind him.

There was, for long stretches, nothing of any interest. He could've been in the American Southwest. The road itself seemed to have been designed by a madman, for it showed no logic in its endless twists and turns. The terrain they were traveling through grew more mountainous; below, a turgid and brown stream rushed through a valley which, in contrast to its surroundings, appeared curiously green and lush.

Periodically, they would pass tanks and personnel carriers, but in the brief glimpses that Hahn got of them, it was impossible to determine whether they were a part of the mullahs' military machine or that of the rebellious army units.

Then, around nine o'clock in the morning, the van came to an abrupt halt. Hahn heard a man's voice, loud and guttural, and instinctively withdrew to his protected place among the barrels. There he waited in the gloom. He assumed that they had run into a roadblock of some kind.

His surmise was confirmed a few minutes later when a man wearing a khaki uniform, with a beret shadowing his face, came around back and began to inspect the steel drums, making an enormous racket as he banged first one drum, then another to check whether there was really fuel inside them.

Through the narrow space between the drums, Hahn could discern the small and indistinct face of the soldier as if it were seen from the wrong end of a telescope.

While he did not for a moment believe it to be a good idea, he removed his .32 from inside his jacket and kept it securely in his grip. There were doubtless other soldiers in the vicinity, and should he attempt to resist capture, he'd be shot on sight. Better that, he thought, than imprisonment and torture, followed by what he assumed would be a grotesque execution.

But the soldier was apparently satisfied that no contraband, even of the human kind, was being carried, and the van was allowed to move on.

As it turned out, the roadblock was only the beginning. The closer they approached to the capital, the more dangerous it became. What from a distance sounded like peals of thunder from a mountain storm, revealed itself to be artillery fire. Puffs of gray smoke appeared over the mountains to the east. From time to time planes passed overhead, most likely drones on reconnaissance missions.

Progress on the highway into Teheran was slowed by the many vehicles that lay in charred ruins along it. American Centurian and Soviet T-62 tanks alike had been destroyed in what must have been a fierce battle for control of the road. In many cases, the tanks were still smoldering, and, from what Hahn could tell, the hideously burned corpses around them were no more than a day or two old.

Hahn would've given anything to know who, if anyone, had won the battle, but his escorts were all sitting up front in the cab and there was no way he could elicit their attention.

On the outskirts of Teheran, the van stopped and the man with the sliced lips came around and removed enough of the drums so that Hahn could crawl out.

"A bus comes here that will take you to the center of the city," he said. He pointed to the stop where a cluster of people were already waiting.

Before Hahn could thank the man, he'd leaped back into the cab and the van was in motion.

With his small travel bag in hand, Hahn crossed the street and joined the people at the stop. The neighborhood he was in was obviously poor; the houses were put together with clay and stucco and mud and roofed with corrugated sheet metal. Everywhere there was the sound of children crying and dogs howling and, above all, the rattle of automatic fire. To Hahn's surprise, the people waiting for the bus showed no reaction to the shooting. They had the stunned and deadened expressions he'd seen on the faces of patients in mental wards. They regarded Hahn without curiosity. For the next several minutes, until the bus pulled within view, not a single word was spoken by anyone.

The Hilton was a Hilton in name only because ownership had long since passed into the hands of the government and was now used exclusively to put up official visitors and the usual assortment of trade delegations seeking oil and lucrative arms deals.

Because of its importance, it was no surprise to discover a generous security presence both outside and in. No one was allowed to enter the hotel without offering their handbags for inspection and without being subjected to a thorough frisking.

Hahn had no choice but to surrender his gun. Possessing one was not considered suspect in itself, since the need for protection in Teheran was so overwhelming. He was assured that he'd get it back upon his departure from the hotel, but he found this little consolation.

Approaching the desk, he told the clerk that his name was Marcel Takim and that he'd made reservations for a week's stay.

"May I see your papers, please?"

He presented the false documents to the man.

The clerk perused them but seemed satisfied that they were genuine. He told Hahn that the hotel would hold onto his passport until he checked out. In its place, he was given papers indicating that he was legally registered at the hotel.

In less than five minutes, both his gun and his passport had been taken from him. It was not what he'd anticipated. But because the situation was so fluid there was no way that anyone in Triad could have prepared him for it.

The first thing that Hahn did after checking into his room was to return downstairs and inquire after "Bill Gerard," the cover that Zoccola was operating under in Teheran.

Opening the register, the clerk ran his eye over the names of the guests currently staying at the hotel. After a few minutes, he glanced up at Hahn and said, "I am afraid, sir, that Mr. Gerard is no longer with us. He checked out two days ago."

"No forwarding address, I suppose?"

The clerk gave him a strange look, intimating that at the moment no one in Iran was in the business of giving out forwarding addresses.

As soon as Hahn had stepped away from the desk, a little man whose diminutive size was emphasized by his stooped posture addressed him: "Are you looking for Mr. Gerard?"

Hahn glanced at the man with surprise; he hadn't realized he'd been overheard nor did he like it. The man might have been in his fifties; dark-complected, with eyes like agates, and his scalp showing through a sparse thatch of hair, he was the sort of person that turned up only in the Levant. He was wearing a jacket that looked as if it might have been bought off the back of a truck.

"No," he snapped and kept walking. The man followed, undaunted.

The man extended his hand. "Let me introduce myself. I am Muhammed Arif."

Was the name supposed to mean anything to him? Hahn thought about it and decided not. There were people he was to meet in Teheran—Triad operatives—but none of them, so far as he knew, went by the name of Muhammed Arif.

"I happen to know Mr. Gerard," he went on.

Hahn was interested, but his expression didn't change.

"And how do you know him?" He still had no intention of acknowledging that he had any acquaintance with the fictitious Gerard.

"I had some dealings with him," he explained, gesturing Hahn away from the desk. "We were involved in some very delicate negotiations."

"And then?"

Arif shrugged. "And then—poof! He vanishes."

"Do you mind my asking what sort of dealings you had?"

Arif screwed up his face. "I don't think that I could reveal such things to you. But if you are a friend of Mr. Gerard then I think maybe you will already know."

Hahn was noncommittal. "Anything's possible," he said.

Arif smiled broadly. "I believe that you do know him. Listen, my friend, I have some Scotch in my room, if you'd care to join me. Unhappily, ever since Khomeini it is impossible to obtain a drink in this town."

Hahn, reasoning that he had little to lose by continuing the conversation, agreed.

Arif's room overlooked a rubble-strewn lot. "There was a building there," he explained. "Then it was shelled so badly by the army that they decided to tear it down."

The Scotch was genuine, Johnny Walker Black, and Arif was extraordinarily generous with it.

"I represent many interests here in Teheran," said Arif. "I am only an agent. No politics. The communists come to me and if they give me a good price, I will do some business with them. The Americans, the British, the French, the same thing."

"It's nice to know somebody who doesn't discriminate."

Arif failed to detect the irony in Hahn's voice.

"I think Mr. Gerard is the same way. We get along. We become good friends."

Hahn doubted this. But he knew Zoccola well enough

to understand that he could make people believe he was an intimate friend, a confidant to whom you could entrust your deepest secrets without fear.

"Tell me, Muhammed, do you know some people by the name of Harry Weber and George Selim?"

These were two of Triad's most important assets in the capital, and it was likely that Zoccola would have been in contact with them. Hahn too was counting on the help of these two men, because without them he was very much alone in the country.

Arif frowned in puzzlement. He repeated the names.

"Weber's British, been here for years," Hahn continued. "Selim is Iranian, used to work for a newspaper in Isfahan until the Shah closed it down. It's possible that Bill might have had some dealings with them too."

This further information brought forth a measure of recognition from Arif. "Ah, yes, I think I know who these people are. I saw these two men with Mr. Gerard. Possibly one was your Weber and one was Selim. I am not certain."

"You wouldn't know where I could find them, do you?"

"I do not know about the Englishman. But this Selim, the police came to the hotel and rounded up several people and he was one of them. I do not know what happened to him. But I hear that many of these were executed."

"By Shastri's men?"

"No, this was before Shastri. On the day of the coup. These were Revolutionary Guards. They were making—how do you say it?—a purge. But later, some people who survived these Revolutionary Guards were rounded up by Shastri's people. So in the end it doesn't matter who you are for; you are marked for death."

"What about you?"

Arif smiled sheepishly. "Everyone needs me, so no one shoots me. One day this will change, and if I am not on a plane out of here, you will make me a visit in Evin Prison."

"Have you any idea what might have happened to Bill? Did he say anything about where he was going?"

Arif shook his head. "He tells me nothing, but I think he went across the Blue Line."

"The Blue Line?"

"That is what we call the border between the area controlled by the rebels and the area controlled by the mullahs. It changes all the time, so you never know from one minute to the next when you are across the border and when you are not. But I think that Mr. Gerard was doing business with the mullahs. If you like, I will make some inquiries and maybe tonight I have some news for you. I am in room three-twenty, by the way."

With Zoccola gone, Selim arrested, and Weber nowhere to be found, Hahn decided that he might as well use Muhammed Arif. Not that he even remotely trusted Arif; it was just that he was the only lead he had.

True to his word, Arif phoned him in his room at a quarter to nine that evening, waking him from a restless sleep. The streets were now in darkness and the view out his window disclosed only the silhouettes of what looked like office buildings across the street. He remembered that a curfew was in effect in the capital from eight o'clock on.

"Come to my room," Arif said. "I think I have some news for you."

"About what?"

"There's no need for you to play this game. Come right now."

But no sooner had Hahn stepped out of the room than he was confronted by a pair of men in uniforms without identifying marks.

"May we see your identification papers?" one demanded.

"By whose authority?"

Hahn noticed now that one of them had produced an automatic and had it sighted on him. That was where the authority lay. He handed over the papers the hotel had given him.

After studying his identification for a moment, the man said, "I am afraid you will have to come with us, Mr. Takim."

"Why?"

"These papers are not in order. You must come with us."

"Where are you taking me?"

These were obviously men who were in the habit of

asking questions, not answering them. They took hold of his arms and roughly steered him in the direction of the elevators. Glancing back down the corridor, he happened to see a small stooped figure in the dimness. He realized it was Muhammed Arif. Their eyes met, but there was not one bit of visible reaction from Arif as Hahn was led away.

5

APRIL 7
THE GOLUL DAGH MOUNTAINS, IRAN

It was James Lisker's second day in Iran. He'd been parachuted at night from a U.S. reconnaissance plane flying from a base in Anatolia, Turkey, and spent the following day, the sixth, traveling several miles on foot to rendezvous with a contingent drawn from what was known as the Ninth Iranian Freedom Brigade. Composed of 600 men, this brigade had been stationed—until Shastri's uprising—on Turkish soil, waiting for an opportunity to return home. Many of the men had served the Shah and been driven into exile when Khomeini had assumed power.

This particular contingent was charged with reconnoitering the border area on behalf of Shastri's government, its objective to see whether or not the Soviets were planning an invasion of the country. The only evidence they could discover so far was the constant overflights by Soviet reconnaissance planes, usually modified Yak-28's (code-named Brewers by NATO). These planes came and went, unopposed by either antiaircraft fire or Iranian aircraft.

Commanding this particular fifteen-man unit was a man named Mansour Arayad, a sullen, bearded man of thirty-three. A student of philosophy at the University of Teheran before his studies were cut short by the revolution, he had been suspected of antigovernment activity because of his interest in such Western philosophers as Kant and Spinoza, the latter a Jew.

When Lisker joined them, Arayad made it clear that he did not especially welcome Lisker's presence among his men. "This is an Iranian problem, all Iranian," he declared to Lisker. "We do not want outside interference from you Americans or from the Russians."

Lisker suspected that it wasn't only the fact that he represented the United States that so disturbed the Iranian commander. He also seemed to resent him for disguising himself as an Iranian peasant. While admittedly he didn't look like most Iranians—for one thing, Lisker towered over most of them—he'd made an attempt. He had dyed his hair dark as bootblack and dressed himself in drab, ill-fitting clothes, complete with an olive-green skullcap. Arayad, however, acted as if Lisker were mocking them with his masquerade.

Nonetheless, he recognized that he was stuck with the American for better or worse, and so Lisker continued to accompany Arayad's unit as it proceeded to reconnoiter the border terrain.

While Arayad was certain that the Soviets would not dare to attack Iran, even if the mullahs wished them to, he did not entirely rule out a series of border incursions by the Red Army—provocative actions, as he termed them.

The unopposed overflights by Soviet reconnaissance craft, like the Yak-28 whose flight path lay almost directly over their patrol, had been going on for the last several days, according to villagers who lived close by.

Thus far, Arayad's party had found no evidence of ground forces crossing the border at any point. That provided Lisker with no reassurance, however. Only that morning he'd received confirmation from Triad headquarters, via the microwave transceiver he carried, that fourteen of the twenty-four available divisions drawn from the Southern and Central Military Districts of the U.S.S.R. had been mobilized and were being deployed at points close to the border. Another two divisions, part of the six currently posted in Afghanistan, had been ordered from the Herat region and deployed at positions on the Afghan side of the Afghan-Iranian border.

Afghanistan didn't much concern Lisker. He reasoned that the six divisions already in that country had all they could handle suppressing the rebels without also committing seasoned forces to a new invasion, which would leave the Afghan city of Herat open to capture.

Although the forces of the United States, and forces of Iran sympathetic to U.S. interests, might be outnumbered by such an overwhelming number of Soviet troops, the advantage did not entirely lay with the Russians.

For one thing, Lisker knew there were approximately a dozen surface arteries from the U.S.S.R. to Teheran—rail lines and roads—and each one had to pass through formidable mountain ranges.

Because of the configuration of the terrain, these arteries all had their "choke points," places where the artery could be completely blocked or else obstructed for a protracted period of time. The result in either case would be to retard the advance of Soviet forces overland; their supply lines would be taxed or else cut off entirely.

Lisker believed that the basic problem was not in impeding a Soviet thrust overland, but in judging whether or not it would occur in the first place. With no proof of a Soviet threat, any attempt to sabotage the arteries would in itself be taken as an act of war and might lead to the very thing the sabotage was intended to avoid. On the other hand, to delay too long was to risk losing the opportunity and leaving the roads and rail lines open to a Soviet juggernaut.

Lisker realized that he wanted to find Soviet troops on the Iranian side of the border. He already had in mind the strategy he would execute, beginning with the road from Ashkhabad, then moving on to the five roads over the Elburz Mountains to Teheran and Qazvin. It would be no problem to destroy the railroad from the Caspian to Teheran either, and surely roadblocks and air bombardment could shut down the road from Jolfa, just across the Soviet border, to Tabriz in Iran. But all this would have to be done quickly and would mean running into the opposition of Iranian troops loyal to the mullahs as well as the Soviets.

Unfortunately for the United States, Shastri's forces were more interested in defeating the fundamentalists than they were in preparing for a Soviet invasion.

Given the lack of time involved and the critical nature of the situation, Lisker had radioed back to Drexell, requesting permission to begin the squeeze on the choke points at the first sign of direct Soviet intervention. The request was naturally sent encoded and he made no mention of it to Arayad.

Arayad really had no idea why Lisker was with his party; he'd simply been told by Shastri's command in Teheran that the American was a liaison officer and adviser whom he had to put up with if he were to continue receiving American largess. For long stretches of the day, he ignored Lisker completely, keeping his men going at what amounted to a forced march, a pace that he probably hoped would exhaust Lisker, who was some years his senior.

But Lisker had fought in many more battles than Arayad and in terrain equally rugged. He was easily able to keep up with Arayad's patrol, maintaining an even, loping pace that belied the difficulty of their mountainous climb.

At 8:45, Teheran time, hours after darkness had fallen over the Golul Dagh Mountains, the patrol arrived at a point just above the Ashkhabad-Mashhad Road. The road went through the Dash Arasy Gorge, whose sides at times reached heights of 200 to 300 meters. At certain junctures the road itself narrowed to a width of three to four meters. As Lisker had surmised from his study of the relevant topographical maps of the area, it was a road that could easily be cut off.

Arayad gave orders to make camp for the night, but just as the men began doing so, the steady drone of an approaching aircraft reached their ears. It was six hours since they'd last seen any Russian planes. They raised their eyes toward a sky that had become bright with a nearly full moon and trained their field glasses on the northern horizon until the plane came into view.

It was not, as they'd originally suspected, another reconnaissance plane, but a Sukhoi-19—a ground-attack aircraft, identifiable by a large nose cone and code-named Fencer.

Because the patrol had been under aerial surveillance from time to time in the last few days, there was little doubt in Lisker's mind that their position was known to the Soviets. However, as they obviously posed no direct military threat to anyone and were still on Iranian territory, he hadn't thought that they would come under attack.

But his assumption was wrong. The Fencer, swooping low at an estimated speed of 950 m.p.h., descended rapidly from its normal service ceiling of 60,000 feet and discharged an air-to-ground missile. The missile detonated at the base of an escarpment less than 150 yards from the encampment. Pieces of the mountainside flew into the air, carried aloft by a spectacular ball of flame bright as the sun at midday. In its light Lisker could see men flung into the air, limbs twitching violently in death throes.

The Fencer dived in, machine gun sputtering, causing Arayad's men to flatten themselves against the ground. Tracer bullets found their way into half a dozen soldiers, and their screams echoed through the gorge far below.

Forty seconds after it had begun, the attack ended and the Fencer rose into the air, vanishing over the mountains in Soviet territory.

The men remained on the ground for some moments, however, awaiting a second sortie. But it did not occur. They began to pick themselves up and tend to the wounded.

Arayad appeared very much shaken. "It is the mullahs' doing," he said to Lisker. "The mullahs cannot command the loyalty of the air force and so they call in the Russians." He spat to register his disdain.

But Lisker did not for an instant believe that the Fencer had attacked them at the behest of the religious leaders of Qum. On the contrary, he was sure that this marked the beginning of a general Soviet air assault on positions all along the border, the first step in softening up any resistance that Soviet ground forces could be expected to encounter.

Why else fire on a reconnaissance patrol in the vicinity of the Ashkhabad-Mashhad Road unless that road was going to be used for a Soviet advance?

As far as Lisker was concerned, he had all the proof of Soviet intentions that he needed. Slipping off on his own, he lifted his transceiver from his pocket and began to punch out the coded message to William Drexell, requesting permission to initiate sabotage operations.

6

APRIL 8
TEHERAN

John Zoccola knew he was in Teheran, but beyond that, he had no idea where he was. The room he'd been kept in for the last three days was commodious enough, but since he wasn't permitted to leave it, he might just as well have been confined to a prison cell. There was one window, but it had been bricked up. In the late afternoons the sound of children playing penetrated through the walls, and in the evenings their mothers would make themselves known, commanding the children to come home for dinner. Nights were full of howling dogs and the occasional rattle of gunfire. But from these sounds Zoccola was able to conclude nothing save that he was obviously in a populated area of the city.

Ever since he'd been taken at night to the village of Barquijan, some thirty-five miles from the capital, to meet with a man who'd identified himself as Osman Khalif, his life had been out of his control. He'd gone to Barquijan with a woman who had the body of a belly dancer and the face of a Madonna, convinced that he was being summoned by Harry Weber. The woman had all the right passwords and seemed well acquainted with Weber. In retrospect, Zoccola believed it was possible that she did, at one time or another, know Weber.

But as soon as he arrived in Barquijan, he sensed that something was amiss. To Zoccola's trained perceptions, Khalif was obviously a man whose life was spent in the shadowy world of intelligence and wet operations (assassinations). After a few words from the other man, Zoccola realized that he enjoyed a role high up in the ranks of the government, where secret information would function as the principal unit of currency. Zoccola also understood that in spite of Triad's best efforts, his cover had been blown and that, probably from his very first hour in Teheran, Khalif had known he was not an arms dealer but an operative of the United States Government.

Apparently Khalif had waited until he'd needed Zoccola for some purpose before placing him in custody. Or maybe he'd only learned who Zoccola was shortly before the American was taken to Barquijan. It was possible that Weber or Selim, possibly both, were double agents or had been made to turn. In any case, without further explanation Zoccola had been bundled back to Teheran and imprisoned.

The reason didn't make any difference now. After five days of excruciating confinement, he prayed that, whoever Khalif was working for, he would decide to do something with him soon. He didn't think he could tolerate a protracted imprisonment. His isolation was near total, and was interrupted only three times a day for meals which, while not unpalatable, were certainly monotonous and in serious need of seasoning. He had the use of a bathroom, what in this part of the world were called low-level facilities because they had no toilet, but rather a hole carved out of the floor.

Zoccola was not a man who could long be separated from other people without lapsing into a state of melancholy bordering on depression. He thrived on people, their company, their conversation, the intricate chemistry of ambitions, desires, intellects, and instincts. He was part negotiator, part haggler, part hustler, moving with fluid ease among the several strata of society. It was no problem for him to confer in the morning, stiffly formal in black tie, with an envoy from the Holy See; idle away the afternoon with an alluring woman; and then spend the night dodging incoming shells with an insurgent leader in a refugee camp. He was equally at home in every situation—except for this one involving a single room with a blocked window.

With no books to read, no newspaper, no radio, he was obliged to entertain himself. But as vivid as his imagination was, he grew increasingly bored and morose. His captors, represented by a man with an M-16 which he was forever polishing, refused to give him the slightest hint as to when a change in his situation might be expected to occur.

He thought a lot about women. Over the years his looks had gotten him in a great deal of trouble—though not as much as his clandestine trade had—but he recognized that he had done nothing to avoid it. Women, even the wives of good friends, gravitated to him because he was not only handsome, but radiated charm and vitality. It was as if they believed that their lives would improve simply by being exposed to his presence. There was something exotic about his features too, suggestive of a Mediterranean heritage, Italian or Spanish perhaps, with sensual lips and dark eyes that glinted with a strange light.

Women might respond to him instinctively, but once they decided that they wanted him for more than a few months—or, in rare instances, for a year—they were inevitably disappointed. Even if he hadn't a secret life to lead by virtue of his profession, he was hardly the sort of man for a woman to count on for the long term. With his mercurial personality and profound restlessness, it was impossible for him to stay in one place for too long or to commit himself to any one woman—although he might occasionally contemplate such a prospect.

This was the case now. Feeling far advanced into his thirties, he almost felt the need for domestication. Cut off from the world with his future so uncertain, he fell into a reflective state that was completely uncharacteristic of him.

There was one woman in particular whom he was in love with—or thought he was, at any rate. She was practically impossible to attain, which was all the more reason why Zoccola desired her. Her name was Adrienne Calenda. She was married to the foreign minister of Indonesia, a murderous, power-hungry man who, having perpetrated the massacre of several thousand suspected communists, would surely not suffer any pangs of conscience killing a rival for his wife's affections. They had met in Morocco during a convention of foreign heads of state, had then initiated an affair in Europe, and then continued it in Martinique and Venezuela. Zoccola had arranged their meetings the same way he had with Triad assets: in secret, through coded messages and cutouts (operatives who acted as go-betweens). There was always the possibility that Zoccola would die, not for having spied on any enemy state or for carrying out the sabotage of a strategic installation, but because he was consorting with the wife of another man.

As excellent as Drexell's sources of information were, he had no idea how deeply involved Zoccola had gotten with Adrienne. It wasn't only Foreign Minister Adam Meureudu whom they'd had to keep in the dark, but Zoccola's own employer. No wonder he meant to pursue her when and if he ever emerged from captivity in this anonymous room in Teheran; she presented a challenge the likes of which he had seldom encountered. Besides which, he might actually be in love with her.

Sometime during the afternoon of the eighth—Zoccola could only estimate the hour by the noise outside, since his watch had been taken away—his guard suddenly threw open the door. Since it wasn't time for dinner, Zoccola sensed that something was in the offing.

The guard muttered a command which Zoccola could make out only through an exercise of his imagination. He rose and followed the guard out the door.

The long corridor was painted a dull, clinical green; he had seen it the night he was first brought here. But now, with sun pouring in through the slitted windows that lined the wall to his right, he could see that the corridor wasn't so long as he'd thought. It swung sharply to the right, then terminated at another door. This door was opened by the guard and Zoccola found himself standing in an office.

There was a portrait on the wall directly in front of him. He couldn't identify the man in the portrait, but from the epaulets gleaming on his shoulders and the stern visage he presented to the painter, it was clear that he was a high-ranking military man, perhaps a general. Resting on the floor in a corner was a second portrait which had no doubt been recently removed from the place of honor now accorded the nameless military man. The deposed portrait was of the late Ayatollah, wreathed in black crepe as a sign of mourning.

Zoccola realized that whoever had previously occupied this office was no longer in charge. Either that or he'd decided to switch loyalties overnight in keeping with the tenor of the times.

Sitting behind a semicircular desk cluttered with telephones, a digital computer console, and stacks of papers and books, one of them a red leather-bound copy of the Koran, was Osman Khalif. His hands clasped before him, he had the air of a priest resigning himself to hearing another tedious confession from one of his parishioners.

It was Khalif who spoke first, after motioning Zoccola into a chair. As he began, the guard who'd escorted the American here nodded once at Khalif and withdrew from the room, closing the door silently behind him.

"I am sorry, Mr. Zoccola, for the inconvenience."

Zoccola noted that he used his name tentatively, as if, after all this time, he still wasn't sure Zoccola was who he thought he was.

Zoccola saw no point in denying his identity; it now made no sense for him to maintain that he was Bill Gerard of Beirut, arms supplier to the world. He chose to remain silent and hear Khalif out. Until he could get some handle on the man, it would be dangerous to speak openly.

"But, you understand, we first had to check out your credentials. We have learned that you represent the highest authorities in Washington and that you are empowered to speak on behalf of these authorities."

Zoccola shrugged. What he said wasn't exactly true, but better to be powerful than to be dismissed as an errand boy. "I have some good connections," was all he admitted, but in such a way as to suggest that these were very good connections, indeed.

"Since the Ayatollah seized power, our relations with the United States have not been good," said Khalif.

"That's putting it mildly."

"My people are interested in pursuing closer relations now that the mullahs are no longer in control here, but we must do this by unofficial channels. We are not like those who are in Paris or Turkey. They are tainted; we are pure."

He spoke this with so much conviction that Zoccola was almost ready to believe him. "Who, may I ask, are your people?"

"I am addressing you as a member of the provisional government of Colonel Shastri." He made a vague gesture toward the portrait hanging above his head.

"I see."

"Colonel Shastri is, as you may know, the leader of our revolution against the mullahs. He is anxious to restore full diplomatic relations with your country—but not yet. It cannot be thought that our revolution was in any way assisted by the United States. There are still, regrettably, many people in my country who regard the United States as an evil force. This attitude cannot be changed overnight."

All this was very well and good, but the question that prayed most upon Zoccola was of less universal significance: "Tell me, Mr. Khalif, do you think I could have my freedom back? I really can't act as a channel for you—unofficial or otherwise—if I'm going to be locked in that damn room you've put me in."

The remark appeared to offend Khalif. "I told you, this was something we did while we made sure who you were. But now that we know, of course you are free. I would like you to come with me and meet with the colonel."

"Shastri?" Zoccola stole another glance at the portrait; he wanted to be prepared when he came face-to-face with the man.

"Yes, that's correct. Colonel Shastri."

Khalif said that he would personally escort Zoccola to Shastri's office. There was something in his manner, however, that provoked Zoccola's curiosity. He seemed to have something he wished to impart to his American guest that couldn't be discussed in his office.

As they began walking, Khalif said, "It is a very bad time in my country. We have our hopes, but there are problems."

Zoccola acknowledged that this was true without having any idea as to where the discussion was leading.

"I have a very large family. Many cousins. They live in the country where there is no work. They depend on me to support them."

Now he knew where it was leading.

"A little extra on the side never hurts," Zoccola said.

Khalif smiled. "Indeed, no."

"Of course, it means a little more work on your part."

"Of course."

Zoccola pretended to consider his next sentence. "Well," he said, "there are some people who might be interested in your services. As you are so close to Colonel Shastri, you might be able to help them out."

He needed to get no more specific than that.

"I think this is quite possible," Khalif said. "If we can agree on terms."

And so it was that in a walk lasting no longer than ten minutes, Zoccola had enlisted yet another operative for Triad.

As it happened, Colonel Shastri was only a short distance away. He'd established himself in the presidential compound, occupying the executive offices that had, up until five days ago, served as the headquarters of Rashid Nasreddin's staff.

To reach his office they'd had to walk through the compound. Many of the buildings were in an advanced stage of deterioration, with walls punctured by incoming shells, leaving awesome gaps, and roofs caved in from the air attack. Rubble and debris were strewn everywhere in their path.

A T-72 tank was positioned directly in front of the president's offices. Soldiers in khaki and green camouflage uniforms were stationed at close intervals throughout the compound, their nervous expressions betraying an anxiety which belied Khalif's confident avowals that Shastri was firmly in control.

Machine gun nests, Zoccola saw, had been placed on the rooftops and along the top of the perimeter wall. In order to shore up fortifications, coils of barbed wire were being unrolled and sandbags installed by men under guard. Whether they were common criminals, political prisoners, or captured Revolutionary Guards, Zoccola couldn't say. But they all looked young and sullen.

Colonel Ibrahim Shastri looked much like his portrait, except that he was considerably smaller than Zoccola had expected. He could have been no more than five-two or -three.

Three guards were in attendance, standing erect with Uzis cradled in their arms. They gave Zoccola sour, deeply aggrieved looks, as if it were only with the greatest forebearance that they could keep from shooting him.

Several medals and a pair of colorful ribbons adorned Shastri's chest. The phones on his desk never ceased ringing. He never touched them; presumably a secretary in one of the outer offices was answering them. Before Zoccola could be formally introduced by Khalif, they were interrupted by a messenger with an urgent written communication.

Shastri's expression never changed as he read it. He appeared to be a man whom nothing could touch and on whom nothing would be lost.

"Sit down, Mr. Zoccola," he said after the messenger had left. His voice seemed strangely calm in the middle of all the commotion that continued around him. "May I order you some tea or coffee?"

Wanting neither, Zoccola politely requested the latter.

No sooner had Zoccola taken a seat than Shastri stood up. In spite of his surface air of calm, he was obviously quite agitated, unable to sit still. He walked to the other side of the room. Zoccola followed him with his eyes. Then he pressed a button set into a walnut panel and the panel slid back to reveal a map of Iran and her neighbors.

With his finger he pointed to three locations on the northern border, two in the Elburz Mountains, one in the Golul Dagh chain. "Last night Soviet jet fighters made an attack at all these points," he said. "Red Army forces are being massed in preparation for invading us. Already the radio of the mullahs is saying that the Russians are welcome. They are saying also that when the Russians come, they will drive on to Teheran and capture it in two days, maybe three."

His English was labored and there were moments when he hesitated for long intervals, perhaps unsure as to what word he wanted next. "With the mullahs," he continued, "there is no problem; these people we will eventually put an end to." He made a slashing gesture across the base of his throat. "The mullahs are kaput, finished! Many of these mullahs, they hate the Russians. They would have nothing to do with them except that they are afraid that they will be thrown out altogether. Listen to me. There are nearly two hundred thousand mullahs. These people dispense food-rationing and fuel cards and business permits, they run the courts and collect taxes and issue loans interest free. Until I came, they were unchallenged. Now that they face a threat, they do not know what to do. They did not ever think that the day would come that they would lose everything. They've killed hundreds of thousands, they have sent young boys to march through mine fields, boys who are led to believe that they are lucky to become martyrs for the Imam. These mullahs are terrified that they too will become martyrs. Not all of them are so prepared to die for the Imam!" He exploded with laughter. "And they are right to have this fear. I will march *them* across the mine fields and watch them die.

"But against the Russians," Shastri went on, "what can we do? We are not so many and we do not have the arms to hold them off for long. Also, we have had many casualties in the last few days. The fighting has been heavy, here in the capital and in the countryside where it continues."

"Excuse me, Colonel, just how much of the country are you currently in control of?" Zoccola asked.

With a blue Magic Marker, Shastri drew a circle around the capital, another about Isfahan, another, larger one, about the oil center of Abadan, and others about Shiraz, Tabriz, and Rasht on the southern edge of the Caspian Sea. "These are the cities we now control," he said. With a green Magic Marker he indicated what he called "spheres of influence."

Huge swaths of the country were left outside these spheres, Zoccola noted. Basically, army units loyal to Shastri held power in the population centers while most of the country-side and the smaller cities and towns lay outside their jurisdiction. Zoccola asked who was in control of these areas.

"Some are in dispute, others are loyal to Nasreddin and the mullahs," Shastri conceded.

What was particularly disturbing was that almost the entire northern part of the country which lay along the Soviet border was in the hands of the mullahs. Thus, if the Soviets did advance there would be minimal opposition, perhaps none, because they would be coming in at the invitation of the mullahs.

This revolution of Shastri's was more trouble than it was worth, Zoccola thought, in spite of his readiness to make sub-rosa peace with the U.S. Before Shastri acted, the mullahs enjoyed enough power in Iran so that they didn't need the Kremlin's help. Now Shastri had succeeded in driving the mullahs into the arms of the Soviets. It was a fine mess.

But, given his predicament and the fact that his freedom depended on Shastri's beneficence, he decided it was wiser to voice none of his doubts. "When do you anticipate that the invasion will come?"

"In twenty-four hours. Forty-eight, maybe. But, you see, there are so many signs that the element of surprise will be gone if the Russians delay longer. This morning there is a report that generals from the various Warsaw Pact nations are convening in Prague to arrange the final plans. Statements from the Soviet press are full of denunciations of U.S. imperialism. They blame your country for our revolution and say that the mullahs must be put in charge again. It is all the groundwork, you see, for the invasion."

It was possible that the Russians were deliberately sending false signals, hoping that by alarming their opponents they might accomplish their objectives without actually having to use force. If Shastri could be made to capitulate when he perceived the magnitude of the Soviet threat, why then, there would be no need to send in troops and risk the repercussions of a confrontation with the United States.

On the other hand, if Shastri refused to back down, and called their bluff, then it might leave the Soviets no other choice but to go ahead with the incursion in spite of the reservations they must be having. For certainly any military operation of this kind was so hazardous that some in the Kremlin would counsel to hold off.

"May I ask you something, Colonel?"

"Certainly."

"What if this attack by the Russians does occur? What will your position be under those circumstances?"

"We will fight," Shastri replied firmly.

"But you've just told me yourself that your troops are unprepared to take on the Russians, particularly now that you're in the midst of a civil war."

Shastri nodded. "Yes, I know. But that is where your country comes in. For surely you will not permit the Russians to occupy a country so vital to your needs and so close to the Persian Gulf. What you must do is stress to your government the importance of beginning immediately the deployment of your troops. If they are here, on the ground, then the Russians might have second thoughts. If not, then they will come."

"But, Colonel, you just told me that you did not want to be associated with the United States for fear that it will alienate your own people and make you look like collaborators, imperialist agents, or whatever."

"Yes, I said this. I do not take back my words. You will tell your friends in Washington that when your troops are introduced into my country, I will have no choice but to denounce them. I will repudiate them. I will make angry words and send my representatives to the United Nations demanding that all foreign powers must vacate my country." Now he offered Zoccola a knowing smile. "But this will all be for show. In secret, we will cooperate with you. And later when the truth comes out, you will be heroes. You will be the ones who kept Iran free from Russia. Even the mullahs, they hate the Russians. It is only because they are afraid and do not know where else to turn that they call on them."

To Shastri it was all very simple and clear-cut. The only thing that remained was to place U.S. combat forces in the oil fields and ring the capital with them as insurance to keep the Soviets out, and as blackmail if the Soviets did in fact come in. For then the U.S. President couldn't very well summon his troops back home; he'd have to commit more. This was precisely what Colonel Shastri was counting on.

When in doubt, let the Americans bail you out.

"So, Mr. Zoccola," he said, "you will talk to your friends in Washington?"

"I'll talk to them, all right."

"But you should do so quickly. There's no time to lose. Even as we speak, more Russian soldiers are being mobilized."

Zoccola said he understood the urgency of the situation.

As he was leaving, Shastri called to him. "I have always admired your president," he said. "He seems like an honorable and decent man. Tell me, do you consider him a man of his word?"

"As much as the next man with a thousand nuclear warheads at his fingertips," Zoccola replied.

TOP WARSAW PACT LEADERS GATHER IN PRAGUE
(Special to the New York Times)

PRAGUE, April 7—High-ranking officials from the Soviet Union and Warsaw Pact nations began what were termed "urgent sessions" today in the Czech capital. Marshal Valeri Grigorenko, the Soviet Defense Minister, arrived from Moscow early in the day and went almost immediately into consultation with his counterparts from Russia's Eastern European allies. The Czech press stated only that the officials were meeting to discuss "matters of mutual interest" and said that the gathering would last until the end of the week. Sources close to the Soviet delegation, led by Marshal Grigorenko, have informed Western diplomats here that the session's purpose is to consider the latest developments in Iran, where an army-backed coup has resulted in a state of virtual civil war. These same sources maintain that no decision has yet been reached on how to respond to any formal invitation by the fundamentalist regime to send troops into Iran, should such an invitation actually be extended.

SCHELLING WARNS OF SOVIET PERIL IN IRAN

WASHINGTON, April 7 (AP)—Secretary of State Jeffrey Schelling today told Congressional leaders that "there was a very real possibility that Russian forces might choose to intervene in Iran." Before a special session of the Senate Foreign Relations Committee, he indicated that preliminary intelligence reports out of the Soviet Union showed a "massive buildup of forces and war matériel which could well be preparatory to an invasion." In response to a question by Senator Lewis Packhammer (D-Mich.), he said that while the United States was prepared to counter any threat to her strategic interests in the region, he saw no need at present to contemplate the introduction of U.S. forces in Iran.

SOVIET WARNS U.S.: HANDS OFF IRAN

MOSCOW, April 7 (Combined dispatches)—In a statement released today in the Communist Party organ Pravda, the Soviet Union warned the United States against intervening in war-torn Iran. "The Soviet Union, in the strictest possible terms, insists that the territorial integrity of Iran remain free from violation by imperialist forces," the statement, signed by "Observer," said. The pen name "Observer" almost always designates a senior official in ruling Party circles.

The statement went on to say that the Soviet Union has no interest in seeing any spread of violence but will take "dramatic steps," should the situation deteriorate. "Any assault on the legitimate government of Iran will be regarded as a threat to the Soviet Union," the statement concluded. There was no indication as to what, if any, steps Moscow might undertake in the event that the United States did send troops into the beleaguered nation.

EUROPEAN LEADERS CALL FOR SUMMIT

PARIS, April 7 (Reuters)—Leaders of the European Economic Community (EEC) convening here called on both Soviet and American leaders to "put aside their differences and hold a face-to-face meeting at the earliest possible date." In a statement delivered to representatives of the EEC, German Prime Minister Ernst Laudenheld declared, "It isn't too late to stop the crisis in Iran from turning into a ghastly confrontation. We seem headed on a collision course and it simply does not need to happen if Secretary Kadiyev and President Turner would sit down and talk to each other and reason out their differences in a peaceful forum." At the same meeting British Prime Minister Trevor Harington warned against the temptation to equate the policies of the United States and those of the Soviet Union. "I have not always agreed in the past with much of what the U.S. has done, but certainly it cannot stand by and watch idly as the Red Army comes marching through the Elburz down into the oil fields of Khuzestan. The allies cannot permit that to happen."

7

APRIL 9
WASHINGTON, D.C.

It was announced at the beginning of the National Security Council meeting at the White House that the President would be late—his briefing of congressional leaders on the Hill had gone on longer than anticipated—and so the meeting started without him.

Thomas Kriendler, the President's National Security Advisor, a lean, nervous man with a gaunt face and the tiresome capacity to draw out his sentences, began the session at quarter to one on the morning of April 9.

"We've been called together by the President," he said, "to decide whether the situation in Iran is critical enough for us to introduce American combat forces."

"I think the way you phrased it isn't exact enough," Secretary of State Schelling said. "There are a whole range of options available to us, not just the commitment of ground forces, and it seems to me that we have to consider all of them. Putting our boys in Iran is an option of last resort after all the others have been exhausted. Or so it seems to me."

"On the contrary," Defense Secretary Marty Rhiel said, "I think Tom is right. The real crux of this matter is whether we are willing to go with a military option and, if so, at what point do we avail ourselves of it. Right now I'm up in the air. I want to hear what everyone has to say—in particular Mr. Drexell."

Drexell, who seldom contributed anything to these meetings, which he was, in any case, rarely called upon to attend, was sitting at the far end of the table, almost directly opposite from the vacant seat reserved for the President. Only when he felt that his words would carry weight did he ever speak; otherwise he saved his thoughts for the President's ear alone. He felt that decisions made by committee took forever to reach and were too watered down to achieve the original ends.

Because the existence of Triad was known only to the President and those few cabinet officials and advisers who needed to know about it, Drexell's exact position was never clarified at meetings such as this. If any outsider ever asked his function, Drexell was described as just another adviser working with an ad hoc intelligence unit formed to monitor the current crisis.

Stanley Burns, the recently appointed director of the CIA, shot a decidedly unfriendly glance at Drexell. That Rhiel had singled out Triad's leader instead of him only underscored the low esteem into which his agency had fallen of late. Nonetheless, even he would have to admit that the CIA had failed to reestablish its intelligence network in Iran after the fall of the Shah and that Triad had managed to some degree to fill the vacuum.

"Gentlemen," Drexell began, "we have something of a paradoxical situation confronting us. I have received two reports from Triad operatives in the last twenty-four hours, both confirming that a Soviet invasion of Iran may be imminent. But in spite of some sporadic raids conducted by Soviet aircraft along the northern border there's no definite proof that the invasion will occur.

"I happen to believe that no decision has been reached in Prague as to whether the Soviets will risk an invasion. We have to ask ourselves, What would make an invasion inevitable? Because, if the Russians feel that they've got a way out of this mess, they'll take it. They aren't interested in having a war with us unless the benefits outweigh the possible losses. Why did they go in in Afghanistan? To rescue a friendly regime and because they figured that if they didn't, then they might have a hostile fundamentalist Islamic state on their borders.

"But now in Iran they do have a fundamentalist Islamic regime on their borders and that doesn't scare them half as much as the restoration of a pro-Western regime. Better Khomeini's people than the dissident colonels like Shastri. The paradox is that if the mullahs could firmly establish a hold over the country and put an end to Shastri, then the Russians would probably stay put. But if Shastri looks as though he's about to put an end to the mullahs, they may decide to act."

"What you're saying is that if the pro-Western forces go down the tubes there, then no Red invasion," said Roger Parsons, a longtime foreign policy adviser to a succession of administrations.

"That's about it."

"And what do you think of the chances for Shastri to secure the whole country?" Rhiel asked.

"They're not terrific," Drexell said. "But the longer he survives, the more likely he'll attract the opponents of the mullahs. And remember that not all the mullahs want the Russians in. It's probably only a bare majority of them, the ones who are most terrified of losing. And why? Because they suspect we'll eventually put our power behind Shastri. Right now I think we're looking at a protracted civil war, with no side powerful enough to best the other. In another month or so you'll see such chaos in that country that it'll be anyone's guess who the hell's running it."

"The Russians aren't going to sit still and allow that to happen so close to them," Schelling noted.

"No, they're not," Drexell agreed. "I'm just spelling out the scenarios that I see. But it seems to me that a situation's developing where the Russians will feel compelled to go in. Maybe not tomorrow, maybe not next week, but sooner or later."

"What I want to know," said Krlendler, "is how long it would take us to build up enough of a force in the area to counter the divisions the Soviets are likely to commit to an invasion."

"Well, it would really depend on how far the Soviets wanted to penetrate," said Rhiel. "They could content themselves with occupying the northern area or, in the worst-case scenario, they could go right down into the oil fields of Khuzestan and threaten our access to the Persian Gulf."

"We'll go with the worst case," Kriendler said.

"I would say, conservatively, that our own mobilization and deployment time might range up to ninety days."

"Ninety?" Parsons said, astounded. "The Reds could be all the way to Istanbul by that time. Why ninety?"

"We're talking about four divisions," Rhiel said. "We'd have to use Clark Field and Subic Bay in addition to our base at Diego Garcia. We have to assume we'd need a full fleet of eighty-odd C-5A transports, and it's unlikely we can reach that level on a moment's notice. Then we have to arrange for C-141 stretch and aerial refueling. We have to fit out our SL-7's to move our mechanized infantry from the East Coast to the Gulf... It takes a lot of time to fight a war like this."

"SL-7's?" Kriendler asked.

"They're fast sealift ships," Rhiel explained. "But remember, the operational and transport capacity of the Soviet Union isn't all that it should be. They have close to eighty Antonov-22 transports for their troops, but even so they couldn't carry on two major operations at the same time."

"What are you saying, Marty—we should start a diversionary attack somewhere else?" Burns asked.

"We've got enough trouble on our hands. I don't think we need a horizontal escalation right now."

"All right," Schelling put in. "It'll take two, three months, maybe more, to move all our men in there. But what do we do in the meantime?"

"In the meantime, gentlemen, we can take some immediate action," Drexell said. "We need only a small number of men initially, enough to block the access routes that the Soviets would have to take overland."

"Can that be done?" Kriendler asked.

"It can. Many of those access routes go through deep gorges and they can be pretty easily cut off. If we can convince Shastri's people, we don't even have to get involved except on an advisory level. Of course, that's just a first step. It'll impede troop movements by land but won't do a damn thing for the soldiers being airlifted into Iran."

"What do you suggest we do to counter them?" asked Burns, scarcely veiling the skepticism in his voice.

"I suggest that we begin our M and D right now with a view to that sixty-to-ninety-day time frame. If it turns out we don't need the troops, then so much the better; nothing's been lost but some of the taxpayers' money. But to delay longer would be dangerous. I also think that we should institute some kind of war games in the area—in coordination with the Saudis and Omanis, maybe the Egyptians too. Send the *Nimitz* into the Gulf."

"That could be considered a provocation by Moscow," Burns pointed out. "By doing that we could escalate the conflict."

"Possibly, but I believe we have to act decisively in this instance. I'd like to see forces—even a token detachment of the Rapid Deployment Force or a company of light infantry—put on the ground, maybe directly in Khuzestan. That way, the Soviets will be under no illusions as to what risks they'll be running should they decide to go in."

"I don't know," Schelling said, shaking his head in consternation. "All this seems too much like jumping the gun."

"Better to jump the gun," Drexell said, "than have it placed to your head."

The President arrived at the National Security Council meeting at close to two in the morning. An aide then summarized the opinions raised so far, although at times the President, obviously very tired and not in the best of spirits, seemed distracted and inattentive. Several times he asked the members of the Council to repeat the arguments they'd made an hour before. Throughout, he refrained from expressing any view of his own. The meeting dragged on past three in the morning at which time the President decided to accept Drexell's recommendation that war games be initiated in the area as a show of force. On the matter of closing off the overland access routes, he chose to wait until evidence of a Soviet invasion became more apparent. He completely ruled out dispatching any U.S. troops to the area—

even the "tripwire" force Drexell proposed—unless Soviet forces had already launched an invasion. "It cannot be made to look as though we were the first to go in," he said. "We have to respond to something real, not something that's still hypothetical."

There was nothing Drexell could say to the President, either in the meeting or in private, that could cause him to change his mind. He demanded facts that simply were unavailable, and he refused to gamble.

At four that morning, after hearing from Zoccola for the first time in days, Drexell radioed Lisker. He recommended that he meet with Zoccola and together prevail on Shastri to use his men to choke off the land access routes. There was nothing the President could do if the Iranians took it on themselves to carry out the sabotage. He also asked if Zoccola and Lisker could discover what had happened to Hahn. No sooner did he have one member of Triad back than another one seemed to get lost.

8

APRIL 9
TEHERAN

At midnight they came for Hahn, three more men without insignias on their uniforms, and untied him. For several hours Hahn had been secured by a chain to a table in an empty room. The empty room looked as if it might once have been a bedroom. The ceiling was elaborately carved and had a large mirror mounted in it so that, if he cared to glance up (and he rarely wanted to), Hahn could see himself sprawled helplessly on the floor with a silver chain taut about his chest.

No one had bothered to tell him why he'd been arrested. His captors might be Shastri's men or they might be working for the mullahs. But it was equally possible that they represented some other faction in the cauldron of Iranian politics. Whoever they were, they obviously suspected Hahn of being an enemy agent. With his flimsy cover story, he did not doubt that he'd be found guilty.

No sooner had they helped Hahn up than the guards blindfolded him. They marched him down a set of stairs, out a door, and into the chill night. He heard voices around him, the sounds of shuffling feet. Orders were barked out. There was the acrid smell of exhaust fumes in the air, the rumble of motors revving up.

He felt himself being pushed forward, then hoisted into what he judged to be the back of a truck or van. There were a great many other people crammed inside already. He could smell nothing but human sweat and the unmistakable odor of excrement.

Doors slammed behind him. A cry of protest emerged from those packed in, but it was drowned out by the surge of the truck's motors. Who are these people? Hahn wondered. What were their alleged crimes?

It seemed to take hours for the truck to reach its destination although it was probably only twenty minutes.

The truck drew to a stop, the doors were thrown open. As the prisoners streamed out, their blindfolds were removed. Hahn was momentarily stunned by the brilliant lights which greeted him. He had no idea where he was, and his retinas burned with incandescent spots. Gradually his eyes grew accustomed to the light and he saw that he was surrounded by hundreds of people, men and women, who seemed to have been brought to this place in trucks like the one he'd just emerged from.

Straight ahead, looming above the prisoners, was a monolithic structure composed of massive blocks of stone and bathed in the glare of searchlights. Pillboxes, barbed wire, and razor-sharp protrusions of steel dominated the walls. There was no question in Hahn's mind as to what purpose this edifice served.

With machine guns trained on them, the prisoners were herded in through the gates, past still more soldiers whose implacable expressions suggested that no mercy was possible here.

Lined up in a courtyard, they were made to stand at attention until, half an hour later, an officer proceeded to give them numbers. It developed that these numbers designated the cell to which each prisoner was assigned. Any attempt to exchange a word with other prisoners was met with a stern rebuke by the guards.

Voices, plaintive and incoherent, echoed down the long, ill-lit corridors into which they were led. Occasionally Hahn would hear a scream, a cry of such agony that it scarcely sounded human.

At last Hahn was introduced to his new home: a dark, cavernous space whose dimensions he was unable to puzzle out. It was already filled with prisoners. Eyes gleamed like phosphorus in the dark. What air there was smelled stale and was permeated by the stench of urine.

Hahn finally found a place where he could squeeze in. When he put his head back, something wet and gelatinous trickled down on his hair. Some creature, a rat he supposed, darted out from his left, leaped in one majestic motion over his legs, and vanished in the gloom.

The silence was astounding. There might be a dozen or three score people in here with him, and yet hardly a sound emerged from them. Once in a while he'd hear a groan, a wracking cough, a sob that could not be suppressed in time.

He must have dozed off although he would never have thought sleep possible in such a place. When he came awake it was to find a hand on his shoulder. He started, blinked, and saw a man sitting beside him who hadn't been there before.

"I beg your pardon," he said in distinct English, "but would you have a cigarette?"

The man was neither American nor British; he had an accent, though not one that Hahn could immediately identify.

He wasn't certain whether he should acknowledge that he understood English but decided that, under the circumstances, he had very little to lose. "I'm sorry, I don't smoke."

The man nodded as if this was the answer he'd been expecting all along. He was probably used to bad news. Anyone in this prison would be.

"You are English?" he asked.

"Syrian."

There were doubtless spies in the prison and Hahn was not about to oblige his captors by divulging his nationality straightaway.

"Syrian?" He shrugged. "You struck me as an Englishman. But no matter. My name is Farouk. Like the king of Egypt. Only he is dead and I am not—not yet."

Hahn could see that he had a beard that spilled halfway down his chest and wore a caftan that had once been all white but was now stained with dirt and what might have been blood. His left eye, when he looked at Hahn, seemed glazed over; possibly some disease had made him half-blind.

Hahn gave him his cover name, which Farouk accepted without question.

"I am from Kuwait," said Farouk. "But I come here many years ago. Now it does not look like I leave." He sounded vaguely disappointed, but by no means despondent.

"Why are you here?"

"Why is anyone here? There are people in this prison who are from forty different political groups. Some support Khomeini when he is alive, some support Colonel Shastri, some support other people. Everyone is for somebody and against somebody else. What does it matter?"

"Who runs this prison?"

"The army."

"Shastri's army or the mullahs' army?"

"It is not so simple. These people who arrest you, they say they are for Shastri, but really they are for themselves."

This was no help at all. On coming to Iran, Hahn had realized the country was in turmoil, but he hadn't any idea that it was going to be this bad. A state of actual anarchy prevailed. There were no rules, no laws; all bets were off. Hahn had never felt so helpless, even more than when he'd been tied to the table in the middle of the empty palatial room. At least then he'd nurtured some feeble hope that he might obtain his freedom. Now he recognized that he could be hauled off tomorrow and shot and no one would be the wiser. His body would turn to ashes in a nameless grave.

"Did they charge you with a specific crime?" he pressed.

Farouk looked momentarily bewildered, as if to say that this question was so absurd that he could not be expected to reply. But then he said, "They say that I am a friend of the people in Qum. They say that I am a spy for the mullahs."

"Are you?"

Hahn certainly didn't expect an honest answer, but he was interested in seeing what the man's reaction would be.

Farouk smiled broadly and then threw his head back and laughed, a sound so unusual in this environment that it caused the other prisoners around them to glower at him in reproach.

"Maybe I am," he said. "Maybe I am."

A long silence passed between them; neither knew what to say to the other.

The silence was broken by Farouk. "I had important friends once," he said wistfully. "I know everybody in Teheran."

"What did you do?"

"I am a businessman," he replied cryptically. "What business I did is not so important. I know Nasreddin. I know the Russian Ambassador. I know everybody." His manner was not boastful, but rather matter-of-fact. "That is why they put me here."

"How long have you been here?"

Again a shrug. "A month maybe. I lose track. I tell you a secret."

It was probably a secret he'd shared with everyone else in the cell, but Hahn was certainly willing to listen to it.

"The Russians plan to kill Nasreddin."

"What? What are you saying?"

Farouk grinned; he liked the effect of his remark on Hahn.

"Listen to me. Like what they did in Afghanistan, they will do here. They wish for their own puppet. They will kill Nasreddin, then install somebody they can give orders to."

What Farouk said about Afghanistan was exactly true; the head of state, despite his communist sympathies, was assassinated and replaced by a man more acceptable to Moscow shortly after the Soviet invasion.

"Are you telling me that if the Soviets invade—"

"Oh, they will invade most definitely, my friend, do you doubt it? Once they enter our country, then they kill Nasreddin and put a man they like to rule. He will not be so much for the mullahs as for the Kremlin."

"How do you know this?"

"I have many friends, I am telling you. Even in this prison people come with information. I know what goes on in the world outside even if I cannot leave here."

"Does Nasreddin know about this?"

"Maybe yes, maybe no. But he must not believe that the Russians would dare do such a thing to him. Because otherwise he would fight them, no? He would not invite them to come into his country to make war against Shastri and the army."

It occurred to Hahn that if he could somehow get to Nasreddin and convince him of the truth of Farouk's words, then perhaps there was an outside chance he'd reconsider his alliance with the Russians. Even if Shastri and he were bitter enemies, maybe it was possible for all factions in the country to unite as one against a Soviet invasion.

Of course, he could not dismiss the possibility that Farouk was a liar, a complete fraud. But if he was on the level his information was of considerable importance to Triad. If Nasreddin could be prevailed upon to denounce the Soviets, his word would carry great weight among the Iranians who adhered to the tenets of the late Ayatollah. He might be merely a figurehead, but no one could accuse him of serving the interests of the United States. As such, he made for a more credible spokesman than one of the exiled Iranian leaders in Paris whose moderate views went ignored inside Iran.

Unfortunately, now that he had such potentially vital information, Hahn could do nothing with it. He was stuck in a prison, without charges, without a lawyer, and without hope of release any time soon. There must be some way out of here, he thought, but he could not for the life of him figure out what it might be.

U.S. ANNOUNCES WAR GAMES IN GULF

WASHINGTON, April 9 (UPI)—Secretary of Defense Martin Rhiel announced today that the United States, in conjunction with Oman, Egypt, and Saudi Arabia, would begin a week of war games in the Persian Gulf this coming Monday. The war games will involve units of the Sixth Fleet, ordinarily based in the Mediterranean, including the flagship carrier, U.S.S. Nimitz. Mr. Rhiel denied that the war games, code-named Orange Star, have anything to do with the crisis in Iran. "These war games have been planned for several months," he stated, "long before the strife in that country erupted."

WARSAW PACT MEETING ENDS

PRAGUE, April 8 (Agence France Presse)—Defense ministers from the Warsaw Pact nations, meeting in Prague for consultations, returned home today following the conclusion of three days of talks. A statement released by the Soviet press agency Tass described the talks as "fruitful," adding that "agreement was reached unanimously on several issues of mutual concern." Although there has been considerable speculation that the purpose of the meeting was to consider military action in Iran and the Persian Gulf, no specific mention of the Iranian crisis was cited in the Tass statement.

Excerpt from a CBS Nightly News Broadcast, April 9, by correspondent Patrick Kramer in Moscow.

"Sources close to the Kremlin have told CBS News that a decision has been reached to carry out a limited invasion of Iran by Soviet troops sometime the next week. This decision emerged from the just-concluded meeting of Warsaw Pact military officials in Prague, according to these sources. While spokesmen for the Kremlin continue to deny that they have any plans for launching an invasion, reports reaching the Russian capital from the southern regions of the country indicate an unprecedented buildup of troops and a recent surge of activity on military and civilian airfields. Our sources said that while the decision has been made, it isn't final and it could be reversed depending on future developments in the area. 'Either the invasion will come next week,' one source said, 'or it won't come at all.'"

9

APRIL 10
TEHERAN

While he was waiting for James Lisker to return to the capital, John Zoccola undertook to find Hahn. He'd learned from Drexell that Hahn was supposed to have registered at the Hilton under the name of Marcel Takim, and it was at the Hilton that he began his search.

Marcel Takim, he found, had indeed registered, but the clerk at the desk claimed not to know what had become of him. "If you do see him," he told Zoccola, "tell him that his bill has come due and he will lose his room if he doesn't pay it immediately."

Zoccola assured him he would do so.

The clerk regarded him strangely.

"Are you not one of our guests?" he asked in bewilderment.

It was as if Zoccola had returned from the dead. Zoccola supposed that most of those who vanished during the night seldom made a reappearance a few days later.

"I used to be."

"Mr. Gerard," the clerk said, recognition finally dawning.

Zoccola nodded.

"You look well." The clerk obviously could not understand why, if Zoccola had miraculously survived a roundup, he did not have the haggard, stricken air of a tortured man.

Zoccola left the Hilton, but half a block away he realized he wasn't alone. He discovered none other than the gnomish Muhammed Arif trailing along at his side.

Like so many other hustlers, middlemen, assassins, spies, and profiteers who'd come to Teheran to capitalize on the chaos, Arif would never reveal his true objectives. It was difficult to decide whether he was a potential asset or liability. But on the other hand, Zoccola too was playing at a dangerous game, and so there was good reason for Arif to be suspicious as well.

"It is so good to see you, Mr. Gerard. I never thought I would lay eyes on you again."

Zoccola shrugged.

"Maybe we can do some business together," he said. "I have many Katyusha rockets to sell. Perhaps you would be interested?"

"Perhaps," Zoccola said noncommittally. He was really not anxious to pursue any kind of relationship with Arif and hoped the Iranian's legs would soon grow tired of the effort of keeping abreast of him.

Arif seemed to sense his impatience. "I have met a friend of yours," he said, "a man who was looking for you."

This stopped Zoccola in his tracks. "Who?"

"A Syrian Frenchman. His name, I think, is Marcel."

"Takim?"

Arif nodded happily. "Yes, that is the one. Four nights ago he comes to the Hilton and asks for you and your friends Selim and Weber. I tell him everyone is gone. I offer to take him over the Blue Line if he is interested. But then they come for him in the night and take him away."

"Who, goddammit?"

Arif could be infuriatingly obtuse, something he had probably been trained to do.

"Soldiers who think he is a spy. They take him to the prison last night."

"How do you know all this?"

Arif looked offended by the question. "It is not so important. He is in the same prison where your friend Selim is. Weber is in no prison. Weber is dead."

Although Zoccola had had only a marginal acquaintance with the Triad operative, the news of his death still came as a shock. Weber had seemed so sure of himself, almost cocky, as if he'd mastered the art of survival in war-torn Iran so well that he no longer needed to take precautions.

"Executed?"

"What else?"

"What prison is Marcel in? Do you happen to know?"

"He is in Khomiteh Mushtarak, I think. From there maybe he goes to Munafek Abad."

Zoccola gave him a puzzled look.

"It is where they bury the bad people, Munafek Abad. Traitors, rebels, criminals, they all end in Munafek Abad."

This could hardly be called reassuring news. "Is there any way to get someone out of this place?"

A sly smile formed on Arif's lips. "There is always a way," he said. "Always."

Lisker arrived in Teheran that afternoon, having taken the most circuitous route possible form the Iranian-Soviet border. He had traveled at night by car, jeep, truck, and bus, the latter a temperamental vehicle that stalled repeatedly.

Triad had arranged for a safe house situated not far from the Archeological Museum, which until a week ago had been patrolled by Revolutionary Guards and was now patrolled by soldiers loyal to Shastri. One window of the safe house overlooked the museum; the other held a view of a wall papered over with slogans and posters and crumbling portraits of the late Ayatollah.

There were three rooms and a bathroom in the safe house. It had once belonged to a merchant who lost his life to revolutionary excesses, and insofar as the authorities were concerned, the current owner was a shopkeeper who ordinarily stayed in Isfahan running a family business.

Zoccola was there, exhausting a pack of cigarettes and a couple of bootlegged Carling beers as he awaited Lisker. When Lisker arrived, Zoccola had someone with him, a little man with an odd, disagreeable face whom Zoccola introduced as Muhammed Arif.

"What happened to Hahn?" Lisker asked as soon as he'd taken a seat.

"Mr. Arif here says that he's been thrown in prison by the army."

"Shastri's men?"

"They have no discipline," Arif explained. "They take who they want and tell Shastri they are arresting traitors—supporters of the mullahs. What does Shastri know?"

"It's possible that they'll execute him as a spy," Zoccola said. "We have to get him the hell out of there."

"You've talked with Shastri. Can't you persuade him to order Jerry's release?"

"I've called him, but I can't get through. I'm told he's on an inspection tour outside the capital. They won't say where. Everything's classified information. We don't have the time to wait for him to get back. And there's no guarantee he'd oblige us in any case. It seems to me he might not have very much control over his own men."

"What do you suggest then?"

"Break him out."

"The question is how," Lisker said.

Arif spoke up. "I think I might have your solution. It all depends."

"On what?"

"On whether you have a lot of money or only a very little."

Lisker and Zoccola exchanged a look that Arif could not interpret. "Muhammed is an arms dealer," Zoccola explained.

"Money," Lisker said, "is available. What have you got for us?"

"I can get hold of whatever you want," Arif said, "with the exception perhaps of an aircraft carrier or a nuclear bomb."

"That's all right. We have other sources for that sort of thing," Lisker said.

Arif paused; he might have realized that Lisker was telling him the truth and that the people he'd decided to do business with were far more important than he'd suspected.

His eyes bulged with excitement; the prospect of drama and catastrophe—not to mention a lucrative sale—clearly delighted him.

"I have some Semptex. As much as you want. One ton, two tons, three... We could blow up Khomiteh Mushtarak—no problem. I have enough Semptex to blow up ten Khomiteh Mushtaraks—no problem."

Semptex was a Soviet-manufactured ultrahigh explosive, capable of exploding at nine miles per second. Known in the United States by its equivalent designation RDX, Semptex had been used by Shiite fanatics against U.S. Marine and French military bases in Beirut, with the consequent loss of close to 300 soldiers.

"Could you provide us with some manpower too?" Lisker asked.

"I have friends. They would be willing to give some help."

"We're going to stay on you, Muhammed," Zoccola warned, "because we don't want you to have the opportunity to fuck up on us. You get out of line, it's your ass. You realize that?"

Arif understood. "I would not have stayed alive this long in this place if I did not," he replied.

10

APRIL 11
BERLIN

By midmorning the sun had disappeared completely, obscured by menacing rain clouds that rolled in from the east. A chill wind that carried too many memories of the bitter winter just past accompanied the clouds. It was no day to take a stroll.

William Drexell, seemingly oblivious of the cold, his coat open, was waiting for a woman to bring him back his passport. The woman was, like all the customs officials and border guards in this sector of Berlin, coldly efficient, as intimidating in appearance as she was in manner. Tall and buxom, with a face to terrify small children, she could have been a man in drag. It was impossible to imagine anyone ever making love to her, though she was probably not more than thirty years old.

Behind Drexell's car, an anonymous-looking Plymouth, loomed buildings vacated by their occupants. Now and then Drexell noticed the curtains shift in the windows as the Volpos—the border guards —peered out.

Now the woman emerged from the customs house and strode over to the car. His passport was stamped; he was now cleared for entry into East Berlin. His visa gave him the right to stay in the city for twenty-four hours, though he would not have to avail himself of all that time—not if everything worked as he hoped.

In spite of his years, he was as vigorous as a man two decades younger. Several consecutive sleepless nights and a transatlantic crossing had tired him but had scarcely sapped his strength. The only time he would begin to fade was when boredom set in, when there was nothing for him to do but settle back and wait.

But this was not such a time. He had an appointment to keep, an appointment so vital that in the absence of Triad's other members, he'd left Washington to come here on a moment's notice.

He had been in East Berlin before, that time to help plan a secret tunnel bored underneath the Wall from the west which would serve as a listening post and an escape route. He was under no illusion now that he wasn't known to the East German security people.

From the instant he pulled out of the security zone, as the buffer area around the Wall was called, he realized he was being followed. It would not do to have his tail—a man with a wire-thin mustache and a narrow chin who drove a pale blue VW—be present when he kept his appointment.

It had not been his idea to come to East Berlin to meet Maxim Kolnikov, whom Triad had code-named Mr. Clean in honor of his bald and shiny scalp. It was entirely Kolnikov's decision, announced in an urgent coded message cabled to an office that served as a Triad drop in Geneva. The message had arrived only twenty-four hours before, giving Drexell no opportunity to see if alternative arrangements in safer precincts could not be made. No explanation as to the choice of East Berlin for a meeting had been appended to the message.

Drexell soon found a parking space for the Plymouth, something much easier to do in this part of the city than in the west where the traffic was far heavier. He left it conspicuously on Karl Marx Allee. This was one of the oldest parts of Berlin, having escaped the ravages of Allied bombing toward the end of World War Two.

A minute later the VW pulled up and his tail parked. With a casualness of step that belied his purpose, the man began to follow him, always being sure to maintain half a block distance between them.

Drexell started back the way he'd driven, continuing onto Marx Engels Platz and along the Unter den Linden, the main boulevard in the eastern sector. To all the world he looked as if he were simply out for a stroll although this was obviously no day for a stroll, with cold drops of rain beginning to fall and the wind strong enough to shake the bare branches of the trees that gave the boulevard its name.

He walked and his tail walked. He had a couple of hours to kill and, after purchasing a copy of the English-language *Moscow News,* he slipped into a café and ordered a draft of beer. One thing communism had not interfered with, he noted, was the German ability to brew excellent beer.

The world might well be going to hell, but the *Moscow News* gave little hint of it. Filled production quotas and new five-year programs for heavy industry dominated the front page. The recent Warsaw Pact meeting was mentioned only in passing, and while Iran was regarded as significant enough to warrant a long editorial—in which, inevitably, the United States was vehemently condemned—there was no indication that the Soviet Union was prepared to do anything about the crisis.

His tail remained outside the café, but Drexell could see him periodically through the window, nervous and cold and looking rather unhappy with the way his assignment was developing.

At nearly half-past one, Drexell walked from the café, leaving behind the copy of the *Moscow News,* and proceeded farther up the Unter den Linden. His pace was somewhat accelerated now that he had started on the business of shaking his tail.

In recent years he'd been in the field like this only rarely. But for all the administrative work he was saddled with, he'd not forgotten the tricks of a trade mastered more than thirty-five years before. Even in a half-empty department store, he managed to leave his trail standing in an aisle of perfumes, looking vastly bewildered.

He now found a tram that would take him far from his destination just in case there was a second tail shadowing him. It was sometimes a practice of intelligence services to use one tail as a decoy to hide the presence of a second.

Over an hour was exhausted in losing someone who might not have been there in the first place. Eventually Drexell reached his destination: the Pergamon Museum.

He found Kolnikov waiting in front of the Market Gate of Miletus. The Russian was pretending to be absorbed in the study of the ancient gate, which was one of the principal attractions of the Pergamon.

As Drexell came up beside him, Kolnikov registered his presence with a slight nod but allowed several moments to pass before he spoke.

"I didn't think you were coming."

"I'm precisely on time."

"Yes, I know. But I still did not think you were coming."

Kolnikov was now a colonel in the GRU—Soviet military intelligence. Being acquisitive by nature and inclined to envision a rosy future as a defector in the West, he'd offered his services to Triad almost two years before, during the Moroccan crisis. At the time, he'd been posing as a trade representative, though his actual mission involved stirring up leftist insurgents throughout North Africa.

Kolnikov's plan of betrayal was meant to be executed in two steps. In step one the idea was to become rich, trading secrets for money and gold, most of it to be deposited for him in a numbered account in Zurich. In step two he would—when the moment was ripe, but not too ripe—defect so that he could take advantage of all his accumulated wealth.

The information he'd supplied to Triad about Soviet intentions in Morocco and Tunisia, and later about their intentions in the Balkans and in the violent dispute between Venezuela and Guyana, had been invaluable. The price that Triad had been compelled to pay was, understandably, very high. And not only in money which, after all, was contributed unwittingly by the American taxpayer. Once, to allay his fears that his superior had caught onto him, Drexell had had to order the superior assassinated. It was against practically all the rules of intelligence operations (unwritten though they might be) to go around killing off your opposite numbers. To do that invited a futile, and very bloody, underground war that accomplished nothing. But in this case, Kolnikov was too important an asset to risk losing. Fortunately, the assassination carried out by Lisker was so consummately engineered that American involvement in it was concealed.

It occurred to Drexell that the only reason Kolnikov would have summoned him here was because he again felt in danger. Only desperation would have led him to take such a risk.

They began to walk in the direction of an adjacent hall filled with stark, monumental Sumerian artifacts. A guard observed them with indifference. Out of uniform, with a fur hat to protect his bald head from the drafts, Kolnikov did not excite any attention. Nor did Drexell. They could have been two businessmen with an occasional interest in the history of the ancient Near East.

"It is time I go over," Kolnikov said, his voice barely a whisper.

This was what Drexell had been afraid he would say. "Why? What's happened? There was nothing in your last report to indicate anything was the matter."

"Then, I didn't know. Now I do. I have received word that at any moment I am to be called back to Moscow and there placed in custody. I will, of course, be shot."

"Have you been able to verify this information?"

Kolnikov shook his head. "If I did anything like that, I would only make trouble for the people who've alerted me."

"So it might not be true. Your position might be just as secure as it was a few months ago."

"Anything is possible, but a warning like this you don't ignore."

"Certainly not." Drexell understood the importance of reassuring the man. "But it would be senseless to act precipitately if it turned out that the information was baseless."

His real concern was not Kolnikov's well-being as much as the prospect of losing Triad's highest-placed agent, particularly at a time when he needed to know what exactly the Soviet Union meant to do in Iran. On the other hand, if it was true that Kolnikov's life was in peril, then his usefulness as an agent had come to an end and arrangements would have to be made to get him out. Under torture, Kolnikov might confess his involvement with Triad and in that way expose other Triad operations and agents to danger.

Drexell tried to draw the Russian away from the subject of his own safety to the one that was uppermost in his mind.

"Have you heard anything about the Warsaw Pact meeting?"

"Rumors, shreds of information, not very much. Since my posting here, I have had little contact with those who plan operations in Moscow. What is happening in Tashkent and the Transcaucasus I can only speculate on. If you want my personal opinion, it is that there definitely will be an invasion. But that doesn't help you."

Even in the best of circumstances Maxim Kolnikov could look melancholic with his peasant face set in an expression of permanent dismay, but today he was especially morose. Contemplation of his imminent demise at the hands of the KGB, which was never on the best terms with its military counterpart, could hardly be expected to improve his disposition.

"Is there any way you could find out what will happen in Iran?"

Kolnikov's bushy eyebrows shot up. Right away he sensed the meaning behind Drexell's words. "You're telling me you will decline to help me unless I first obtain for you this information?"

Drexell was bluffing. For the security of Triad, he would have to get Mr. Clean to safety in the West—if the situation was as grave as Kolnikov seemed to believe it was. But since he was clearly a very desperate man, it was possible he might agree to undertake even greater risks than those he was now running if he thought that this was the only way he could secure help.

But all Drexell said now was, "What happens in Iran is the most crucial matter we have to deal with right now. I want to help you, but you have to get us this information . . ."

"What are you saying?" He'd gotten so upset that he let his voice rise loud enough to attract the notice of one of the guards. Drexell gave him a look sufficiently stern to quiet him. "Haven't I done enough for you already? In Morocco, in Venezuela? Have you forgotten so soon?"

"I haven't forgotten. Not at all. You have close to a million dollars sitting in an account in Zurich. And more is added every month. That alone should convince you we haven't suffered a lapse of memory."

"But I can't get at it," he said unhappily.

"By your own volition. You were the one who proposed the arrangement and the disbursement of funds. Now you're the one who has the problem with memory."

Kolnikov was staring into the stone face of some long-dead Persian potentate. "So what would you have me do? Acquire the war plan of the Red Army for the invasion of Iran?"

"As much of it as you can get."

Kolnikov continued to fix his eyes on the bust. He didn't seem to want to look at Drexell. "And then if I do this, you will get me out?"

"Immediately. When you have the plan, we'll have you—and the plan—on the other side in a matter of hours. I assure you that Triad will do everything it can to have you free and enjoying that million dollars. And I'll make it even more attractive for you. If you can get us that plan, we'll throw in another quarter of a million."

"Half a million."

Drexell hesitated, unsure he could obtain authorization for such a large expenditure. Even the smaller amount was going to cause him difficulty. "All right, half a million extra."

For the first time since they'd met, a look of satisfaction came over the Russian's face. Turning away from Drexell, he said, "I will be in touch with you by the usual channels."

"When can I expect to hear from you?"

"Forty-eight hours from now I shall let you know of my progress."

"And if I don't hear from you?"

"Then you may safely assume I am either in Lubyanka or dead."

11

APRIL 12
TEHERAN

The truck, loaded with a ton and a half of Semptex, left the garage where it had been loaded and headed along the Tarasht Highway in the direction of the prison. The driver of the truck, an intense-looking young man barely past his twentieth birthday, drove at breakneck speed, slowing only when a roadblock loomed ahead. Concealing the high explosive was a mountain of garbage which emitted a fierce stench. The soldiers manning the roadblocks were disinclined to undertake an exhaustive search and invariably waved the truck on.

The driver, whose name was Abolhasan, was Muhammed Arif's brother-in-law. Until the revolution a week ago, he'd been employed as a garbage collector. But now the garbage lay uncollected since no one in authority had seen fit to delegate the responsibility for picking it up.

It had not been Abolhasan who'd loaded on the Semptex and so he had no reason to believe that there was anything but garbage in back; to the soldiers who stopped him along the way he appeared perfectly innocent because, in a fundamental sense, he was.

Several miles away, in the north of the city, not far from Argentine Square, Arif was waiting in a maroon Citroën with Zoccola on one side of him and Lisker, in the driver's seat, on the other.

They would wait until twenty of ten at night, by which time Abolhasan should have reached a point two blocks away from the Khomiteh Mushtarak. Sitting behind them in a Buick were four of Muhammed Arif's friends, men who in any city in the world would be classified as criminals. Their faces were scarred, and there was a strange and menacing glint in their eyes. Unlike Arif's unwitting brother-in-law, they knew exactly what they were up to; three of them had been confined in the Khomiteh and they could not have been happier to see it destroyed and its inmates freed.

Zoccola was nowhere as confident as Arif appeared to be that this operation would succeed. Although Lisker had planned it with a military precision that marked every enterprise he embarked upon, so much depended on chance that Zoccola was sure something would go wrong.

Lisker's plan called for the truck to plow straight into the prison, detonating on impact as soon as it struck the gates. Then he and Zoccola would proceed into the courtyard and begin the search for Hahn while Arif kept the car motor running. At the same time, the second team would initiate a diversionary attack on the rear walls. Lisker believed that, with the chaos ensuing from the explosion, they'd be able to get in, find Hahn from among the thousands of other prisoners, and get out with him before anyone caught on to what was happening. Zoccola had gone along with him, but he remained dubious as to the prospects for success.

Often in operations like this, the very first step would go wrong, causing the whole plan to fail. So no one was more surprised than he to find that Abolhasan had left the truck exactly where he was supposed to. That was all that he'd been required to do: to park the truck and go home. Arif intended that Abolhasan retain his innocence.

For the most part, the streets were pitch dark though lights shone from some of the windows. While the curfew had been cut back, it was still in effect and by eleven o'clock patrols were free to shoot at will anyone found on the streets. Every so often the sound of muffled gunfire would reach the members of the rescue party, but it was so distant that no one paid any heed to it.

One of Arif's criminal friends took the wheel of the truck while the others proceeded on in the Citroën and Buick, one heading around to the rear of the prison while the other moved up behind the truck in the front.

There was no mistaking the location of the Khomiteh; it was brilliantly floodlit and surrounded by machine-gun-wielding soldiers.

The rumble of the garbage truck's motor was what first alerted the guards. However, there were always trucks and personnel carriers moving through the area and so initially they took little notice of it. But when it came into view they realized it was not a military vehicle at all. The smell of waste was so overpowering they understood at once that it was a garbage truck and took no action against it.

Both the Citroën and the Buick were equipped with CB radios so that there would be no problem coordinating the attack by the two teams.

It amazed Zoccola that Lisker should appear so unconcerned about the danger they faced.

"It's going too smoothly," Zoccola said. "I don't like it when it goes too smoothly."

Lisker thought this remark rather funny. "Would you like it better if some crazed militiamen put us under arrest right now? Would that make you happier?"

"All I said is that I don't like it. We're moving on this thing too quickly; we're relying on people we don't know, with no time to do our own reconnaissance..."

Hearing this, Arif said, "Not to worry, not to worry. You see, everything is fine!"

"Was I speaking to you?" Zoccola said.

Lisker was laughing quietly.

"I'm just saying we might have taken one more day and figured out another option."

"Jerry might be dead in another day," Lisker noted.

Lisker's face was expressionless, his blue eyes focused straight ahead, hands clasped firmly on the wheel. The PPKS Walther rested in his lap.

The direction the truck was taking could leave no doubt in the minds of the soldiers at the gate that it was headed directly for them. Lisker abruptly slowed the Citroën so that it wouldn't be caught up in the explosion.

They heard a burst of gunfire.

"Where the hell is that coming from?" Zoccola asked, instinctively lowering his head below the level of the dashboard.

The truck in front of them was accelerating.

"Must be going at seventy, seventy-five miles an hour," Lisker said. It was now within half a block of the prison gates.

Another burst of gunfire. The soldiers were scrambling, trying to get out of the vehicle's path. Some were firing as they did so, aiming for the tires, the windshield, and the engine. The truck continued to barrel straight ahead.

Now the driver flung open the door—the truck was less than a quarter of a block from the gates—and proceeded to leap out of the cab. His left leg caught on something, though, and he found himself being dragged along with the truck. His head smacked hard against the pavement, then his leg pulled free and he was hurled to the ground.

"Dammit, the son of a bitch waited too long!" Lisker said.

But when Zoccola looked at him, he noticed no change in Lisker's expression. Arif, squeezed between them, viewed the spectacle with indifference.

One of the front wheels visibly sagged, punctured by repeated rounds, but the damage wasn't enough to retard the forward movement of the truck. The windshield was blown apart and several of the rounds continued all the way through, causing the rear window to shatter as well.

The driver lay motionless in the street, a gathering pool of blood by his head. The truck bounded up on the pavement and struck the steel gates. There was a great clamor of shrieking metal and the gates heaved and gave way, but there was enough resistance to cause the truck to stop dead. Trapped among toppled steel supports and dislodged bricks that had collapsed along with the gates, it resembled a prehistoric animal in its death throes. Its wheels kept spinning uselessly, and the motor protested its paralysis.

The soldiers, surprised and relieved that no explosion had occurred, approached it cautiously. Garbage, fallen from the back of the truck, was strewn everywhere, lending a farcical touch to the event.

Unnoticed by the prison guards, Lisker drew the Citroën off onto a side street. Putting the motor in neutral, he took hold of the CB, switched it to channel 2, and contacted the leader of the second team:

"Are you in position? Over."

There was a burst of static, then the answer: "We are in position. Over."

"You may proceed. Over."

"Read you. Over and out."

A moment later Lisker switched the radio to channel 3 and then depressed a small toggle switch on the side of the instrument.

An enormous roar that sounded like the end of the world to Zoccola followed in less than a second as the Semptex detonated.

A vast sheet of blinding white light filled the sky, completely emptying the night of darkness. It seemed to expand as they watched, mesmerizing them.

"Let's move," Lisker said.

"May God go with you," Arif added, to which Lisker responded, "If you're not here when we get back, I'm going to search the whole damn country until I find you."

Arif seemed to be resigned to unkind words from strangers. "I know," he said. "I'll be here."

Here and there Lisker and Zoccola could see shadowy figures staggering about in the smoke. But otherwise there was just death. Charred corpses, many of them lacking limbs and heads, were scattered everywhere, some carried by the explosion far from where they'd been standing. It was not uncommon to spot a severed arm or leg lying among the debris, the wound bloodless because it had been cauterized by the intensity of the heat.

They set off at a run, Lisker with the Walther, Zoccola with a P-210, a single-action, self-loading, short-recoil pistol which held eight 9mm Parabellum rounds. He had secreted it into Teheran in his luggage. Made by a respected European firm, Schweizerische Industrie-Gesellschaft, it was an expensive piece of weaponry, retailing at about $1,500. Zoccola had only used it for practice before, never in a combat situation. It remained to be seen how well it would perform, but Zoccola was reasonably certain of its efficacy.

They'd now reached a point, a block from the prison, where they could view the extent of the damage the explosion had caused.

Not a great deal remained of the wall adjoining the gate on either side; it had fallen away in enormous chunks, resulting in the destruction of the pillbox mounted at the top. Of the truck almost nothing was left; it had virtually disintegrated. But the devastation had spread beyond the prison walls. Buildings on the other side of the street had been almost completely leveled by the blast and fires raged in their ruins. Smoke blanketed the area and to the previous stench of garbage was added an acrid odor composed partly of the ignited Semptex and partly of burning flesh.

With no time to meditate over the destruction they'd perpetrated, they proceeded in through the gap in the prison walls. Automatic fire cracked overhead, causing them to zigzag and occasionally drop to the ground, but it was sporadic and so badly targeted that it failed to stop their progress. From somewhere far in the distance a siren blared crazily.

Directly inside the prison, in the outer reaches of the courtyard, they discovered still more bodies. Those guards who'd survived were in many instances covered with blood. One man had fallen to the ground and was watching his intestines ooze out of a wound in his gut, not with horror, but with detached curiosity.

None of those still alive so much as looked at Lisker and Zoccola. They were simply too traumatized. Nor did they react to the rattle of gunfire coming from the rear of the prison where the diversionary attack had gotten under way.

In much better condition were the prisoners now piling out of their cells, unsure as to what had happened but obviously gratified to be released. Much of the prison was constructed of stone so solid that the explosion had done little more than scoop chunks out of it. But renegade soldiers, secretly sympathetic to the prisoners, had taken advantage of the spreading chaos to unlock the cells. The prisoners, finding themselves suddenly free, began to thread their way with shuffling gait down the dank, narrow corridors leading to the courtyard. As Lisker discovered, the generator must have cut out for there were no longer any lights to see by. In the confusion, guards were throwing off their uniforms, mingling with the prisoners, obviously fearing that they would be taken prisoner themselves by whoever was attacking them.

More and more prisoners emerged, some shielding their eyes against the floodlights that were still functioning along the part of the walls left intact. Most were emaciated, and they walked in a shuffle that suggested they were using muscles they hadn't called on for some time.

Lisker and Zoccola separated as they moved into the prison proper, looking for Hahn. They found the prison baffling in its construction, with successive subterranean levels, one darker and more cavernous than the next. Brackish water, smelling of urine and excrement, flowed along at their feet. Gunfire echoed back and forth, reverberating in the closed confines of the corridors so that it was impossible to determine its origin. For a few minutes Lisker and Zoccola were able to keep sight of each other, then Zoccola became submerged in the darkness of one vast cell whose black metal door, showing a mangled lock, had been thrown open. Lisker called out to him, heard no response, then spotted two oncoming soldiers training M-16's on him. Hoping only to slow them down, because he himself was moving too quickly to take accurate aim, he fired his Walther. The acoustics of the place made the gunshots sound like hand grenades going off. The soldiers flattened themselves against the wall, leaving Lisker time to escape. He kept running, growing wet with the water splashing him, until he found himself again in the courtyard.

Not all of the soldiers garrisoned here had been killed or incapacitated by the explosion. With every passing minute the danger increased. As the surviving guards recovered from the initial shock, they began to retaliate.

There was no telling from what part of the prison they'd come from, but all at once Lisker spotted three soldiers armed with machine guns which they sighted on the mass of prisoners. Taking up positions close by the ruptured gate, they opened fire.

There was a great cry that filled the air, a cry that welled up from hundreds of throats, as the gunfire tore into them. With so many prisoners in the yard, there was little room for movement. A score of them, Lisker guessed, must have been mowed down in the initial fusillade.

While he was temporarily out of the line of fire, he realized that he would not be safe for long. He feared that he might lose Zoccola and be forced to flee alone—and without ever knowing what had happened to Hahn.

Just then a shot was fired close enough to singe his ear. Without a moment's hesitation, he dropped, whipped about, and, sighting the opposition out of the corner of his eye, fired the PPKS Walther twice. The guard lurched to the side and then vanished in the throngs of prisoners.

Gunfire was intensifying at the rear of the prison. Flares burst repeatedly above the prison walls and sirens wailed in bitter cacophony. It was sheer madness.

Boxed in by the crowd, Lisker could do nothing but allow himself to be swept along with it. Suddenly he spied Hahn. Zoccola was with him, gripping his arm to lend him support. They were still too far away for Lisker to make himself heard. The important thing now was to keep them in sight.

As far as he could tell, they were moving toward the jagged hole that the bomb had created in the front wall of the prison. Gunshots continued to ring out, and pandemonium ran like an electric current through the prisoners. Just visible outside was the turret of a Centurian tank being moved into position. The gun swiveled on its mount, then discharged.

Several people went down near the break in the wall, disappearing in a plume of smoke. The crowd opened up, and for a moment there was room to escape. Which was exactly what Lisker did.

With no idea of what had become of either Hahn or Zoccola, Lisker made his way through the collapsed gates of the prison and ran into the street. A number of others had managed to do the same. Tracer bullets followed them and felled a few more prisoners.

The Citroën was where he'd left it, the engine idling, exhaust pouring from its tailpipe. He threw open the door and slid himself inside. Already in the seat was Arif, who appeared vastly relieved to see him. Now Lisker realized that the back seat was occupied.

He turned, seeing Zoccola and Hahn. "Goddamn," he said, "where the hell did you two come from?"

Without waiting for a reply, he released the emergency brake and shot the Citroën out into the street.

ATTACK ON TEHERAN JAIL BLAMED ON ISLAMIC TERRORISTS

TEHERAN, April 12 (Reuters)—A fast-moving truck, armed with more than a ton of powerful explosives, penetrated the compound of the notorious Khomiteh Mushtarak prison here last night, destroying much of the surrounding walls and killing at least 25. The prison, packed with several hundred political prisoners, was nominally under the control of a dissident faction of the Iranian army. The attack, which was blamed on Islamic fanatics that have regularly used suicide trucks to strike military bases and sensitive political installations, came just after the imposition of the curfew at eleven o'clock, Teheran time.

After the blast, sources here say, many of the prisoners attempted to escape in the confusion. Soldiers, armed with automatic weapons and backed by at least two tanks, halted the mass escape by directing heavy fire against the prisoners. There are no official estimates of casualties among the prisoners, but informed sources believe they may be as high as 50 dead and many more seriously wounded. There are reports that several prisoners did succeed in escaping and troops stationed in the capital have been put on alert in an effort to round them up.

12

APRIL 13
QUM, IRAN

There was on Rashid Nasreddin's forehead a prominent knob, red and smooth as a slab of polished wood. While it resembled a bump that one might sustain in an injury, it had actually developed because of the Iranian president's religious devotion. Five times a day, in accordance with Moslem tradition, he would bow down in the direction of Mecca and pray. With his head continuously pressed to the ground day after day, month after month, year after year, the knob had appeared and begun to grow. Nasreddin didn't mind; he considered the blemish an honor.

Others, like Bani-Sadr, who'd been entrusted with running the ship of state in the early days of the Ayatollah Khomeini's regime, had not been so fervently religious and as a result had lost their power—and sometimes their lives. Nasreddin had never been under any illusion as to where the real power in his country lay: with the Grand Ayatollahs of the holy city, who'd obeyed the Ayatollah Khomeini during his life and attempted to follow his precepts now that he was gone. The Grand Ayatollahs governed by committee, deliberating in secret council and then handing down their decisions to the government of Nasreddin, which in turn executed them. The government, with all its panoply of ministers and bureaucrats, was, of course, the political equivalent of a Potemkin village, a stage play where all the actors, Nasreddin in particular, recited lines written for them well in advance.

But because the policy views of Nasreddin and the mullahs usually coincided, he had no objection to this arrangement. In fact, he appreciated the fact that the responsibility for making the hard decisions was left to someone else.

Although physically he gave the appearance of being in command, he really was a very frightened man. He'd been chosen to serve as head of state because he was malleable; there was little likelihood that he would embarrass the fundamentalist leaders by suddenly declaring his opposition to them.

Driven into exile by the revolution of Colonel Shastri, Nasreddin had become the mullahs' symbol of legitimacy. Therefore, his life, which no one had previously placed a very high value on, was now considered worth saving. Disguised, in one humiliating instance as a peasant woman, he was brought out of the besieged capital by Revolutionary Guards and transported clandestinely from one village to another until he was finally in territory controlled by forces loyal to the mullahs.

The morning of April 13 found Rashid Nasreddin in his new presidential office in Qum. The windows to this office looked out on one of the largest mosques in this city of mosques; in the sunlight its white facade, edged with lime green, made for a dazzling sight.

Aside from issuing proclamations calling for the overthrow of Shastri, there was little for Nasreddin to do in Qum. This was truly the political and spiritual center of the country and he was out of his element here. He longed for Teheran, but going back there would mean the agony of interrogation and a brutal end at the hands of Shastri's firing squads.

Yet he recognized how important it was for him to remain here, to continue to broadcast over the Voice of the Islamic Republic. While his speeches had hinted at the necessity for calling on Soviet support to keep him and his fundamentalist backers in power, he had absolutely no intention of actually going ahead and requesting the Kremlin's aid. He firmly believed that it was well within the capacity of the Revolutionary Guards, as well as those army and air force units loyal to his government, to quell Shastri's rebellion.

It had been the Ayatollah's conviction that the Iranian people could defend themselves against all outside forces—communists as well as imperialists and Zionists. To summon the Red Army would be a confession of weakness, evidence of lack of faith.

In comparison with the threat that Iraq had presented, the one posed by Shastri was relatively inconsequential. Most of Nasreddin's military analysts were convinced that, in a few months' time, the status quo would be restored, Teheran would once again be theirs, and the only decision left to Shastri would be whether or not to wear a blindfold at his execution.

The problem was with the Ayatollah Ghafferi, the man who now had assumed Khomeini's place as the ruling religious authority of the country, the man who wished to become the Velayat-e-Faqih—the supreme theological leader. He was the one who commanded the majority of the Grand Ayatollahs to support the introduction of Russian forces. While he contended that the Soviets were necessary to protect the integrity of the state and prevent it from falling into the corrupt hands of Shastri (who was, according to Ghafferi, nothing more than a puppet of the United States), Nasreddin had only lately begun to suspect that his true motive lay elsewhere. It was just possible that Ghafferi had been a Soviet sympathizer from the very beginning of the revolution in 1979 or, worse, that he was a Soviet agent planted long ago in Khomeini's entourage. For years he'd been building up a base of support among the 180,000 mullahs who ruled in Iran. Now he was calling in his debts.

Restless, Nasreddin refused to stay any longer in his office. The high-pitched, ululating voice of the muezzin outside his window momentarily disrupted his train of thought. No matter how urgent the situation, Nasreddin could never ignore the call to prayer. This morning he decided that he would walk across the street to the Friday

Mosque and say his prayers there, rather than pray in his office as he generally did.

The security surrounding the president was tight; any movement on his part precipitated an immediate mobilization of no less than twenty guards assigned to protect him. Mostly armed with AK-47's, they deployed themselves all the way from his office on the third floor, down the stairs, across the colonnaded walkway to the Friday Mosque, and inside as well.

A man in his late fifties, he walked nimbly, with a purposefulness he often didn't feel of late. Two aides, bearing classified documents in briefcases, accompanied him. Both were armed with revolvers, which he declined to carry, insisting that it was undignified for a head of state to appear armed in public. He was a president, he said, not some guerrilla leader who'd just come down from the mountains.

As he emerged from the colonnaded walkway onto the plaza that immediately adjoined it, he stooped down to unlace his shoes. His aides did the same. It was not permitted for anyone to enter a mosque with his shoes on.

In the instant that he switched his hand from his right shoe to his left, he saw the shadow of a running figure from the corner of his eye. It was so quick that he did not at once react to it. Glancing up, he found himself gazing into the eyes of a man wearing a checkered kefiyah which partly shielded his face.

He didn't even see the gun the man held, only realized it was there after the first shots rang out. He heard someone cry out, then understood that it was his voice, that he was hit.

There were more screams, not his own, and more gunshots. He staggered mindlessly.

He began to feel pain; it clawed at his entrails and reached into his heart like a grasping hand, grasping at him, tightening its hold until he could scarcely breathe.

He saw that he was on his knees and that there was a surprising amount of blood on the tiles, more all the time. Blood had soaked through his shirt and he could feel it oozing out of his lower back. I am dead, he thought, this is what it is like to die.

The sun looked as though it were darkening in the blue morning sky over Qum. About him was a circle of men, but their forms were indistinguishable; he felt hands on him, probing his wounds.

This is unnecessary, he wanted to say, it is too late.

But he could not get out the words. A spasm shot through him. He gasped once, his eyes, engorged with blood, bulged hideously in their sockets, and then Rashid Nasreddin was no more.

13

APRIL 14
SOUTH OF TEHERAN

Zoccola and Hahn were on their way to the holy city of Qum, now the capital of the territory controlled by the fundamentalists. Muhammed Arif was doing the driving, but he seemed less interested in the road up ahead, fraught with ever-changing perils, than in spinning the dial on his car radio. The radio included a short-wave band which picked up everything from air traffic to maritime stations. But it was a news broadcast Arif wanted, and he eventually found one. Whatever the announcer, a woman with a beautifully lilting voice, was saying in Farsi, it obviously held some importance for Arif, if the concentrated expression on his face was any indication. When the news was over, he translated for his two passengers.

"President Nasreddin has been shot to death by an unknown assailant who was cut down by security soldiers," he said.

"It's always an unknown assailant," Zoccola said. "It's better that way; you can make him out to be anything you want."

"Yes, this man, the mullahs say, was acting for Shastri."

"What else do they say?" Hahn asked.

"The ruling council of the mullahs has decided to appoint Seyyed Jalili as its new president."

Zoccola and Hahn looked at each other, but neither had seen this man mentioned in any of the documentation on Iran that they'd studied recently.

"Another figurehead, I'll bet," Zoccola commented.

"I know who this man is," said Arif. "For some time he served as a trade representative to the U.S.S.R."

That gave them some clue as to where Jalili's loyalties might lie. Arif continued:

"It seems that the ruling council, through the new president, has decided to invite into the country an advisory force of Soviet military personnel. They say this is necessary because of the threat that Shastri's people pose to the Islamic Republic."

Turning to the noon broadcast of the British Overseas Service, they learned that two Antonov-22 transport craft had already landed at a military airstrip outside of Qum, bringing in the first contingent of the purported "advisory force."

Both Hahn and Zoccola believed that Nasreddin's assassination had paved the way for the direct intervention of Soviet troops. From the conversation that Hahn had had with Farouk in prison, he knew that Nasreddin's murder had been planned well in advance. It was unfortunate that they couldn't have gotten to him before the attempt on his life took place. As the symbolic head of state, he would have proven an invaluable ally to the West—particularly because he'd earned his antiimperialist credentials. No doubt he'd been taken out because he opposed those elements in Qum that hoped for Soviet backing.

In a sense, with the arrival on Iranian soil of 250 Soviet advisers armed with light weapons and hand-held rockets (according to reports reaching the BBC), the invasion had already begun. It was just that it was being accomplished in stages, with a gradual buildup that would, several months down the road, conclude with a Soviet occupation of the entire country. This same kind of course had been taken by the Soviets in Syria where nearly 10,000 advisers and technicians, in addition to combat forces, were deployed for the purpose of thwarting Western influence in the Middle East. But in Iran larger stakes were involved, both for the Russians and the Americans.

"If President Turner doesn't act now," Hahn said, "he should be replaced."

Lisker, installed in the safe house in the capital, was still waiting for Shastri to provide the men and equipment necessary to cut off the overland access routes from the Soviet Union. But as of that morning, when Hahn and Zoccola had left Teheran, Shastri was still vacillating, uncertain that such an operation might not divert needed troops and supplies from the conflict with the Revolutionary Guards.

"The thing that none of them understand," Hahn said, "is that in a few weeks it won't matter who's got the upper hand—the army or the fundamentalists. It'll be irrelevant. All the shots will be called in Moscow—that is, if we don't move quickly."

For lack of a better alternative, Hahn and Zoccola had decided to make do with their original covers: Hahn would continue to pose as Syrian-French businessman Marcel Takim, while Zoccola would remain Bill Gerard, arms importer from Beirut.

The objective of their mission, undertaken at Drexell's request, was first to discover the extent of Soviet penetration—political as well as military—that had already taken place in Qum. If possible, they were to determine how vulnerable the holy city would be to a seizure by either Shastri's forces backed by U.S. troops, or by U.S. troops directly. A contingency plan had been devised at the Pentagon which called for the kidnapping of the mullahs and using them as leverage against the Russians. It was one of the more preposterous plans the Pentagon had come up with, however, and it was unlikely ever to be executed.

The second part of their mission was more difficult still. Drexell wished to know whether there was anyone in the ruling circles of Qum who was prepared to negotiate a settlement with the United States, even if it were to be done in secret, in exchange for arms or money or power—whatever was required. From the intelligence reports that Drexell had read about the late Iranian president, just before his death, Nasreddin had begun to have second thoughts about inviting the Soviets into his country. Had he lived, he might have been useful to Triad as an anti-American and a fundamentalist who nonetheless opposed the Soviet Union. But Nasreddin had been too weak, too vacillating, and he had never had either the power or the following that Drexell felt would be optimum for his purposes. What he was hoping for was another Nasreddin, but a Nasreddin with influence and cunning who could advance Western aims in the area. Both Zoccola and Hahn were dubious as to the prospect of finding anyone like this.

Having proven his reliability to Triad during the prison breakout of two nights ago, Arif had now enthusiastically assumed the current assignment on its behalf, an assignment even more perilous than the first: taking Hahn and Zoccola straight into the heart of enemy territory.

Arif claimed that he was known in Qum and that he had many friends among the top echelon of the army that remained faithful to the cause of the mullahs. "I have sold them everything you can imagine—BM-27 multiple rocket launchers, 130mm guns, S-60 antiaircraft guns, combat vehicles, Malyutka rockets, M-16's . . ."

"A veritable smorgasbord," remarked Zoccola.

Arif gave him a quizzical glance. "What do you say?"

"Nothing. Go on."

"So they are friends of mine. And I will tell them that you are my friends. And they will accept you, no problem."

Like arms dealers the world over, Arif had no particular interest in ideology. He did not care one whit whether the fundamentalists or the army came out ahead or whether Iran fell under the American or the Russian sphere of influence. All that mattered was that he have a good market for his products and the opportunity to make an enormous profit. His side was the side that was paying him the most money. At the moment it was Triad. But because that could change tomorrow, Hahn and Zoccola were not prepared to place much trust in him.

They continued on the same highway, absorbing continual shocks and the clatter of pebbles ricocheting off the car, a Moskova which had the habit of making ominous clanking noises that grew louder as the journey continued. Arif, who seemed to have an access to as many different types of cars as he did weapons, had abandoned the Citroën used the night of the prison raid. He believed that where they were headed, a Russian car might provide them with safer passage than either an American or French one.

Qum lay approximately 100 miles to the south of the capital. The so-called Blue Line which separated the two clashing armies ran roughly along the Qareh Su River. The river was very close to Qum, not many miles to the north of the city.

Arif had warned his passengers that the Blue Line was more theory than fact, that just because the Blue Line followed the Qareh Su yesterday did not necessarily mean it did so today. Although an informal cease-fire was in effect—mostly for the purpose of allowing both sides to recoup and bring up reinforcements—it was only sporadically in force. Troops were constantly fighting or at least lobbing a few shells across the cease-fire line lest anyone become too complacent. Consequently, the Blue Line was always shifting back and forth.

Army checkpoints were to be found all along the major routes in and out of Teheran: on the Karaj Highway, on the Vanak Highway, and on the Tarasht Highway. It was impossible to proceed for more than fifteen minutes before stopping again to have documents examined anew.

Thirty miles or so north of the Qareh Su, though, they encountered no further checkpoints or roadblocks. Ahead of them black smoke belched from gun emplacements, but at such a great distance that there was no way for those in the Moskova to tell whose guns they were or whom they were firing at.

The road itself was gutted by shells that had fallen in previous days and there were long stretches where Arif had to abandon the road for the rock-strewn strip of land that ran along its shoulder. Here and there they'd spot a rusting tank or personnel carrier that had taken a direct hit. But Hahn noticed no corpses as he had on the way into the city several days before; somebody had obviously seen fit to remove them, if only to conceal the number of dead.

What they found most disconcerting was that there seemed to be no military presence at all for miles on end. It was apparent that they'd entered a kind of no-man's-land. There was no doubt in any of their minds that they were being observed—probably by both sides—with high-powered binoculars. There was no other traffic on the road once they passed the final army checkpoint, leading Zoccola and Hahn to believe that no one else was foolish or demented enough to try to go from one side to the other right out in the open like this.

Looking for some sort of reassurance, Hahn turned to Arif and said, "You've come this way before, haven't you?"

Arif replied, "Yes, I did, but that was many days ago, and now everything has changed. So I know no more than you what to expect."

That was no reassurance at all.

The road ended without warning. It came to an abrupt halt at a roadblock constructed out of dead tanks and scrap metal cannibalized from other damaged military vehicles. A squadron of Revolutionary Guards, bristling with semi-automatics, materialized as if from out of nowhere. They were young and exceptionally nervous, and as soon as Arif applied the brakes to the Moskova, they raised their weapons as if they meant to fire. Several of them approached the car and began rapping on the windows until Arif lowered his. At that, one thrust a Makarov pistol through the opening, placing it within a few centimeters of Arif's head.

Seeing how resolute the Guards looked, Hahn grew afraid. "Looks like we're fucked," he muttered.

Zoccola nodded. "How lucky do you feel today?"

"Not very."

"Too bad. Neither do I."

The man with the Makarov, hearing their exchange but not comprehending it, glared at them.

Very cautiously, Arif reached into his jacket pocket and produced his papers. Zoccola and Hahn did the same.

The documents were taken by the one who seemed to be in charge of the roadblock, a bearded man with a livid scar that appeared to be quite recent. He stepped away from the Moskova and began to scrutinize the papers. His expression bewildered, he began shouting wildly to those under his command.

Both Zoccola and Hahn had the same thought—that here, twenty-five miles from Qum, there was no law other than the one these Revolutionary Guards decided to enforce. They could as easily execute them here and toss their bodies into the trackless desert as they could place them under arrest.

At last the officer returned to the car. "You are Muhammed Arif?" he demanded.

Arif acknowledged that he was.

"You have here a laissez-passe from the Ayatollah Ghafferi?" Arif nodded. "And these men, they are your friends?" He narrowed his eyes at Zoccola and Hahn, probably unable to understand how a man of Ghafferi's importance could have such men as friends.

"Yes, they are my very good friends," Arif assured him.

"And where do you go to?" the officer inquired.

Arif replied he was on his way to Qum. "We have business there."

"With the Ayatollah Ghafferi?"

"Yes, with the Ayatollah Ghafferi."

The officer deliberated for a moment longer as if there were something else he felt needed saying. What he finally said was, *"Allah akhbar*—God is great."

Arif quickly gave his assent to this declaration and, with a peremptory wave of his hand, the officer gave him permission to go ahead.

As soon as Arif put the car in motion the barrier of tanks, metal, and barbed wire was opened to let them through. Not once, however, did the Revolutionary Guards relax; their guns remained fixed on the Moskova for as long as it was within range.

Although there were other roadblocks established farther on in the direction of Qum, they were not stopped again. Somehow the information must have been passed along that the people in the Moskova were to be allowed through to the holy city.

At quarter past three, they reached the outskirts of Qum. Far in the distance, they could make out a jet coming in from the north. But as small as it was in the great expanse of sky, its shape was unmistakable. It was yet another Antonov-22 transport jet conveying still more Red Army advisers and guns into Iran.

"This is a great day for an invasion," Hahn said.

"Whose?" Zoccola asked, following the descent of the Antonov with his eyes. "Theirs or ours?"

14

APRIL 14
OVER THE ELBURZ MOUNTAINS

A Transcript of a conversation between Soviet pilots identified by code numbers 148, 230, and 755. All times are in Greenwich Mean Time.

2005: 148: Roger, course 60.
2008: 230: Course 100 in a climb to 9.
2009: 148: I am executing.
2010: 148: There it is. Course 100 at 9,000.
2011: 755: Roger. Repeat course.
2011: 148: Course 100 at 9. I'm executing.
2012: 230: What is your fuel?
2013: 148: Three and a half tons.
2014: 755: Course 70 in a climb to 9.
2014: 148: Should I turn on the weapons system? The target has turned. It is 90 degrees on my right.
2019: Yerevan Ground Control: 148, turn on weapons system.
2019: 148: I am executing. Course 210.
2020: 755: Roger. I see it visually and on radar.
2021: 148: Executing 20 right.
2021: 755: I have dropped my tanks. I am executing.

2022: 230: I see it. I'm locked onto target.
2023: 148: The pilot isn't responding to I.F.F.
2023: 755: It might be U.S. The target's course is 240.
2023: 148: Roger.
2024: 230: My fuel remainder is 3,100. I have enough speed.
2024: Yerevan Ground Control: What is the target's course, 148?
2024: 148: The same. 240. Azimuth 1,001 meters. I have it in sight.
2025: 755: I can still see it. I am closing in on the target. There are no A.N.O. burning. I'm certain it's an American reconnaissance.
2025: 230: I'm at 7,500 now and climbing.
2025: 755: Roger. Target is climbing to 10,000. Estimated speed 2,500 kph.
2025: 148: I am flying behind the target at a distance of 70. My Z.O. is lit.
2026: 755: I need to get closer to it. I am at about a distance of 50 kilometers and climbing.
2028: 148: What are instructions?
2028: Yerevan Ground Control: Can you get abeam the target?
2029: 148: It's traveling too fast for that.
2030: 755: I am falling behind. 80 kilometers. Target's altitude 11,500 and climbing.
2031: 230: Roger. I am flying behind at 130. I have visual contact. My Z.O. is lit. I am turning 45 to my left.
2033: 148: I am approaching again. 30 to target. On a course of 80. The wing tank indicators are lit.
2035: 230: I am executing left to a course of 160.
2038: 148: Course steady at 80. Distance to target 45. What am I to do now?
2039: Yerevan Ground Control: Switch to channel 5.
2040: 148: Executing. Channel 5. Altitude now 11.
2043: 755: Climbing to 11. Distance to target 140 and closing.
2047: 755: Executing. On a course of 240. What are my instructions?

2048: Yerevan Ground Control: Do you have the target in view?
2050: 755: Visual and radar contact, Roger.
2052: Yerevan Ground Control: Fuel remainder?
2053: 755: Fuel remainder 2,800. Course 270 now.
2054: 148: Roger. I have around 2,800 and have dropped my tanks. There are clouds below me, but I don't see any ahead. Distance to target 20.
2055: 755: I am in a right-hand turn. The clouds are below me too. I cannot determine the cloud base.
2057: 148: Z.G. Distance to target 12.
2058: 755: Z.G. Distance to target 40.
2059: 230: I am climbing to 11. Target is on my left at 45.
2101: Yerevan Ground Control: Execute launch, 148.
2101: 148: Roger. I am executing launch.
2101: Yerevan Ground Control: Execute launch, 755.
2101: 755: Roger. I am executing launch.
2102: 148: Target is hit.
2102: 755: Target is destroyed.
2102: 148: I am breaking off attack.

PENTAGON ADMITS DOWNING OF SPY PLANE
(Special to the New York Times)

WASHINGTON, April 15—A Pentagon spokesman announced today that a Lockheed SR-71A high-speed reconnaissance plane was shot down over Iranian territory at 1:32 A.M., Teheran time, by Soviet fighters. The two pilots on board the craft were presumed lost. The Pentagon spokesman, James Fischer, said that the reconnaissance plane had taken off on a routine overflight from a U.S. base in Anatolia, Turkey, when it was intercepted and fired upon. He said that the downing of the craft was "in violation of international law" and maintained that its presence over Iran was known to the authorities in Teheran and had their sanction. This was the first time that a high-level official in the administration has acknowledged that there was any military or diplomatic cooperation between the newly installed regime of Colonel Ibrahim Shastri and the United States. This would seem to confirm the impression of various Western diplomats that Shastri's provisional government is considering at least informal relations with the U.S. in view of a potential Soviet intervention in that country. So far, Moscow has remained quiet on the incident.

15

APRIL 16
TEHERAN

James Lisker, oblivious of the cold wind coming out of the mountains to the north, stood on the tarmac of Doshen Toppeh military air base and watched as the first C-130 Hercules transport plane made its landing. The plane was arriving from Oman where the United States had previously established a base for units of the Rapid Deployment Force.

The RDF, under a military command centered in Tampa, Florida, was formed, according to Defense Guidance, its five-year classified master plan, "to assure continued access to Persian Gulf oil and to prevent the Soviets from acquiring political-military control of the oil directly or through proxies."

While there were only 125 men in this first contingent, their arrival was of far more significance than their number would suggest. This marked the first time since the Ayatollah Khomeini had overthrown the Shah that the United States and Iran—at least a part of Iran—were cooperating on any level. Authorization for this airlift had been granted by the President less than twenty-four hours before in response to the introduction of a large Soviet advisory force into the holy city of Qum. And it had only been in the last twelve hours that the government of Colonel Shastri had publicly sanctioned any U.S. military presence.

From what Lisker had been told by Drexell, via encoded radio transmissions, a total of 4,000 paratroopers would be landed in the Teheran area in the next couple of days. There was no indication as to whether this force would be supplemented or remain at that level indefinitely.

Officially, the President would announce that the first contingents of paratroopers would be acting in the capacity of an advisory force and would not engage in any combat operations unless it was required for self-defense. In other words, the arrangement was intended to match the Soviets' move into Qum. Any effort on their part to conduct military operations would be matched by the Americans.

According to Drexell, though, the President had no intention of leaving these first contingents of U.S. troops in Iran simply as a passive tripwire to heighten the prospective risks in the event that the Soviets began moving some of their available twenty-four divisions south into Iran. The general situation in the area was so volatile that as soon as word got out that the Americans were in Iran, anti-American demonstrations were bound to erupt throughout the Arab world. It was thus necessary for the U.S. to use these forces as soon as possible.

That very same night Lisker was to confer with Brigadier General Hal Sunderland, whom he'd encountered twice before, in Saigon during the height of the Tet offensive, and again in Washington eight years later at an armed forces subcommittee hearing. Of the 1,000 paratroopers that would be landing tonight, 400 would accompany Lisker to the north and begin the task of closing down the overland access routes—especially the rail lines—that the Russians would presumably use in addition to the Antonov fleet of transport carriers.

Sunderland was a confident and unorthodox military man. He was built like a linebacker and had a face that looked as though it had been worked into place by a blacksmith on a bad day. Upon debarking from the first C-130, he quickly greeted his Iranian counterparts and made his way across the tarmac to Lisker, whom he'd quickly spotted.

Wasting no time, Lisker conducted him inside one of the

barracks where, on a gray steel table, he unfurled a topographical map, drawn up from surveys and satellite recon photos, that showed the whole of the Soviet-Iranian border area.

"We have approximately a dozen surface arteries—roads and rail lines," Lisker began. "Of these, there are five roads over the Elburz Mountains to Teheran and Qazvin that have to cross bridges over precipitous faults or go through narrow gorges. The intelligence we've received so far indicates that the Russians are so concerned we'll knock these roads out they've taken an inventory of all their draft animals—horses, camels, donkeys, and mules—in case they have to use them to make the crossings."

"I'd like to see that," Sunderland said. "A whole Red Army division on camelback. Make a good picture, don't you think?"

Lisker nodded and continued. "Three of those roads, unfortunately, lie in territory now controlled by the mullahs. To get to them we'd have to do battle with Revolutionary Guards. The other two are more easily accessible, and I suggest we take those two out first. Now, if you'll look here—" He was pointing down from the Elburz chain toward the Zagros Mountains in the south. "Here is the only rail line running from the Caspian Sea to Teheran. While much of the line is in the control of the mullahs, I think it's vital that we take it out, because if the Soviets try for a drive on Teheran, that's the line they'll use. They'd love to seize the capital and then turn it over to the mullahs. It would be a big coup for them and deprive us of an important base. Only Red Army troops have the power to wrest the capital from Shastri's forces at the moment. If the Revolutionary Guards could have, they'd have done it before now."

"I agree with your assessment," said Sunderland. "Can we accomplish this by air?"

"Absolutely. There are some parts, though, that aren't as easily observable from the air as in the lowlands near the capital. For the less visible areas we might need to authorize ground forces—small parties of saboteurs—to go in and cripple the line directly."

"No problem there."

"Finally, we have the northwest—Iranian Azerbaidjan—where a single road crosses from Jolfa on the Soviet side to Tabriz in Iran. If we strike by air at Km 22 on this road, right where the Daradis Gorge begins, we can successfully choke off access. Place explosives in the right places and we can doubly insure it's blocked by creating landslides."

"I like the sound of that. Is the Jolfa-Tabriz road Shastri's or the enemy's?"

"Mostly the enemy's, I'm afraid."

"Shit. But we'll manage somehow. If we can't defeat the Revolutionary Guards, what chance do we have against the Red fucking Army? Tell me, when do we start on all this?"

"How does tomorrow sound to you?" Lisker asked.

"Tomorrow suits me just fine."

THE DEBUT OF THE BLACKJACK

New Soviet Fighter Poses A Threat To The West

In the midst of the turbulent events of last week in Iran, even many military analysts overlooked the premiere appearance of a new Soviet fighter, the Blackjack bomber, a swept-wing aircraft with a combat range of 4,550 miles. According to senior Pentagon officials, at least three Blackjacks were involved in bringing down a Lockheed SR-71A reconnaissance plane, which up until now has been regarded as the fastest military aircraft in the world, its maximum speed of 1,980 miles per hour marking a record. When it was shot down over Iranian territory with two pilots on board, Pentagon analysts were baffled at first since they believed the SR-71A would have easily outdistanced any Soviet fighters sent up to intercept it. It was only later, when it became known that Blackjacks were used, that the U.S. military began to understand the potential threat they were confronting. The Blackjack, according to a Defense Department aide who spoke to *Time* under the condition that his name not be used, "is armed with air-launched cruise missiles and is faster than our B-1B. While we've long known about it—the prototype was developed in the early part of this decade—we've never seen it in action before. There's no telling what will happen in Iran, but I'll say one thing for sure: the use of Blackjacks against an American plane means that the Russians now believe they have superiority in the air. It doesn't take much imagination to figure out the implications of that one."

—*Time*, week of April 21

16

APRIL 17
BERLIN

The call came at half-past seven. Drexell had fallen asleep and his first thought was that the jangling phone belonged in his dream. It took him several moments before he understood that the phone was real and so was the call, which was the one he had been waiting for.

"The Metropol Hotel?" the caller said. "Do you know it?"

Drexell said that he did.

"Be at the restaurant there at ten tonight."

Drexell was unable to identify the voice on the other end, but he assumed that it was a cutout Kolnikov was using to protect himself.

"There will be a piano player there," the caller went on. "Are you familiar with 'The Way We Were'?"

"I know it."

"Good. If you hear it, you will know that everything is going well. Please leave the restaurant when you hear this song and go to the lobby. Pretend to use the rest room. Return to your table after five minutes' time. Is that understood?"

"Yes, it is."

"If some problem develops, the piano player will play

'A Ghost of a Chance.' You know this?"

It was an old ballad and Drexell knew it well.

"If you hear this song, then you leave the hotel immediately and return to the western sector."

That said, the caller hung up.

True to his promise, Mr. Clean had contacted him on the thirteenth, within the forty-eight-hour deadline they'd agreed on at their meeting in the Pergamon Museum.

Drexell had been disappointed over the delay; it meant that he had no choice but to remain on in Berlin even as the crisis in Iran worsened. The President wanted him back in Washington, probably because he distrusted the advice given him by his cabinet members and military experts, but Drexell maintained that his presence in Berlin was absolutely necessary and that he'd get back as soon as he could. He didn't wish to say why he had to stay in Berlin; the transaction with Kolnikov, involving as it did the top-secret war plans the Kremlin had drawn up for Iran, could not be discussed with anyone, even the Chief Executive. Not that Drexell believed for a moment that Turner would leak the information deliberately, but there was always the possibility he'd drop a word to his chief of staff, Morse Peckum. There could be a breach of security anywhere; one slipup and Kolnikov could be lost—and so too would the war plans.

All he had been able to do over the last few days was to run Triad from his hotel room, in this instance, a tidy, white room in the moderately priced Bremen.

If he was frustrated at being stuck in a city he did not especially care for to wait for a telephone call that might never come, he at least could derive some satisfaction from the fact that the President had at last agreed to dispatch U.S. troops to Iran. So far it was just a token force, but if the situation deteriorated, as he strongly suspected it would, more troops would be forthcoming. Drexell was only grateful that it was the President, and not him, who had to contend with Congress and the War Powers Act.

Now he realized that he might be walking into a trap, that by going back into East Berlin and appearing at the Metropol, he might be placing himself in jeopardy. But while he could always have sent in an intermediary, he was determined to go himself. For one thing, Kolnikov might refuse to deal with anyone else; for another, Drexell was not about to avoid a mission simply because it could be dangerous. That had never been his style and he did not believe that either his age or his seniority gave him any right to change now.

He made a short phone call to a Triad operative who went by the name of Helmut. "I have heard from my good friend Karl," he said. "I'm meeting him at the Metropol at ten. Have your people ready."

Helmut said that his people would be at Drexell's disposal.

Karl was the code name Drexell had used to identify Kolnikov. Helmut didn't know who Karl was or why he was important. All that he'd been told was that he was someone who might have to be smuggled out of East Berlin at a moment's notice. Drexell stressed that Karl was to be given top priority in getting across. Helmut and Drexell had worked on the secret tunnel under the Wall together, and from time to time they had also gotten refugees out in the trunks of cars, in hot air balloons, in small motor launches, and occasionally on foot. To Helmut, extricating one more refugee or defector was all in a day's work.

For all Drexell knew at the moment, though, Kolnikov might have decided that he was safe for the time being and had given up the idea of defecting. Whatever Kolnikov decided, Drexell hoped that he'd have the war documents. That was the only thing that finally mattered.

Driving his Plymouth, he didn't get to Checkpoint Charlie until nine; he had no special interest in hanging around in the east. He just wanted to get in and get out. Unlike the first time he crossed over six days before, the inspection of his passport consumed an inordinate amount of time. Though he presented a calm outward appearance, the delay made him apprehensive, as he supposed it was meant to. There was nothing to stop the customs officers from keeping him waiting past ten o'clock. From previous experience, he knew that if he should fail to turn up at the meeting place on time, the whole thing would be blown.

The border police, intimidating figures toting AK-47's, were clearly silhouetted in the harsh glow of lights near the Wall.

At half-past nine the customs man returned from the shed and handed back Drexell's passport.

"Enjoy your stay," he said.

That was something Drexell very much doubted he would do.

In the rear-view mirror he noticed the inevitable tail; he might have been disappointed had one failed to materialize. This one was driving a Fiat, perhaps a model made under contract in Russia.

The Metropol, on Friedrichstrasse, was one of the city's newer motels, designed to pick up a tourist trade accustomed to Hiltons and Intercontinentals in the West. What it mostly got were trade and sports delegations from Prague and Budapest, with an odd assortment of Europeans on their way to points east.

By quarter to ten Drexell was seated in the dimly lit, uncrowded restaurant one floor above the lobby. Just as the mysterious caller had said, a piano player was in attendance, rendering perfunctory versions of old standards. Drexell kept listening for "The Way We Were" or "Ghost of a Chance," but neither one had been played by the time his order came.

On the wall opposite him was a particularly lurid mural, with an assortment of men, women, and animals contorted in suspect positions: a strange sight to encounter in the usually puritanical context of a communist hotel.

There were too many waiters for the number of diners; they loitered in the darkness with the uneasy expressions of people who realize that their services are no longer needed.

Glancing out the window, Drexell had a view of Friedrichstrasse, which was eerily empty of traffic and pedestrians save for a couple, a soldier in uniform and a young woman who were embracing in the glow of a street lamp.

In the corners of the room, partially submerged in darkness, the other diners sat, talking low, their faces dimly perceived in the flicker of the candles on their tables. The clatter of silverware made the loudest sound. Which one of them, Drexell wondered, is watching me? And more important, which side is he on?

He lacked an appetite. It was all he could do to take a few bites of the chicken he'd ordered. His entire attention was fixed on the piano player, a tall, balding man in a tux, who seemed indifferent to the tunes that emerged from his instrument.

It was twenty past ten when he was finally able to identify one of the songs he'd been told to listen for.

It was "The Way We Were."

So far so good, he thought. He looked over to the piano player, but the man failed to meet his gaze. The title song from the Streisand-Redford film of several years ago seemed to inspire him no more than the previous numbers. Drexell waited a moment, then rose from the table and casually walked from the restaurant, proceeding down to the lobby where he assumed the rest rooms to be.

In spite of the care he took not to elicit attention, he still could not avoid scrutinizing the people he passed. It was his nature to regard life as a perpetual masquerade where no one was given to revealing his true feelings or motives. The ones he suspected the most were those who affected to open up to him; the more intimate the details they revealed, the more he discounted their veracity. Here, in the lobby of the Metropol, there was no such pretense. If every other person looked like an agent or an informer, that was probably because he was an agent or an informer.

He found the rest room, lingered there for the mandatory five minutes, then returned to the restaurant.

The table was just as he left it, with the half-finished chicken and the drained glass of Burgundy. The piano player was improvising a variation of "Long Ago and Far Away."

He sat down, his eyes searching for something—anything—that might be out of place. Maybe, he thought, Kolnikov had decided the risk was still too high and had balked at the last moment.

Furtively he glanced underneath the table, but there was nothing there either.

What a goddamn waste, he thought. He called for the check and paid it, leaving an unreasonably large tip because he had to do something with all the extra East German money that had been forced on him in the currency exchange at the border, and departed. No one, he noticed, made any attempt to follow him.

It was chilly out. Drexell buttoned up his Burberry coat and thrust his hands in his pockets. It was then that he felt something buried deep in the right pocket. It was about the size and shape of a 35mm film canister. Microfilm.

He didn't dare remove it. Instead, he continued walking to where his car was parked.

There was no sign of Kolnikov. If the Russian intended to defect, this didn't seem to be the night he'd chosen to do it.

In any case, Drexell's primary concern was getting whatever was contained inside the canister back to West Berlin. He knew very well that he couldn't carry it in; he fully expected to be searched at the border. That was where Helmut's people came in. Prepared to smuggle a defector to the West, they were now only obliged to smuggle something that could be carried in a coat pocket.

There was one problem. Helmut's people, who Drexell knew by sight, were not anywhere nearby. They should have been there, waiting for him somewhere in the vicinity of the hotel, but the street was empty. Even the lone couple under the street lamp had vanished. He almost longed for the sight of a tail. The silence and emptiness oppressed him.

He couldn't wait; the longer he remained in East Berlin, the more he exposed himself to the danger of arrest. He resigned himself to bringing the microfilm across the border himself.

He drove directly to the checkpoint, watching all the while to see if there was anyone behind him, but no vehicle followed him.

Armed Volpos motioned him to stop well before he reached the Wall. Drexell had steeled himself for the inevitable encounter with these people, and so his manner betrayed none of his disquiet. The impression he meant to convey was one of a man from the West who'd gone to meet someone at the Metropol, perhaps a lady friend, and who'd left disappointed that that person hadn't shown up.

He naturally presumed that the officials at the checkpoint were well aware of his movements that evening.

One of the Volpos took hold of his passport and gave it a cursory examination, noting the visa issued just an hour and a half previously. "You will wait here, please," he said in English and went back into the shed. His companion, however, stayed put, eyeing Drexell from a distance.

About five minutes later, there was a disturbance off to his right, just out of his line of sight. There were running footsteps, shouts, the cry of "Halt!"

Then two figures appeared, racing in the direction of the Wall. What surprised Drexell was that they were both in uniform. Volpos. It seemed that they'd chosen tonight to try to escape.

Drexell knew that to go over the Wall at this strategic point was nearly impossible. Ever since the Wall had been constructed, the East German authorities had been making improvements on it, refining the technology of obstruction, until it was virtually impregnable. Lengths of pipe now lay across the top of the Wall so that even if someone managed to claw all the way up, he'd have little purchase at the top and be sure to slip off.

Either these Volpos had found a vulnerable point in the Wall or else they'd been discovered and rather than face arrest had decided to make a run for it.

One of the escapees still had his AK-47 with him; the other must have thrown it down. But the Volpo with the gun turned slowly and opened fire. Drexell heard a scream, then saw a body flung up into the air.

More Volpos emerged from the shed, their automatics brandished.

Windows in the deserted tenement building across the way from him on the eastern side were thrown open and other border policemen appeared in them, their guns protruding, as they sought to identify the source of trouble.

Now the unarmed Volpo began to clamber up the Wall; several bursts of automatic fire tore into him. He hung at a point midway up the structure for a moment, then toppled off. His friend, though, had not been hit and now, crouched low on the ground, was directing his fire at his pursuers.

The Volpo who'd been watching Drexell had begun to move toward the traitor. But before he could sight his gun he was cut down.

Drexell glanced up in the direction the shot had come from. He saw a movement in one of the windows in the tenement building.

Now, almost too late, he realized what was happening. This incident was being staged for his benefit. The lives lost were irrelevant so long as the microfilm was delivered to the West. Only one person could have arranged this escape attempt: Maxim Kolnikov.

He hesitated only a second longer, then turned the key in the ignition. The gunfire grew more heated. More shots rained down on the Volpos from the tenement.

Keeping his head low, Drexell gunned the Plymouth forward, gradually increasing the pressure on the gas. Just as he passed the checkpoint, the second would-be defector spun around and went down, his blood spattering the side of the Plymouth.

The rear window shattered as several rounds pierced it and glass fragments exploded throughout the interior, one catching Drexell in the back of the neck. He didn't realize he was wounded until he felt blood trickling under his shirt collar.

Gunfire was now directed at him from the front. The hood popped open and steam began pouring out, but the car remained functional. As Drexell accelerated to over seventy miles per hour, the side window directly to his rear came apart. He was hunched over so much he could scarcely see where he was headed.

Checkpoint Charlie loomed just ahead. The left rear tire went flat and the car bucked and sagged but kept on going. The din from all the rounds striking the chassis was like hail.

Then, abruptly, the firing ceased. Drexell was in West Berlin.

Two hours later, after the formalities with British and American intelligence officials were over, Drexell was back at the Bremen Hotel, the canister of microfilm safely in his coat pocket. He'd told the intelligence officials only that he'd panicked when gunfire had broken out and had simply bolted. The officials were canny enough to realize that he was not telling them the truth, and they would have liked to keep interrogating him had not a phone call come in from Washington insisting that he be released immediately. A stern note of protest from the Soviet representative to the four-power commission that administered the divided city went ignored. Ignored too was a demand by the East German authorites for the return of William Drexell.

All that he'd lost was a good car and a valid passport.

Not long after he'd gotten back to the Bremen, he received a phone call. This time he had no problem identifying the voice on the other end. Mr. Clean.

"Did you enjoy tonight's show?" he asked.

"I found it a little too melodramatic for my taste, but I appreciated the outcome. I presume you were the one who did the choreography."

"Not bad for something done at the last minute, no?" Kolnikov sounded buoyant, far more confident than he had the other day in the Pergamon.

"Not at all."

"So you still have the program?"

Drexell said that he had; Kolnikov was clearly referring to the microfilm.

"Only half the program is there. The other half will be forthcoming when I can get hold of it. In the meantime I expect my payment . . ."

"No problem. Half will be deposited—"

"Not half. The full amount."

The full amount was half a million. In essence, Kolnikov was asking for all the money before he'd delivered all the goods.

"Let me see what the first half of the program says. Then I'll contact you through the usual channels."

There was a long silence on the other end. At last Kolnikov said, "All right, that will be satisfactory."

"What about you? Are you in good health?"

"I seem to be. But I will let you know should my health suddenly deteriorate."

"Be sure and do that," Drexell said. He waited, but Kolnikov had nothing further to say. The line had gone dead.

17

APRIL 18–19
THE TEHERAN-DEZFUL RAILROAD

The first rays of sun glinted off the wings of the five A-6E Intruder low-level attack bombers as they proceeded over the city of Dezful. The bombers, all part of the 354th Tactical Fighter Wing of the United States Air Force, had been in the air since 0500 hours, when they had taken off from Doshen Toppeh air base outside Teheran. Their mission: to knock out the one rail line linking the capital to the Caspian Sea, thereby denying its use to the Red Army, should it decide to come in.

As the planes continued their sorties, dropping five-hundred-pound bombs guided by television and radar, anti-aircraft fire erupted all about the periphery of Dezful. Smoke cascading up from the bomb blasts almost completely shrouded the city. The planes dived in, sweeping down to avoid the fire directed from ZSU-23 and ZSU-57 self-propelled radar-guided guns.

To take out the guns, the Intruders made use of the TRAM (Target Recognition Attack Multisensor) system which relied on a turreted electro-optical/infrared capacity matched with laser-guided weapons. Harpoon active-seeker missiles soared through the air, speeding with dead certainty toward the guns, demolishing them long before anyone could move them to safety.

All of the Intruders returned safely to Doshen Toppeh where they were refueled and were back in the air again by 1108 hours, this time to pound the rail line farther north in the Elburz Mountains.

"A limited mission is being undertaken by units of the Iranian Air Force against the traitorous Jalili regime," Teheran radio announced ten minutes later. This was regarded as a joke by most of the listeners to the state-controlled radio station, since the only Iranian air force to speak of was the one the United States was supplying.

But because of the sensitive nature of the crisis, it was thought best not to make explicit reference to American involvement in the air strikes.

This time the Intruders were met, not just with self-propelled guns, but by heat-seeking SA-9 missiles.

The Intruders were designed to give the pilots in the two-seater craft an excellent view in all directions through a broad sliding canopy. At the same time, the navigator could keep control of all the navigation, radar, and attack systems that were now registering the threat posed by the missiles.

Hundreds of bombs began descending, blowing craters out of the mountains, mangling the railroad ties, obliterating stations, power lines, sidings, and any structures that happened to be in the vicinity of the tracks. A twenty-three-car train crawling north toward the border was struck by no less than three bombs, which blew up half the cars and irreparably damaged the rest. The pilots in the Intruders could see flames racing down the tracks for miles, fanning out into the trees and brush that grew nearby.

But antiaircraft fire came with increasing frequency. The SA-9 missiles (some, it was assumed, launched by Soviet crews assisting the fundamentalist troops) continued to come, and in such numbers that the Intruders kept having to alter their course to elude them. But then, at 1224 hours, a missile caught one of the craft in its tail, shearing it off. A split second later, the Intruder erupted into flames and plummeted into the Elburz Mountains.

Another missile raced in the direction of a second Intruder, struck it close to one of its turbojet engines. One of the pilots succeeded in ejecting himself just before it too spun out of control and went into a dive.

An hour and a half later the Voice of the Islamic Republic in Qum announced the capture of the pilot, Lieutenant Arnold Baxter of East Lansing, Michigan. He was reported to be in excellent health and unharmed except for a few minor abrasions. By the end of the day, he would make his appearance on television, appearing haggard and bewildered. His eyes blinking frantically under the glare of klieg lights, he was permitted only to speak a few words: "I am being treated well by my captors and I hope that they can forgive my actions this morning against the Islamic Republic." It was not clear whether he'd said these words on his own or had been forced to do so by the Revolutionary Guards who'd seized him.

Two other American bodies were located in the Elburz not far from the wreckage of their planes. One other was presumed dead, though his body was not recovered. The Qum regime announced that the bodies would be returned to representatives of the U.S. government, a gesture intended to underscore the fact that the Islamic Republic was now engaged in a war with the United States and would have to rely on Soviet assistance if it were to survive.

A statement issued by the State Department in Washington soon after Iran's initial announcement of Baxter's capture read as follows: "The State Department was informed just a short while ago that a U.S. Air Force officer, Lt. Arnold Baxter of the 354th Tactical Wing, was shot down and captured by hostile forces while flying a mission over Iran. A second plane, an A-6E Intruder, was also reported lost in the same combat mission. All other planes involved in the operation, which was successfully executed, returned safely to base. The mission conducted by the U.S. Air Force is consistent with fulfilling our current objectives in maintaining the stability and territorial integrity of Iran. Efforts are now under way to secure the return of Lt. Baxter and recover the bodies of the other officers lost today. The Government of the United States deeply regrets the loss of life and offers its sincere condolences to the families of the airmen concerned."

The statement was read at a special State Department

briefing and copies of it were distributed to the press. No questions were taken by the department spokesman.

Despite the embarrassment and political complications that U.S. participation in the bombings set off, Brigadier General Hal Sunderland was pleased. The rail line had been pulverized in so many places, with bridges taken out over the Qareh Su and Shur rivers, that it was, to all intents and purposes, useless for military or civilian transport in either direction.

With three roads over the Elburz Mountains choked off by sabotage—one more than Lisker thought possible—the crippling of the rail line insured a particularly difficult crossing for the Red Army. Only one major artery—in Iranian Azerbaidjan, in the northwest corner of the country—remained to be closed.

An air strike at Km 22, at the beginning of the Daradis Gorge, was ordered by Sunderland for 0430 hours the following morning. He also ordered a detachment of 200 Rangers to be dropped into the area at 0600 hours to sabotage whatever parts of the road the bombers had not been able to destroy.

Lisker offered to accompany the Ranger detachment although Sunderland argued that his presence was hardly necessary. "I could better use you here in Teheran," he insisted.

But Lisker was unmoved. "I'm tired of sitting in war rooms, following the fighting on tactical maps. The only way I'm ever going to get a feeling for what's happening out there is by going into the field."

As Sunderland held much the same view, he did not persist in trying to talk the Triad operative out of his decision.

"If something happens to you, it'll be my ass. You know that."

"You don't have to worry, General. I'll be back."

At midnight Lisker, using his microwave transceiver, radioed Drexell to keep him abreast of developments. He was connected to him through the communications facilities of the National Security Agency; consequently, he had no idea where Drexell was when the conversation was initiated.

"The war plans I referred to before have fallen into our hands," Drexell said without going into specifics. "We're still working on the translation, but so far this is what we've found."

He then proceeded to outline the Soviet military design for the conquest of Iran. It was to begin with an advance through northern Iran, over the Elburz, Qareh Dagh and Golul Dagh mountains, to the Teheran line. This would be followed in turn by the seizure of the city of Qazvin to the northwest of Teheran. As Qazvin was principally in the hands of Revolutionary Guards, this was not regarded as a problem. It was expected that Qazvin would open its gates for the Soviet troops.

Phase two of the war plan called for the Red Army to advance south through central Iran, securing Dezful at the southern base of the Zagros Mountains preparatory to a final thrust into the province of Khuzestan on the Persian Gulf where Iran's main oil and shipping facilities were situated.

The plan hypothesized that the trans-Iran rail line from Dezful to Teheran would still be in existence. "After today," Drexell said appreciatively, "I expect that the Kremlin's strategists are burning the midnight oil trying to come up with an alternative supply route."

There were certain reassuring details to be found in the plans: of the possible twenty-four divisions available for the invasion, half of them were at Category B, meaning they were between half and three-quarters strength; another quarter of them were at Category C, about one-quarter strength; and only a quarter were at Category A, full-strength with complete equipment. No matter how quickly the Soviet generals acted, they could not bring up all their divisions to Category A or B if the invasion were to be launched, as the plan specified, no later than April 20.

"The twentieth? That's the day after tomorrow," Lisker said.

"Exactly. I've informed the President. It's still possible that it might not come off. My source hasn't given up the whole plan so we still don't know what contingency plans the Soviets have drawn up. Somewhere there must be a scenario that resembles the situation we have now, with at least some U.S. forces on the ground and U.S. bombers in the air. That kind of deterrent force might convince them to stay on their side of the border. On the other hand, they might figure that they've gone this far already, so why not go all the way? Especially as the mullahs will start screaming bloody murder if the Soviets fail to move after all this."

"What was the President's reaction?"

"He said that he thinks he's doing all he can. Having already authorized the use of troops in Iran and mobilized the RDF, he's convinced that he now has to devote his attention to the political sphere. I can hardly get a minute with him; he's been on the phone consulting our allies, trying to put together a united front. He's particularly disturbed about reports that the Soviets are reinforcing troops and theater nuclear weapons close to the Fulda Gap."

The Fulda Gap, Lisker knew, lay on the East German border. NATO analysts long believed that in the event of an invasion of West Germany, Red Army forces would first strike through it. "Does he believe that the Soviets are opting for a horizontal escalation here?"

Horizontal escalation was the term used to denote a retaliatory action carried out in another region strategically equivalent to the one where the fighting had begun. Thus, American efforts to respond to a Soviet threat in Iran might be met, not necessarily with a Soviet drive on Iran, but rather with a heightening of tensions, and possibly an outright invasion, in Europe.

"He says that he's prepared for anything," Drexell replied. "Myself, I don't think we're going to see any actual fighting in Europe. Moscow's behaved fairly cautiously on this one—they're testing the waters, as it were—and they're not about to risk an all-out global escalation of hostilities at this juncture. My sense is that they'll confine any military action to Iran. We might see some moves on the part of the Syrians against Israel and Lebanon or some disturbances in North Africa and the Caribbean using surrogate forces. But if there's to be any confrontation with the Red Army, it'll come only in Iran."

Drexell was about to put an end to the conversation, but Lisker had one more question.

"In the war plans you have, does it say anything about the Soviet force bringing nuclear weapons in with them?"

Drexell hesitated before responding. "Well, in fact there is some indication here that any long-range bombers used in an invasion will be equipped with nuclear weapons."

"But their long-range aviation force is stationed in Europe and the Far East," Lisker said. "So the use of nuclear weapons would have to remain hypothetical at this stage."

Even Lisker, who was known for his sangfroid, did not want to contemplate a war that would get so far out of hand that nuclear weapons were employed. That would change the nature of the game so much that no one, either in the Pentagon or in the Kremlin, would know how to react.

"If we'd been speaking this morning, Jim, I'd say you were right. But both SIGNIT and IMINT received in Washington today leave no doubt that one of the three air armies available to the Soviets, the one based in the Ukraine, has been transferred to the Caucasus."

SIGNIT (signal intelligence, including communications and electronics) and IMINT (imagery, including radar and photointelligence) were regarded as the two most important sources of information for U.S. intelligence services. (It was in the third, HUMIT—human intelligence sources ranging from spies to newspaper clips—that the U.S. had been most deficient, and it was precisely that deficiency that Triad had been created to rectify.) So there could be no question that the long-range bombers had been moved. And because it was unlikely that the Soviets would deplete their air force in Europe so drastically unless the Kremlin thought it essential, the conclusion was obvious: Nuclear weapons were being made ready for the war in Iran.

When Lisker was silent for several moments, Drexell said, "No sense worrying about the implications of this right now. I suppose we'll have to cross that bridge when we come to it. Right now, let's just worry about taking out the Jolfa-Tabriz road. One thing at a time, okay?"

PRESIDENT DECLARES U.S. ROLE
IN IRAN "LIMITED"

CAMP DAVID, Md., April 19 (AP)—Speaking to reporters at the Camp David retreat, President Creighton Turner said that the role the United States was assuming in Iran was "limited to rendering assistance to the Shastri government until such time as it is able to function successfully on its own." Citing the Soviet threat to Iran, the President maintained that the United States did not wish to get drawn into "the quagmire of Iranian politics" that, since the death of the Ayatollah Khomeini three weeks ago, has turned into a virtual civil war between the Iranian army and Shiite fundamentalists.

"Both the rival factions in Iran," the President continued, "have an overriding interest in preventing a Soviet attack on their country. The United States and her allies appeal to all peoples in Iran, whatever their ideology or religion, to unite in the face of the monstrous threat that the Soviet Union presents to their country." In response to a question, the President said that he had, in accordance with the law, submitted to the Speaker of the House and the President pro tempore of the Senate a report pertaining to the introduction of U.S. military units under the War Powers Act. If Congress does not declare war or else extend the time limit, the act mandates that all troops must be withdrawn from the conflict within sixty days.

Excerpts from the President's April 19 news conference.

Q.: Mr. President, three aircraft, one a reconnaissance plane and the other two jet fighters, were shot down by the Soviets and their fundamentalist allies in the last few days. Are we going to see this happening with greater frequency? Do we have the technology to fight a war?

A: In any conflict you're going to see casualties and the loss of aircraft and tanks and what have you. There's no way to avoid it. I've seen statements by doomsayers asserting that the United States is inferior in the kind of weapons we have available in our arsenal. This has no basis in truth. Although there's always a need for improvement—and I'm sending a new emergency defense budget request to the Hill early next week—there's no question that the United States has the capacity and the will to defeat any aggressor. Next question?

Q.: Mr. President, from the events of recent days, it looks as though we might get into a situation where our forces are going to end up confronting Soviet troops. Isn't this paving the way for a third world war that could lead to a nuclear catastrophe?

A: While we have ample intelligence data revealing that the Red Army is prepared to launch a preemptive attack on Iran, the fact is that right now that attack hasn't come. We have repeatedly urged the Soviet Union by every channel available to us—and I myself have written several appeals to First Secretary Kadiyev—to show restraint. Believe me, I have no desire to see our boys fighting the Russians and I am as aware as anybody of the danger of such an eventuality occurring.

Q.: Excuse me, Mr. President, I'm not sure you understood the question.

A.: I understood it perfectly well.

Q.: What I meant was that if the Red Army does invade, the fact that our troops are already in Iran makes the situation that much riper for a direct confrontation. I don't think there's anybody in America who'd doubt that something like that could easily get out of hand and lead to a global conflict.

A.: Believe me, Jack [Remington of the *L.A. Times*], we are going to do our best to see that something like that doesn't happen. Terry [Cooper of the *Boston Globe*]?

Q.: Mr. President, isn't it possible that our actions in the last week or so, putting men at Shastri's disposal, knocking out the trans-Iran railroad, blowing up passes through the Elburz Mountains, won't be used as a pretext for a Soviet invasion? Aren't we going to create the very event—namely an invasion—that we want to avoid by taking these actions?

A: There's always a risk in anything of this sort, of course. And none of the operations we've conducted so far—either on the diplomatic or the military level—have been undertaken without a great deal of forethought and consultation with our allies. We hope that by our taking these actions the Soviets will understand how gravely we view the situation in Iran and will reconsider sending their troops into that country.

Q: You said earlier, Mr. President, that you had—and I quote—"ample intelligence data revealing that the Soviet Union is prepared to launch a preemptive attack on Iran." Where have you gotten this data from and is it reliable?

A: I am not at liberty to disclose the sources for such sensitive material, but let me assure you that it is reliable.

Text of appeal sent to Alexei Kadiyev by the U.S. (Released by the White House, April 19th)

THE WHITE HOUSE
1600 Pennsylvania Avenue
Washington, D.C.

Dear Mr. Secretary,

I am once again saddened by your failure to respond to my last letter (of the 15th), calling on your government for reassurances that no Soviet incursion is contemplated against Iran. On the contrary, during the past few days there has been every indication of a continuing Soviet buildup in the sensitive border region with Iran.

Consequently, I am obliged to remind you that the United States would view any Soviet military action as a direct threat to its vital interests in the Middle East and would act accordingly. It is crucial that all parties involved in the present conflict in Iran act with the utmost restraint. Any precipitate action on behalf of your government would only lead to a spillover of the conflict resulting in unpredictable consequences.

Given the grave nature of the situation confronting us, I would urge you to reply immediately and to do all in your power to ease the crisis facing us all.

I remain yours,

Sincerely,

(signed)
Creighton Turner,
President of the United States of America

18

APRIL 19
IRANIAN AZERBAIDJAN

Airlifted into Iranian Azerbaidjan by Boeing Vertol CH-47 Chinook choppers, the 200 Rangers put down at a little before six in the morning under a cloud cover that blanketed the Qareh Dagh Mountains north across the Soviet border. Except for sporadic antiaircraft fire, the American force met with no opposition. An hour and a half before, Intruders and A-7E Corsair II's, armed with air-to-ground antitank and antiradar missiles as well as general-purpose bombs, had inflicted heavy damage on the Jolfa-Tabriz road. At Km 22 the road had been made impassable; the Daradis Gorge, practically all seven kilometers of it, was filled with rocks and debris which had been blasted away from the rock face on either side.

The Rangers were going in to make certain that the road remained impassable and to remove any opposition force that might try to repair the road or construct an alternate route. It was to be an operation lasting no more than twenty-four hours, what Sunderland called a "swift surgical strike."

Jake Long, the strapping commander of the Ranger unit assigned to conduct the strike, watched as his force, in fifteen-man squads, piled into pneumatic assault boats brought in by the Chinooks and began setting out across the small but treacherous river that separated them from their objective. Lisker stood by his side, scanning the wooded terrain directly across from them, trying to spot any sign of opposition.

Long, checking his stopwatch repeatedly, seemed most interested in how rapidly the operation was proceeding. So far he was satisfied. "Two minutes on the button," he said as another assault boat was pushed out into the churning water.

"Damned if I can make anything out, though," Lisker muttered.

Early-morning mist hung over much of the farther bank, obscuring all but the tallest trees. Otherwise everything was a blur of grays and browns.

Lisker would've given anything to disengage himself from the life jacket strapped around his waist. Complete with an M-16 secured to it, the jacket was too bulky and uncomfortable for his liking, but Long had insisted he wear it, and he was, after all, the commander.

All along the river, Lisker could see M4T6 rafts moving light mortars, howitzers, and personnel carriers to the other side. Overhead a pair of AH-64A—Apache—choppers hovered noisily, their pilots scanning the terrain for potential sources of trouble beyond the river.

Just moments before the first pneumatic assault boat reached the shore, Lisker heard the sound of automatic fire. It seemed to be coming from the bank to the south. Long turned and strained to identify its origin through Steiner field glasses. All that Lisker could discern were sporadic flashes of light accompanied by gray puffs of smoke dissipating swiftly in the air.

"I'd make it at two o'clock," Long said.

Water was shooting up in geysers about the small armada of assault boats still crossing the river. The Rangers replied with 12.7mm machine guns and 35mm grenade launchers. Meantime, directed by Long from the ground, the Apaches went into action. They swept low over the forest, and air-to-air missiles swooped down from them against enemy batteries. The detonations of the missiles were followed in an instant by a flash fire that raced through the trees and brush. For the time being, the enemy guns were stilled.

But no sooner had the boats made it to the other side than batteries positioned downriver from Lisker began to open up on the landing force.

Long radioed the Apache pilots. "Abel Victor, this is Hobby Horse. Come in, Abel Victor."

"Abel Victor. Over."

"Enemy fire at eleven o'clock. Over."

"Confirm. Eleven o'clock. We're going in. Over."

"Over and out, Abel Victor."

At that, the two Apaches swung across the river, heading toward the source of opposition. While few of the mortar rounds were accurately targeted, they had the effect of halting the Rangers' advance from the shoreline. Until the barrage ended, there was no way that they would be able to start the march overland toward the Jolfa-Tabriz road.

As the Apaches, in tandem, veered in for the kill, a ZSU-23 antiaircraft gun, consisting of four 23mm guns, responded. The ZSU-23 was capable of delivering up to sixty seven-ounce shells a second. The ferocity of the fire did not retard the Apaches' approach, though. Among the most modern of U.S. choppers, they were built to withstand hits from these particular shells. Still, they could cause enough damage to eventually put them out of commission.

Spattered with mud and sprawled face down on the ground, the Rangers sensed that the Apache pilots were scared, for they suddenly slewed off to the east, away from the fire. Yet their capability was such that they didn't need to be in close. Four air-to-surface missiles launched from the craft, one right after the other, slammed into the zone specified by Long. The explosions rocked the earth and tore scores of trees up by their roots, jettisoning them into the river.

Fire continued against the Rangers from both sides of the river, but so sporadically that it could no longer hamper the advance of the Rangers.

Long told Lisker, "I'm sure it's the army we're dealing with here, not the Revolutionary Guards."

Since at least half the Iranian army had remained loyal to the Grand Ayatollahs, and since this attack had been so well orchestrated, Lisker was inclined to agree.

After Long and Lisker crossed over to the Rangers in the last assault boat, the force began to move out. In the meantime, the wounded had been fitted into pickup suits, which consisted of heavy canvas to which a parachute harness was attached. Using red gas handles, the injured could inflate a dirigible that would make them identifiable to the CV-2 Caribou Skyhooks that would be dispatched to airlift them back to army hospitals in Teheran. They would be retrieved by a 300 foot line extending from under the Caribou's belly while the Caribou was doing 125 miles per hour.

There were others with lower priority who'd be airlifted out later. These were the dead, and they numbered seven.

The Rangers had scarcely gotten under way when an advance patrol radioed back the disturbing news that there was far more opposition ahead than had been assumed. And the opposition was not Iranian, but Russian.

"It looks like we might be looking at a detachment of airborne assault troops," the patrol leader said. "I can see one Mi-26 from where I am and maybe a hundred troops taking up position on the western slope of the gorge."

The Mi-26 was a heavy transport helicopter; a squadron of Mi-26's was attached to every brigade of Soviet airborne assault troops.

"If that's true," Long said to Lisker, "I think we might have to get the hell out of here."

Each brigade consisted of sixty-four helicopters and three airborne rifle battalions. They were employed as the main axis of advance of a front, along with a tank army under cover provided by the air army. For a force of Rangers already depleted by the initial attack on the river, a confrontation with such a force would be the height of folly. Moreover, the Rangers had no authorization to engage Soviet soldiers in combat.

Long was so preoccupied by the situation on the ground that, unlike Lisker, he failed to appreciate the implications of the recon patrol's report. As they were well within Iranian territory, the presence of a Soviet airborne brigade could only mean that an invasion, however limited in scale, had begun. The fate of the Jolfa-Tabriz road was secondary to the real problem the United States faced: How was the Red Army to be contained.

The Rangers were brought to a halt half a mile from the shores of the river they'd traversed. Long radioed back to Sunderland at the base in Teheran, and proceeded to apprise him of their situation.

"It sounds like it could become untenable," Sunderland agreed when he'd finished. "We've been picking up a lot of electronic and radar activity all along the border this morning. There's been a definite shift in troop deployment too, from the most recent satellite photos we've seen. Right now, the dispatches we're getting from the border through The Elburz and Golul Dagh are sketchy, but it sounds like a big front has opened up in the north. I think we're going to have to pull you out of there. Can you get back across the river?"

"It might be difficult, but I believe we can do it. We'll call in the Apaches again to give us air cover."

"You get back on the other side, and we'll pick you up in the same place we dropped you."

"I'll keep you posted," Long said.

"You begin taking heavy fire and find you can't make it, we'll work out some other contingency."

Already they could hear the roar of planes overhead. A few moments later visual contact was made with them, a pair of MiG-25's.

The MiG-25's were simply designed, easily mass produced, and yet were among the most efficient aircraft in the world. Bound for points farther south, they posed no threat to the Americans winding their way back through the forest to the shoreline.

These were followed in turn by Tu-22M's—Backfire jets—which were used for low-level penetration and reconnaissance missions. Soon the Rangers could see MiG-29's, code-named Fulcrum, which Lisker knew to be employed for ground attack. But what struck him most in this astonishing display of aerial strength was not a military aircraft, but a transport plane. It came out of the north last and was astonishing in its size. Coming closer, it revealed itself to be an Antonov-400, code-named the Condor. Capable of carrying 200 fully equipped troops, it was one of the largest airplanes in the world.

Long could not believe his eyes and kept shaking his head in awe. "Jesus Christ, will you look at that mother?"

Lisker, who'd heard about the Condors but had never seen one before outside of intelligence photos, was equally impressed.

There could be no question that this represented the first wave of an invasion. This was not the type of military power you brought to bear if all you meant to do was create a provocation on the border.

"Well, it's begun," he said. "Now we're going to have to see how it'll end."

Long turned to him. "What did you say?"

He was evidently still thinking of this conflict on a local level. His objective was to move his men out and get them back to Teheran intact. He did not realize that this could be the start of a catastrophic war.

WAR ERUPTS IN IRAN ON SEVERAL FRONTS
Red Army and Air Force Begin Assault in North
(Special to the New York Times)

TEHERAN, April 19—The Soviet Union launched an all-out attack on Iran early this morning at 5:00, local time. Several divisions of the Red Army, supplemented by a massive show of air power, began moving south across the mountainous border region separating the Soviet Union from Iran. Initial reports from the area indicated that very little opposition to the assault was encountered by the Red Army forces. While witnesses tell of the downing of at least two MiG fighters from antiaircraft fire, in most parts of the country, antiaircraft fire was either light or nonexistent.

Muslim leaders in the city of Qum today welcomed the Soviet moves, terming the military operation "limited in scope with the objective of restoring the legitimate authority of the Islamic Republic." Since the death of the Islamic Republic's founder, the Ayatollah

Khomeini, a month ago, Iran has been torn by civil discord, with fundamentalist Moslems pitted against a dissident faction of the army under Colonel Ibrahim Shastri, a man considered by Washington to be moving toward alliance with the West. It was the threat posed by Shastri, whose troops seized Teheran on April 3, that precipitated the invitation for Red Army intervention from the religious leaders based in the holy city of Qum.

Echoing the statement out of Qum today, Radio Moscow, monitored in Teheran, also said that the troop movement would be limited and that no Soviet troops would remain in Iran once the "traitorous elements under the warmonger Shastri are crushed."

In Teheran, a spokesman for Colonel Shastri's provisional government denounced the Soviet attack, calling it "premeditated aggression," and vowed that all the patriotic people of Iran will unite to drive out the "Godless invaders," as he termed them. While he made no mention of American military or political assistance, it is common knowledge that substantial U.S. military aid has been coming into Teheran in recent days along with a military mission whose number is expected to reach four or five thousand. U.S. fighters and bombers have also gone into operation against supporters of the regime in Qum.

Excerpt from a special live NBC News bulletin, broadcast at 8:15 P.M., April 19:

"The White House has just released a statement calling for the immediate withdrawal of all Soviet forces from Iran. In the first official response to news of the Soviet invasion of that country, President Turner said, 'The United States vehemently protests this act of aggression and demands that all Soviet forces be immediately withdrawn. Failure to comply with this demand will only risk a grave escalation of hostilities.' The statement continues, 'Let there be no doubt in the minds of the Soviet leaders that the United States will take all steps necessary to protect vital American interests in Iran and the Middle East.' White House deputy press secretary Lloyd Hartley said that the President will hold a special news conference on the Iranian crisis at 9:30 tomorrow morning. This is Sam Hyland, NBC News, Washington."

UN SECURITY COUNCIL DEBATES IRAN CRISIS

NEW YORK, April 20 (Reuters)—The United Nations Security Council met in urgent session today to consider the latest developments in the Iranian crisis in light of the Soviet invasion. The United States and the Soviet Union called the meeting, which was attended by representatives of the Qum and the Teheran governments. Both seek to be admitted as the sole representative of Iran. Up until now, only Rassoul Sabesi, UN ambassador for the Islamic Republic, has been recognized by the UN as Iran's official representative. But in a compromise worked out among members of the Security Council, Ardeshir Golam, representative of Colonel Shastri's provisional government in Teheran, will also be permitted to speak.

The first session of the Security Council meeting was marked by acrimonious debate, with the American and Soviet delegates accusing each other of aggression. John Maitland, the U.S. deputy representative, maintained that the Soviet invasion should be condemned by the community of nations and warned that Moscow was running the risk of world war. Andrei Kohevoi, his Soviet counterpart, asserted that it was the introduction of U.S. forces in Iran and "the blatant use of American warplanes against the Iranian people" that created the conditions for the current crisis. "Soviet troops will be withdrawn just as soon as the United States does the same and ceases to prop up the puppet regime of Colonel Ibrahim Shastri." The debate recessed at noon, but will resume in the afternoon when the representatives of the rival governments in Iran are scheduled to present their cases to the Council.

STOCKS DOWN IN HEAVY TRADING

April 20 (Dow Jones)—Responding to current unrest in Iran and the possibility of a U.S.-Soviet confrontation, issues of stocks plummeted on the New York Exchange today. By the final bell, the Dow Jones average was down by 38.5 points. The number of shares traded was at a near record 194.56 million.

GOLD SOARS ON WORLD MARKETS

April 20 (Reuters)—The price of gold soared today to $545 in New York. The price was slightly lower in London. This represents a jump of $65 from yesterday's closing. The markets remain jittery after news arrived yesterday of a Soviet invasion in Iran. One gold broker on the floor of the Commodities Exchange in New York said yesterday that the price of gold would have gone to even higher levels except for persisting rumors that the Soviet Union, the biggest owner of gold bullion in the world, is about to unload a vast quantity of the precious metal on the world market in order to raise cash to fund its war effort in Iran.

OIL UP ON SPOT MARKET

Rotterdam, April 20 (UPI)—The price of a barrel of light crude on the spot market in Rotterdam advanced to $51.50, the highest reported price posted in the history of the spot market. This price is more than $20 more than the current OPEC benchmark price. The mounting crisis in Iran and the looming danger of a direct U.S.-Soviet military confrontation in the Persian Gulf have precipitated the climb in the price of light crude and aroused speculation that movement of oil through the Persian Gulf might be curtailed or brought to a complete halt because of war.

19

APRIL 21
WASHINGTON, D.C.

It was another late night for William Drexell. At ten past eleven Morse Peckum called to summon him to the White House for urgent consultations with the President. He'd been back in the country only forty-eight hours, having left from Hamburg on a special military charter. He'd brought back the Soviet war plans—or at least half of them—in an attaché case which, if opened by an unauthorized party, would blow up, simultaneously destroying the contents and burglar.

The call from the President's chief of staff had preceded only by a few minutes the arrival of a limousine in front of Drexell's Georgetown apartment complex. In a short time he was at the White House.

In 1983, in response to Iranian-backed terrorist attacks in Lebanon, Turkey, Kuwait, and elsewhere, the Secret Service had instituted a variety of security precautions to protect the White House and the President. Concrete barriers set up outside the southwest gate of the White House and painted snow white were reinforced by truck barriers and Stinger surface-to-air missiles mounted on top of the executive mansion. But now that the United States had directly entered the fray in Iran, the possibility of a terrorist attack against major U.S. political and military installations had increased tenfold. Even more sophisticated security precautions had been undertaken recently than in the most paranoid days of the Reagan administration. Devices, sold by the Delta Scientific Company of Burbank, California, were now in place on the grounds of the White House. Composed of movable steel and high-speed hydraulics, these devices were known as Vehicle Arrest Systems and were intended to stop kamikaze raids by trucks loaded with explosives. In addition, digital vehicle loop detectors had been deployed to monitor vehicles that came anywhere near the White House. In the event that one suddenly swerved or dramatically accelerated its speed, the detector would sound an alarm.

There were sniper guards on the White House roof and everywhere on the grounds. And there were rumors, probably unfounded, that the President had taken to wearing a bulletproof vest even in the comparative safety of the Oval Office and his bedroom.

Some of these precautions, so far as Drexell was concerned, were unnecessary. For instance, the Stinger missiles were next to useless. It was estimated that if terrorists were to commandeer an airplane and attempt to bomb or strafe the White House, the guards manning the missiles would have only ten seconds' warning. And ten seconds was hardly enough time to recognize the threat, aim the missile, and fire.

The security precautions extended to Drexell too, and he was obliged to undergo a thorough frisking and pass through a metal detector before being allowed to enter the heavily guarded West Wing of the White House. A special security pass, with a homing device sealed into it, dangled on a chain from his neck. It made him feel somewhat like a suspect on his way to a police lineup.

In the Oval Office he found the President, his chief of staff, Secretary of Defense Marty Rhiel, Secretary of State Jeffrey Schelling, and Thomas Kriendler, his National Security Advisor. Drexell noted that CIA director Stanley Burns was absent; he was still at work at Langley, reviewing the latest intelligence reports from Europe and the Middle East.

Covering practically half the wall in back of the President's desk, just to the right of the Presidential Seal, was a map of Iran and the surrounding states. Bright red arrows designated the latest Soviet troop movements; fifteen of them pointed downward from the northern land mass of Iran. Blue arrows, which numbered only three, represented U.S. military countermoves.

Rhiel began the meeting by presenting an update of the Iranian military situation on the ground and in the air.

"In the last twenty-four hours the Soviets have moved on Tabriz and Qazvin, consolidating their hold over both those cities," he said. "The reason for these initial successes is obvious: There's been practically no resistance, since both the Russians and the mullahs maintain the fiction—which the mullahs might sincerely believe—that they are in the country only to prop up the fundamentalists and will leave just as soon as Shastri has fallen. Elsewhere, Soviet divisions have advanced through the Elburz and the Golul Dagh, forming spearheads meant to effectively cut the country in half, with the purpose of isolating those areas where Shastri is in control. That's the first stage.

"Whether they then intend to go on into Khuzestan Province and seize the oil production capacity of the country, we still have no idea." He looked over to Drexell. "The classified documents that have come into our hands reveal the Soviet battle plan only to phase two, which culminates in a buildup at Dezful and the securing of the southern base of the Zagros Mountains. We don't know what phase three entails—we don't have the relevant documents yet. There may not even be a phase three. How far the Red Army can be expected to go might finally depend entirely on events in the political arena.

"Meanwhile, we have reports of extensive movements on the part of the Black Sea Fleet. In the last seventy-two hours SIGNIT sources report that at least five nuclear subs are in the Persian gulf, with several diesel-electric subs trailing along behind them. We also have evidence that several surface ships will also be in the area, plus marine infantry divisions, the entire component of the naval aviation of the Black Sea Fleet, as well as diversionary SPETSNAZ troops to be used against enemy naval bases and the usual assortment of coastal rocket and artillery troops."

"What it looks like then is that the Soviets are planning to mount a naval and air attack to accompany the land operation we now see going on," Kriendler commented.

"I would have to say that would be the only conclusion we could draw," Rhiel said. Using a pointer, he indicated a strip of Iranian territory all the way from the Gulf of Oman to Khuzestan at the northern end of the Persian Gulf. "I think that within a few days the combined naval and air forces of the U.S.S.R. will try to secure a beachhead along the south with the intent of eventually linking up with ground forces advancing from the north."

"Which would mean that Khuzestan might be in imminent danger of a takeover?" the President asked.

"It's certainly possible, Mr. President," Rhiel answered. "But before that happens, the Soviets may try to interdict our oil carriers."

"I think, in that case," Drexell put in, "that we should provide air cover to all oil carriers going in and out of the Gulf and make it clear that we'll bomb the hell out of any battleship or sub attempting to interfere with free passage of unarmed transport."

"That would constitute an act of war on the part of the Russians," the President acknowledged.

"We'll have the full backing of our allies on that," Schelling said. "Most of the oil coming out of the Gulf is intended for them, after all."

"My impression is that in the next few days we'll see a slowing of the Soviet advance," Drexell said. "Their lines of supply are going to become increasingly strained. But most importantly, I believe that the air and sea threat posed by the Black Sea Fleet may well be a bluff. Depending on our response, the Soviets may decide to consolidate their position on the ground and apply political pressure in hope of ousting Shastri and sending us packing at the same time. That way, they could avoid the sort of losses—political as well as military—that they'd inevitably incur if they tried to advance on Khuzestan."

"What I'd suggest we do immediately," Rhiel said, "is

to mobilize SPIF. We've got 35 B-52H's ready to operate from our bases in Guam, Clark Field, and Diego Garcia. Since we don't have the forces on the ground to provide adequate deterrence—and there's no way we can build our troops up in less than thirty days—I'd go with a tiered interdiction."

SPIF was an acronym for Strategic Projection Force, which was designed some years before specifically for conventional bombing operations in the Persian Gulf region. The plan called for a preponderance of air strikes to be conducted at night.

"I'm not sure I know what you mean by 'tiered interdiction,'" Kriendler said.

"Basically, to use the B-52's to deny Soviet engineers any opportunity to repair the routes and rail lines we've already put out of commission. We can rely on the *Independence* and the *Nimitz* to provide escort for the bombers. And at the same time the carriers could support the tactical air cover for a Marine beachhead in Khuzestan."

"Wait just a minute," the President said. "Are you saying you want SPIF put into effect—*and* a Marine landing in Khuzestan simultaneously?"

"That's right," Rhiel replied.

"I'm not at all certain that escalating the war to that level is going to get us where we want," Drexell said. "It's one thing to keep those bombers in the air and prevent the engineers from restoring their troops' access routes. But as soon as we place Marines in Khuzestan we're virtually challenging the Soviets to come in and throw them out. As I stated before, my feeling is that we can keep this war from getting worse than it already is. Shows of force make sense. Knocking out transportation lines makes sense. Shoring up Shastri against the fundamentalists and their Russian supporters makes sense. What does not make sense is foregoing any opportunity to negotiate an end to this thing by putting Marines in Khuzestan right now. Given the logistical difficulties the Soviets might have by continuing south to the province, they're probably going to stop right where they are."

Rhiel glared at Drexell. "You were the one who counseled taking military action in Iran not so long ago, if I remember correctly."

"On a limited scale. And I still support military action—on a limited scale. But the Russians have transferred one of their air armies from Europe, and we know it has long-range aviation capability. That represents a considerable sacrifice on the Russians' part because it takes away from their ability to handle a threat from NATO in Europe. We have to assume that if they're going to risk a move like that, there has to be nuclear weapons on board those planes. That's why I want to proceed as cautiously as possible here. I'm sure you all share that same desire."

The President nodded abstractedly. It was hard to know whether he agreed or was just being polite.

"We're all anxious not to trigger off a nuclear war," said Rhiel. "But at the same time I wouldn't want us to wake up one morning and find that the Red Army has occupied the oil fields and cut off our access to the Persian Gulf. For all the air and sea power we can deploy in the area, I don't think anything is going to send a message to the Kremlin quite so effectively as putting in the Marines."

Drexell wished that he had the rest of the classified war plans that Kolnikov had promised him. But he'd had no word from the Russian agent since Berlin; the last he'd heard of him, Kolnikov had been transferred to the Southern Soviet Military District. He might even be in Iran now. Drexell believed that the war plans would show that the Russians had no intention of advancing to Khuzestan and taking the oil fields unless they were provoked.

But having to rely only on guesswork, he said, "Don't forget, there are Revolutionary Guards and elements of the Iranian army we'll have to fight if we go in there. Even some of our closest allies will think that our only interest in sending in the Marines is to grab the oil wells for our own convenience, not because we're particularly worried about the Russians. We're likely to lose every friend we have in the Middle East who would otherwise oppose the Russian intervention."

"That's a chance we'll have to take," Rhiel said.

"I think the American people would be behind something

like that," offered Morse Peckum. "For years they've gotten tired of being kicked around by OPEC—particularly Iran. You go in and take those wells—I don't give a damn what the reason is—and you'll find that Americans will back you one hundred percent, Mr. President."

Peckum was no expert in foreign affairs; in fact, he cared little about them. He could not tell you where Vlan Bator or Kuala Lumpur were. Yet he was acutely conscious of the pulse of popular opinion at home, and his only real concern was in making sure that the President didn't commit himself to any policy that would jeopardize his standing in the polls.

"Let's get back to something that Bill said a couple of minutes ago," Schelling said. "You mentioned that there were opportunities you didn't want to see forgone by taking any precipitate military action. What opportunities are you referring to?"

Thinking of Hahn and Zoccola, Drexell said, "I believe that we haven't exhausted all our political options. Despite the assassination of Rashid Nasreddin, I have reason to believe that the mullahs still have mixed feelings about the Russian intervention. I have some men in Qum right now who are attempting to see whether there's any room for maneuver."

"Have you any indication from these men that there is any room?" the President inquired.

"I'm awaiting their reports," Drexell hedged. In truth, he had heard from neither operative in the last thirty-six hours and so he didn't have any idea what the situation was like in the holy city.

"What would you like to see happen, Bill?" Schelling asked. "What's your optimal scenario?"

"I don't know whether you'd consider it optimal in terms of what we'd *like* to see happen," Drexell began. "I have a sense that you have a no-win situation in Iran. No win for us and no win for the Russians. I believe there's still an outside chance that we could establish a neutral government there, one as satisfactory to the Russians as it is to us, and that would represent neither the Khomeini faction, now led by the Ayatollah Ghafferi, nor the provisional government of Colonel Shastri."

"What the hell!" Kriendler cried. "Are you suggesting we ditch Shastri?"

"Only if the fundamentalists ditch the Russians and demand that they leave the country. I think that would be a fair trade-off. I'd go farther and propose a deal whereby we'd withdraw our forces from the ground—not from air or sea—if the Russians would reciprocate. I believe a deal is possible."

Drexell knew that his opinion would be controversial with hard-liners like Rhiel and Kriendler, who saw in Shastri an opportunity to gain back the kind of influence the U.S. had in Iran when the Shah was in power.

But Drexell believed his idea was more realistic. There was no way the United States could regain such influence over the country, not after seven years of rule under the fundamentalists. The majority of the 40 million people who lived in Iran would simply not stand for it. The basic objective, as he saw it, was to oust the Russians and create in Iran a state that was as neutral as possible, one that, like Finland, the Russians did not perceive as threatening to their interests.

The other alternative—to try to turn Iran into a pro-American state—would lead to a full-scale confrontation with the Soviet Union and possibly a nuclear war.

"I think there's something to what you both say," the President said after a long silence, looking first at Rhiel and then at Drexell. "While I don't want to overlook any political option that may avert a costly and potentially catastrophic war, I wouldn't want to see us lose our oil and very likely the entire region, including Saudi Arabia, to the Soviets because we were too squeamish about using all the military power at our disposal." Turning to Drexell, he said, "I tell you what. I'm going to authorize the use of SPIF right now, but I'll hold off on a decision about landing the Marines—but just for another twenty-four hours. I want to hear what your people in Qum have to say about cutting a deal. If it looks hopeless, I'm inclined to go along with Marty and put our boys in Khuzestan. Is that acceptable to you, Bill?"

Seventy-two hours would have been acceptable, forty-eight hours would have been acceptable, but not twenty-four. Yet, seeing as he had little choice, Drexell agreed. Drexell didn't even know whether he could raise Zoccola and Hahn by radio in that amount of time. But it was clear that the President was not about to be any more generous with him.

"Yes, sir," he said, "that will be acceptable."

20

APRIL 22
QUM, IRAN

On the day the first squadron of B-52H bombers began to go into operation from Clark Field in the Philippines and Diego Garcia in the Indian Ocean, Jerry Hahn found himself in a tea shop in the holy city of Qum waiting for an old acquaintance to turn up.

There was no question that he looked out of place in this tea shop, for most of the men at the other tables were clothed in turbans and loose-fitting white garments. The natives eyed him with an interest that bordered on suspicion.

John Zoccola was outside, ready to back him up should trouble develop. For the last few days, ever since their arrival in Qum, the two had been switching residences every night, relying on Mohammed Arif to help find them new quarters. They were on the run, though they weren't certain whether anyone was pursuing them or not. For their own safety they had to assume that someone was.

But despite their best efforts, their presence in Qum evidently had not gone unnoticed. Only that morning a handwritten message to Hahn had been thrust into Arif's hands as he was on his way to morning prayers at a nearby mosque. (Arif believed that if he were to make any headway selling arms to the fundamentalists, he ought to familiarize himself with the customs of his prospective clients.)

Arif told Hahn that the messenger had vanished into the crowd so swiftly that he'd scarcely gotten a glimpse of him.

The message, Hahn discovered, was from none other than his old cellmate Farouk. It said only: "We must meet and talk. It is very important." To this he appended the address of the tea shop and the hour and date of the appointment he wished Hahn to keep. The words were written in English, but clumsily, like a third grader's scrawl.

Hahn told Zoccola that it might be a setup.

While acknowledging that this was possible, Zoccola pointed out that if Farouk had succeeded in contacting him to begin with, he could always find him. "If it really was a setup," he said, "why should he arrange to meet you in some tea shop? He could've tipped off the authorities and there'd be a hundred Revolutionary Guards outside here by now. I say you should go meet him. I'll stand guard for you if it'll be any comfort."

Hahn conceded that he might be right, but he was still reluctant.

"I don't want to force you into this," Zoccola said. "But if this joker has the connections you told me he did, then we might be able to use him. Arif knows people, but only up to a certain level. Farouk might be able to connect us higher—to the Grand Ayatollahs who run the show. He knew what was happening with Nasreddin, he knew he was targeted for assassination at a time when no one else in Teheran did."

Against his better judgment, Hahn assented to the meeting.

The question now that he was actually at the tea shop was whether Farouk would keep the appointment. He was already twenty minutes late. Hahn's only comfort lay in what Zoccola had said; why lure him all the way to this obscure tea shop so that he could be arrested—or butchered? It seemed unnecessary.

But his edginess persisted. At such times he wished that he was a smoker so he would have something to do with his hands. The tea they served him was scalding and yet, in his nervousness, he drank it anyway, burning his tongue.

"I look at you and I see a ghost."

Hahn raised his eyes to see Farouk standing over him. Farouk looked entirely different from what he'd remembered, but then, what he remembered was a haggard, skeletal man in the gloom of an infamous prison. Farouk's face was fuller now, with more color to it, and his beard was thicker, perhaps to conceal the scars.

He took a seat. As he did so he cast his eyes about the tea shop, smiling in recognition. The other men were evidently acquainted with him.

"They see that you are my friend and so there will be no problem," Farouk said.

Hahn was thankful. Any acceptance was welcome.

"To tell you the truth," he said, "I thought you were dead."

Farouk laughed. The notion that he might die in such a fashion must have seemed preposterous.

"No, I got out the same time as you. When it is necessary, I run. I run very quick. The bullets fly, but they do not touch me. And so I come home."

"And this is home?"

"Why not? I have many friends here."

Hahn believed him, but he was anxious to get to the point.

"How did you find me?"

"Qum is not such a large place, and I have eyes everywhere."

It was an answer as true as it was cryptic. But Hahn did not press him. "All right, but why do you want to talk to me?"

"Because I have a feeling you have important friends."

Hahn shrugged. "You're the one with the friends."

Farouk ignored him. "Tell me, do you know the Sources of Inspiration?"

"Sources of Inspiration? Are you referring to the council of the six highest ayatollahs?"

Farouk offered an appreciative smile. "Ah, so you do know something of the political situation here in Qum. Then you also know that now that Khomeini is dead, there is no true leadership, that the supreme authority is invested in the

Velayat-e-Faqih, who rules as a delegate for the Hidden Imam."

This Hahn also knew, having versed himself in the tenets of Shiite Islam. In essence, politics and religion were so intertwined in Iran—just as they were in Saudi Arabia, where a different branch of Islam, the Sunni, held sway—that it was impossible to separate them.

According to the Shiites, the true religious leader was the Twelfth Imam, who in the ninth century disappeared into a cave, which was why he came to be called Hidden. It was said that one day he would return as the Redeemer. Until then, authority was to be maintained by a religious guide—the Velayat-e-Faqih.

At present that post, established by the Ayatollah Khomeini, was held by the Ayatollah Ali Kazem Ghafferi, who was every bit as fanatical as his predecessor, but nowhere near as charismatic.

When Hahn mentioned his name, Farouk grimaced; it was as if he'd bit into a red-hot pepper. "A madman!" he proclaimed, making no attempt to lower his voice.

Instinctively Hahn glanced about him, but none of the men at the other tables gave any indication of having heard him.

"He has no consensus. The Grand Ayatollahs are divided. Ghafferi wants the Russians. He was the one who ordered Nasreddin's assassination when he realized he opposed the Russian intervention. He was the one who put Jalili in power. But his day will come."

"Sooner than later, I hope."

"It is possible. Since you are so knowledgeable about the people who rule my country, you must have heard of the Ayatollah Hadi Zayedi?"

"Yes, I've heard of him—but not for years. Isn't he dead?"

"No, he is not dead. But he is under house arrest."

The Ayatollah Haki Zayedi, a venerable religious teacher who, if alive, was into his ninth decade of life, was known throughout Iran as a man of moderation and wisdom. An opponent of the Shah, he'd turned against the Ayatollah Khomeini once he saw what course he'd embarked upon;

he deplored the executions of suspected dissidents and Bahais whose only crime was to worship God differently. Because he was such a religious authority, a man whose devotion to Islam could not be called into question, he'd been brought from Meshed, Iran's second holy city, and, according to Farouk, was now locked up in a house not far from where they were sitting.

"So many years have passed since he was put under house arrest that everyone in the West forgets his existence. But there are many who have not forgotten. The Sources of Inspiration are so afraid of him they will not let him out, especially now that Khomeini is dead. They think that he will overthrow Ghafferi, replace Jalili as president, and then order the Russians to leave."

Hahn was beginning to see where this was leading. Zoccola had been right; this appointment with Farouk was well worth keeping.

"Does he truly have a large popular following, Farouk?"

"Yes, I assure you, my friend, he has a very large following. Even people who are now loyal to Colonel Shastri would gladly rally behind him. The fundamentalists—except for the fanatics—they would rally behind him."

"But since he's so old now, and it's been years since he's been free..."

"You want to know whether he is capable of leading? Is that your question?"

Hahn nodded.

"I have not seen the Ayatollah Zayedi myself. But there are people who have managed to see him. They receive special permission and they go to pay him their respects. They say that he is in good health and of sound mind and that if he becomes free, he is prepared to lead his people. There have been old men before who have done this. In India, in Yugoslavia. And here in Iran. Zayedi is younger than the Ayatollah, remember."

"If Zayedi were free, do you believe that Iran could then unite behind him against the Russians?"

"And against the Americans. Under the Ayatollah Zayedi, there would be no foreign agents, no foreign armies in our country. No Jalili, no Shastri. Just one Iran."

Hahn was thinking, Zayedi is the key to the solution of the crisis. He is exactly what Triad needs.

But Hahn didn't allow his excitement to show. "Why have you told me all this about Zayedi?"

"I tell you this because maybe you can help arrange his escape."

Hahn frowned. He wasn't ready to blow his cover yet.

"I'm a businessman. What makes you think that I can arrange his escape?"

Farouk looked surprised by the question. "Because you arranged to escape the Khomiteh Mushtarak."

"It had nothing to do with me."

"Please, my friend, there is no need to deceive me. I know you are no businessman. You could blow up the Khomiteh Mushtarak, so you can free Zayedi."

"I might be able to talk to some people," Hahn said, hedging.

"Of course you will talk to some people."

"How heavily guarded is Zayedi?"

"Very many Revolutionary Guards. Machine guns, concertina wire, alarms. The Grand Ayatollahs know what will happen if he is free. They will lose their power."

"Would they kill him if they thought that might actually occur?"

"Yes, I think so. They do not want a martyr because if it is known that they kill him, then the people will rise up against them. But maybe they poison him and say he died in his sleep and quietly bury him. It would not surprise me if Ghafferi is planning this now."

To Hahn all these intrigues were faintly reminiscent of a medieval court where the king saw a conspirator in every prince, where poisonings, beheadings, and executions carried out stealthily in the dead of night were commonplace. But, then, Iran under the Ayatollahs was like a medieval country.

"So you are saying that if anyone is thinking of freeing him, they had better do it quickly."

"I am saying this exactly."

"Where can I find you?" Hahn asked.

"It is not necessary to find me. I will find you. Tomorrow

we talk. And if you are interested, maybe I will show you where Ayatollah Zayedi is being held."

Hahn shook his hand and left him sitting alone, contemplatively sipping his cupful of mint tea. On the street he found Zoccola idling in the shadow of a rug merchant's shop.

"How did your meeting go?"

"Profitably," Hahn said. "It looks like everything we're trying to do here hinges on the fate of an eighty-year-old man."

Zoccola looked intrigued. "An eighty-year-old man?"

"The Ayatollah Hadi Zayedi."

"I thought he was dead."

"No, he isn't dead. He might be soon, though."

"And we want to get to him before that happens, am I right?"

"Exactly."

"Well, then," Zoccola said, "I suppose that means we should have another talk with our friend Muhammed Arif and see what kind of toys he has in stock."

"Something that goes boom in the night?"

"You've got it."

SAUDI ARABIA DENIES U.S. USE OF BASES

JIDDA, April 23 (Agence France Presse)—The Saudi foreign minister, Abdul Hafik Tabriz, said today that the United States would not be able to use military bases or airstrips for refueling nor would any Saudi port be available for U.S. warships. Calling for an immediate cease-fire in Iran, the Saudi minister said that it was vital that the war not spread throughout the Middle East. His statement came at the end of a visit by Philip Drummond, the U.S. special envoy to the Middle East. Mr. Drummond reportedly appealed to the leaders of several moderate Arab nations, including Saudi Arabia, Kuwait, Jordan, and Egypt, to assist U.S. efforts in Iran. In virtually all cases he has either been rebuffed or else had to settle for much less than the kind of commitments he was hoping for.

Mr. Tabriz hinted that his country might provide the U.S. with intelligence and might make available AWACS spy planes along the sensitive border region with Iran. Significantly, Mr. Tabriz is to leave tomorrow for Moscow to continue Saudi mediation efforts in the war.

CONGRESSIONAL DELEGATION ASSAILS ARAB POSITION

TEL AVIV, April 23 (AP)—A visiting U.S. congressional delegation here released a statement deploring the "unfortunate and cowardly position taken by Saudi Arabia and other so-called moderate Arab states" in regard to U.S. military requirements in the Middle East. Composed jointly by Representatives James Hooker (D-Ohio) and Mendel Owensby (R-Nevada), the statement noted that "for many years Congress has voted billions of dollars in appropriations to these countries in military and economic assistance. Now that some reciprocity is demanded to counter undisguised aggression on the part of Soviet troops, these same countries have turned tail and run." The congressional delegation of 18 congressmen and senators is in Israel as part of a fact-finding mission on the situation in the Middle East. Their joint statement demands that the President immediately curtail all foreign aid grants in the pipeline to any Middle Eastern country that refuses assistance to the United States.

FRANCE CALLS FOR NEGOTIATIONS OVER IRAN

PARIS, April 23 (UPI)—Asserting that "the time is now critical," French Foreign Minister Paul Vidal called for an international conference to negotiate an end to the war in Iran. At a press conference here he refused to place the blame for the current situation on the Soviet Union, insisting that "we can't keep raking over the same old coals; we have to move on." "I think it is obvious," he said, "that all parties involved in the conflict have to share some of the responsibility." It is thought that France is edging toward a more neutral position in the conflict to enhance its position as a mediator.

DEMONSTRATIONS ERUPT IN GERMANY

BONN, April 23 (German Press Agency)—Thousands of demonstrators turned out today in cities throughout Germany to demand an end to "outside intervention in Iran." With tensions increasing between the United States and Soviet Union over the crisis there, Germans have become particularly concerned that their own country could be adversely affected by the Middle Eastern strife. A spokesperson for the Green Party, Marthe Schmidt, said, "It is no secret that there has been a buildup of troops and arms on both sides of the border here and that both the Soviet Union and the United States are prepared to turn Germany—East and West—into a second battleground while their respective territories remain untouched and unscarred."

The demonstrations were called by the Green Party, which takes a political position far more radical than either the Christian Democrats or Social Democrats. The largest demonstration was in Hamburg where an estimated 150,000 people turned out. Most of the demonstrations were peaceful, but in Berlin, Munich, and Cologne street fighting broke out between the predominantly youthful demonstrators and police. In Berlin at least 50 people were taken to hospitals with injuries and more than 80 were arrested.

21

APRIL 24
THE PERSIAN GULF

It had long been known that in peacetime Russian ship locations are monitored more precisely than their Western counterparts. A carrier task force, such as the one now steaming into the Gulf of Oman in the direction of the Persian Gulf, was capable of searching over 100,000 square kilometers of area per hour using air and electronic surveillance. Early-warning aircraft could spot the enemy 700 kilometers away. That was why, if the Soviets were to attack, it would be the carriers—in this case the *Nimitz* and the *Independence*—which would be targeted first. Once the carriers were disabled or destroyed, any aircraft aloft would have to come down in a few hours, and the remaining surface ships would become that much more vulnerable to Soviet destroyers and warplanes.

Joining the two carriers now were two venerable World War Two battleships that had been reconditioned and put back into service—the *Iowa* and the *New Jersey*. Several other battleships, including the cruisers *Belknap, Truxton, Biddle,* and *Long Beach,* and the destroyer *Ticonderoga,* along with three nuclear submarines of the Ohio class, were also deployed in the task force.

Although 18,000 Marines were being transported by

the task force; they would be ready when ordered to launch an amphibious assault on the oil-producing province of Khuzestan with the objective of establishing a beachhead there.

Intelligence reports reaching the Air Operations Center on board the *Nimitz* indicated that, in anticipation of just such a move on the part of the Americans, up to 15,000 Revolutionary Guards and units of the army loyal to the mullahs had been dispatched to the area to reinforce the 35,000 troops already there. So far, though, whether because of political decisions taken in Moscow or—more likely—because of the formidable logistical problems involved, no Soviet forces had been airlifted into the area. Of course, this could change at any time. Should a landing of U.S. forces take place, the Soviets might decide to introduce at least some forces in order to up the ante and discourage the invaders from advancing any farther into Iranian territory.

The Sixth Fleet commander, Admiral Jonas Brooks, a crusty veteran of the seas given to bursts of violent temper interspersed with surprising interludes of placidity, was, however, less concerned with the situation on land than with the current position of the Black Sea Fleet. Reconnaissance aircraft had reported that three guided missile frigates of the Krivak class, used mainly for antisubmarine warfare, were sighted less than seventy miles away from the American fleet. The main bulk of the force was only slightly farther behind. In addition, Tu-142's and Tu-22M's, both naval patrol planes, had been buzzing the American fleet for the last thirty-six hours.

Although U.S. and Soviet combat forces had exchanged fire on the ground in Iran—in an incident that had fortunately not yet come to light—the governments of both superpowers were anxious to show some restraint, at least for the moment. As a result, as much as Brooks wanted to do it, no antiaircraft fire was directed at the Soviet planes; they came and went with impunity.

What Brooks feared most was becoming boxed in, caught between the Black Sea Fleet on the one hand and Iranian defense forces in Khuzestan on the other. The only way to prevent this from happening, should the military situation escalate to that point, was to rely on a massive use of air power to keep the Soviet armada at bay.

At 0600 hours on the morning of April 24, Admiral Brooks was on the admiral's bridge in the superstructure of the *Nimitz* (which also housed the Air Operations Center and captain's bridge). With him was the special Mideast envoy, Phil Drummond, a short, pale man whose hurried manner scarcely hinted at his incisive intelligence or his exhaustive knowledge of the politics, history, and culture of the area he was attempting to bring peace to. Also present was Triad's senior officer, William Drexell, who'd been flown directly to the *Nimitz* from Washington to confer with Drummond and Brooks. In addition, he'd be monitoring the operations of his agents in Iran.

Drexell and Drummond had met by chance many times during the last two decades, usually in Washington restaurants and local watering holes. Having worked for no less than five administrations of both parties, Drummond was the kind of man that Presidents recruited as their troubleshooter when they'd run out of other candidates. Because he was shrewd enough to maintain his cool under fire and was singularly closemouthed in front of the press, he aroused virtually no controversy. He also had the advantage of being on good terms with the leaders of most countries in the area. Even when relations between the United States and Iraq were strained to the breaking point, for example, he would still be welcomed in Baghdad. Periodically he would announce his retirement, either because he wished to spend more time with his family or because his health wasn't the best (he'd suffered a serious heart attack five years before), but it was tacitly understood that if the White House ever needed him, he would always obey the summons.

Phil Drummond was not a man who was easy to get to know and, while he was amiable and, in the best sense of the word, diplomatic, Drexell never considered him a friend. But he respected his opinion, for he was a pragmatist who was not, like many of his colleagues at State, a slave to any ideological bias.

The admiral's bridge of the *Nimitz* was an unlikely context in which to discuss prospects for peace in the region, but it was what was available at the moment.

Gazing out at the distant shoreline of Iran, which was just becoming discernible in the first blush of dawn, Drexell asked the envoy if he'd made any progress at all in his shuttle diplomacy.

Drummond shook his head. "There seems little room for compromise. The Arabs are more worried about the war spilling over into their countries than they are about the Russians. In their view, the Russians are less interested in conquering Iran than in keeping us from exerting too much influence there. They genuinely believe that we want a return to the days of the Shah, that Colonel Shastri is really our puppet, and that if he went, the whole crisis would end and everybody could relax.

"Nor are they as afraid of a world war as we are. Their fear is that, with so many different factions and with restive populations like the Palestinians in their midst, the war in Iran could turn into a permanent revolution in which everybody—Shiites, Sunnis, Kurds, Palestinians, Bahais, Phalangists, Alawites, what have you—would be fighting. Everywhere I went, in Amman, in Beirut, in Damascus, in Cairo, it's the same story: If you Americans intervene in Iran, the whole Middle East is going to turn into Lebanon, with endless killing and endless suffering, and all the friends you've made here will desert you."

"So the only friends we can rely on are the Israelis," Drexell said.

"They're the only ones. And of course you realize the danger of allying ourselves too closely with them. We may isolate ourselves so much that, even if we can push the Russians back on the battlefield, we'll end up squandering just about all our political capital. One way or another, we'll lose the war."

"My fear is that we'll lose it on the ground *and* in the diplomatic sphere," Drexell said.

"Well, we really are in something of a no-win situation."

He turned to look desolately on the shoreline of Iran. They were approaching the province of Khuzestan, where the fate of the war might ultimately be determined. A pair of F-14A Tomcat fighters, skulls and crossbones on their tails indicating that they were part of the Jolly Roger Squadron, were headed inland over enemy territory.

It was at this point that Drexell decided to raise the subject of the Ayatollah Hadi Zayedi. Word that the dissident ayatollah was still being held under house arrest in Qum after all these years had reached him only last night, along with Zoccola and Hahn's recommendation that a rescue mission be instituted to save him.

Drummond knew of the Ayatollah Zayedi, but he too was surprised that he was alive. "The CIA said that he'd died of a stroke three years ago," he said.

"You know how reliable the CIA is in Iran," Drexell reminded him. "Anyway, he is alive and, from all accounts, prepared to assume power if both the reigning Ayatollah Ghafferi and our man Shastri are gotten out of the way."

Drummond shot him a curious glance, but said nothing.

"In your considered opinion, would the Russians accept Zayedi as a compromise candidate, that is, if we both pulled our troops out?"

Drummond gave this some thought. "It's possible. Obviously, he would have to be free before we could try and cut a deal with them. The Russians are probably as much behind Ghafferi and his band of fanatics as we are behind Shastri."

"Not so much behind them that they'd begin a nuclear war to keep them in power?"

"From my knowledge of the Soviets over the years, no. No ayatollah is worth a hundred million Russians. But by the same token, they're not about to back down unless they can save face."

Drexell smiled. "Neither are we."

"Do you think we can get Zayedi out?" Drummond asked.

Before Drexell could respond, the sound of artillery fire, like repeated claps of thunder, penetrated the bridge.

Admiral Brooks, who had been listening to the conversation, calmly strode to the window that looked out on the shore of Khuzestan some fifteen miles away. Drexell and Drummond came up behind him.

Batteries all along the shore, manned by Revolutionary Guards and loyal Iranian army units, had begun to open up on the *New Jersey* and the guided missile destroyer *Tattnall*.

Brooks radioed to the commanders of the two craft, which were approximately ten miles offshore, and ordered them to open up "with every gun you've got." The *Tattnall* was equipped with five-inch guns, but the *New Jersey* was more formidably armed, with both its twelve- and sixteen-inch guns. The sixteen-inch guns could lob 1,900-pound shells, which could carve out craters fifty yards across and twenty feet deep. A fire-control system, a Mark 48 shore bombardment model which relied on a digital computer, fed information on the ship's position and map coordinates of the targets into the computer so that the guns were always accurately sighted, regardless of the ship's motion.

There were also armor-piercing shells, weighing 2,700 pounds each, which could be used to bombard fortified targets.

At the same time Brooks ordered six Intruders and an equal number of A-7E Corsairs, with air-to-ground antitank and antiradar missiles, into operation against the shore batteries. "By the time we get through, I don't expect that there'll be much of anything on that beach," Brooks commented.

The planes streaked in low over the beach, dropping 500-pound bombs all along the front. Antiaircraft guns added to the din. Smoke billowed from one end of the shore to the other until visibility was reduced dramatically. One of the Intruders slewed to the right, flames erupting from its tail. A moment later a parachute could be seen opening up, olive-green against the blue morning sky. The Intruder somersaulted, then plunged into the sea where it exploded with a great cascade of water. What happened to the pilot was impossible for Drexell to tell. He appeared to have gone down behind enemy lines.

The guns of the *Tattnall* and *New Jersey* continued to pound away at the opposition artillery. At the eastern edge of the shoreline, the fire was especially heavy, but no American warships were struck.

For fifteen minutes the battle raged until it seemed as if most of the Iranian gun emplacements had been taken out. Most of the smoke dissipated, revealing a lunar landscape pockmarked with craters and crisscrossed with channels. Tangled heaps of metal littered the entire beach, which had turned black with soot. Fires blazed out of control everywhere one looked. Here and there the shelling from the coast continued, but it was desultory and altogether ineffectual.

Admiral Brooks surveyed the scene with obvious satisfaction. "We could move right in now and establish a beachhead," he remarked, "if AFSOUTH would let me."

AFSOUTH stood for Allied Forces of NATO's Southern Command. Of course, authorization would have to come from far higher up than NATO headquarters in Brussels. As Brooks and his guests, Drexell and Drummond, all knew, this wasn't really NATO's fight, however much the United States wanted it to be. Britain had yet to contribute any troops to the effort, West Germany had its own borders to worry about, and Greece and Turkey both preferred to remain out of the fray for fear of endangering their own security. Although in theory the President might try to consult with the allies before sanctioning an invasion of Khuzestan, it was Drexell's opinion that he would end up moving on his own.

But at the moment that sanction hadn't come, and Brooks had to content himself with hammering away at the shoreline.

Twenty-two minutes after giving the order to return fire, he ordered the captains of the *Tattnall* and *New Jersey* to silence their guns. He then instructed the pilots of the eleven fighters still in the air to fly farther inland and knock out any mobile guns that the enemy might be moving up to replace those just destroyed.

Just then he was alerted by intercom that radar had picked up eight jets approaching the coast at close to 2,000 miles per hour. "We have them at three o'clock, just over Hendijan now, coming in at sixty thousand feet," the carrier's captain, Clark Taylor, reported from the Air Operations Center.

Hendijan was a city that lay very close to the coast. At the speed the unidentified aircraft were coming in, they would soon be able to spot them with the naked eye.

Brooks turned to Drexell and Drummond. "I'll lay odds that they're Russian."

A few minutes later the jets came into view, descending so that, as they passed over the horizon, they were at an altitude of about 40,000 feet.

Through Steiner field glasses, Drexell identified them as MiG-25 Foxbats—all-weather interceptors. They would be armed with AA-6 Acrid missiles, radar homing devices with a range of twenty-eight miles.

Their purpose was almost immediately apparent. The Intruders could maintain speeds of less than 500 miles per hour, the Corsairs less than 700. The MiG's could fly higher and faster than either and were soon able to overtake the American craft.

Brooks immediately ordered the planes back to the deck of the *Nimitz*. The MiG's had six air-to-air missiles each, but no guns and no bombs, and it was unlikely that they were going to attack any units of the task force. Rather, their objective was to keep the Americans from enjoying mastery of the air over the coast of Khuzestan Province.

But the planes were simply not quick enough. Brooks ordered four F-16's of the Black Ace Squadron to scramble and intercept the MiG's. At a speed of 1,300 miles per hour, the F-16's were still slower than the MiG's, but they were armed with advanced Sidewinder missiles which could be a persuasive argument in their own right.

No sooner had he radioed the command to the Air Operations Center than the MiG's launched their missiles. Twenty feet in length, they could scarcely be seen from the *Nimitz*. But their effect was not difficult to perceive. Three Intruders, making a frantic rush out into open waters, were hit and exploded in midair before any of the pilots had a chance to eject themselves. Two Corsairs were similarly blown apart, their bodies broken in two.

From every corner of the sky, it seemed, flaming bits of fuselage, wing, and tail were plummeting down into the Persian Gulf.

"Oh, Christ," Brooks muttered.

His face was pale and his expression contorted into a grimace. He was helpless to do anything to help his remaining fliers. The F-16's still weren't off the deck of the carrier yet; everything was happening much too fast.

Six of the American fighters finally made it back. The

MiG's did not follow or attempt to attack the U.S. warships lying off the coast; instead they climbed to almost 50,000 feet and, in formation, made a single pass over the *New Jersey, Tattnall,* and *Nimitz* before turning around and vanishing over Iranian territory.

The message was unmistakable: While the Americans possessed the firepower to subdue Iranian artillery on the beach, they had yet to control the air. The downing of the American fighters was intended to warn the U.S. that the Soviets might well go to the assistance of the Iranians in the event that Marines actually did go in. How much assistance, was another question, but no one on the admiral's bridge early that morning of April 24 believed that it wouldn't be considerable.

22

APRIL 25
QUM, IRAN

Zoccola and Hahn saw the situation in Qum deteriorating by the day. Not only did they have to elude the Revolutionary Guards who were now present in the streets everywhere, but they also had to watch as new Soviet detachments arrived almost hourly.

These detachments included an artillery brigade with five battalions equipped with 180mm S-23 guns and 203mm B-4M howitzers, an airborne assault brigade, an engineer brigade, a pipe-laying regiment, two field and evacuation hospitals, a signal battalion of 1,000 men to maintain phone and radio nets in the area, and a headquarters battalion to plan and coordinate strategy on the Qum front.

But it wasn't just the presence of Soviet forces in the Qum area that was a cause for concern. On the morning of April 25th an Antonov-22 arrived, bearing the commander-in-chief of the Southwestern Strategic Directorate, the commander-in-chief of the Long-Range Air Army recently transferred from East Germany, and the head of the Chief Intelligence Directorate (the GRU).

That so many high-level officials would decide to turn up at once in Qum indicated to Hahn and Zoccola that the

Soviet move into Iran might not be just a temporary effort to apply political pressure, but a more permanent occupation. Consequently, the chance that the Kremlin was seriously contemplating fighting a war with American troops was that much greater. While senior defense officials from Moscow constantly shuttled back and forth to Kabul to coordinate the war effort there, at no time had Afghanistan attracted a military delegation equivalent to this one.

Especially alarming was the appearance of the commander of the Long-Range Air Army, Vladimir Yeremenko, and the Commander of the Strategic Rocket Forces of the Southwestern Strategic Directorate, Alexei Imozentsev, for these were the two men who were in charge of delivering nuclear bombs and tactical nuclear weapons, respectively. Of course they would have to answer to Stavka—the headquarters of the Supreme Commander. The Supreme Commander, in this case, was the Minister of Defense. Also on the Stavka were other high-ranking members of the Politburo and the Party's Central Committee. But that they were there, on Iranian soil, meant that preparations were under way to employ nuclear weapons in the event that the war threatened to go against them.

In Qum proper there was only a scattering of Soviet troops to be seen, mostly military police who'd assumed the role of directing traffic in the ancient city. The traffic primarily consisted of tanks, armored personnel carriers, and towed antitank guns. (Towed antitank guns were favored by Soviet strategists over self-propelled guns for a number of reasons: one was that manufacturing them was easier; another was that, once emplaced, they formed a kind of final redoubt due to their lack of mobility. Thus their nickname: "Farewell, Motherland!")

It was thought that it was better not to give the inhabitants of the holy city the impression that they were being occupied by an enemy force. After all, the Red Army was here at the behest of the Grand Ayatollahs and was consequently to be considered an ally. So the bulk of Soviet troops in the area were stationed five miles outside of Qum.

However, it was becoming a common enough sight to see streamlined black ZIL limousines speeding through the ancient streets, red and blue lights blinking atop their roofs. Inside, concealed from view by tinted windows, were the Soviet commanders, advisers, and intelligence officials who daily made courtesy calls on the ayatollahs.

"They pretend to consult with them," said Farouk when he next paid a visit to Hahn. "But really they don't give a damn what the mullahs say. They will do as they wish. Tomorrow they will open a front and begin the drive on Teheran."

They were seated on the floor of yet another safe house, a cool white stucco structure with windows facing a southern exposure. There were mats and a coal stove and a small chest atop which rested a carved wooden stand for the Koran; otherwise there was no furniture in the two rooms where Hahn and Zoccola had taken shelter for the last twenty-four hours.

How Farouk had found them was a mystery, just as it had been the first time he'd made contact. He insisted that he hadn't been followed, but neither Hahn nor Zoccola was particularly reassured.

"Are you certain that the Russians intend to launch an attack against Teheran *tomorrow?*"

Farouk nodded his head confidently. "My information is always reliable. It comes from the Sources of Inspiration."

What a name for a collection of fanatics, Zoccola thought. It was the kind of name he'd expect a soul group to have.

Obviously Drexell would have to be notified that the Soviets were about to attack the capital. He suspected it might be a diversionary strike, one meant to focus attention on the north of the country when it was Khuzestan that was the true objective. But it was not Zoccola's place to make those determinations. His present mission was to somehow secure the release of the Ayatollah Zayedi.

Farouk had brought with him the plans of the house in which the ayatollah had been imprisoned for the last five and a half years. How he'd managed to get hold of them he would not say. "The only thing that matters is that they are accurate," he said and then proceeded to point out the security posts that were set at regular intervals around the house.

"There are eight Revolutionary Guards on the outside," he explained, "and another six inside. They are armed with semiautomatics and machine guns. But they maintain a discreet presence so that the people who live nearby have no idea that this house is important. Sometimes you see only one or two Guards on the front gate. It is behind the walls, in the courtyard, where most of them are positioned."

"How often are they rotated?" Zoccola asked.

"Every twelve hours. There is so much need for soldiers that they cannot spare more men. Also, except for the commanding officer, they are young. Some of them are maybe sixteen years old, eighteen the oldest."

"Sounds to me like they don't anticipate anyone coming in and trying to spring him," Hahn said.

Farouk gave him a puzzled glance. "Spring him?" he asked uncomprehendingly.

"It means help him escape," Zoccola said.

"Ah, yes. Spring him, what a felicitous phrase. What you say is correct. Many people have forgotten the Ayatollah Zayedi."

"Should we attempt to warn him that we're about to do this thing?" Hahn asked Farouk.

"No, much too dangerous. It is true that messages are smuggled in and out all the time, but there are too many traitors."

Zoccola agreed that it would be too much of a risk. They would just have to surprise the eighty-year-old ayatollah in the same way they did his captors.

"From what you tell me, Farouk," Zoccola went on, "I think we would have to move at night, toward the end of the first shift, half an hour before the next one comes on. We want to hit them when they're tired and inattentive."

Farouk saw the wisdom in this. "Have you found the help you will need to do this?"

Perhaps, Zoccola thought, he was no longer so convinced that he and Hahn could pull off this operation. Certainly they didn't give the appearance of having a great deal of firepower at their disposal. All Farouk could see were two men on the run, sitting on a mat in a safe house. Not a sight to fill someone with very much confidence.

"We're working on that right now," Hahn said.

Farouk nodded, but it was apparent he remained dubious.

"We must do this thing tomorrow night. So you must be ready by then."

"Why tomorrow?" Zoccola asked. This was far sooner than he expected. There was no telling how long it would take their arms dealer friend, Muhammed Arif, to dig up the necessary arms and men to carry out this operation. Zoccola and Hahn had been thinking more in terms of a week's time.

"Because when the Russians decide to move on Teheran, what will Colonel Shastri do? He will begin bombing Qum in retaliation."

"You know this for a fact?" Zoccola was astounded. This man, enigmatic as he might be, was a veritable fount of information. Of course, it might turn out that much of it wasn't accurate. If the guns along the Qum-Teheran front stayed silent tomorrow, he'd reconsider his estimate of the man.

"Believe me, this will happen," Farouk said. "Already the ayatollahs have made plans to evacuate. And when they do, they will take with them their most important political prisoners, including the Ayatollah Zayedi. Once he is moved, we will lose our chance to get him. So you understand how urgent it is to act."

Zoccola and Hahn understood; it was just that they weren't sure what they were going to do about it—not when all they had was twenty-four hours to work with.

23

APRIL 26
TEHERAN

James Lisker awoke to the sound of rumbling. His bed was vibrating crazily and the walls were shaking so badly that bits of plaster began to loosen from them and drop to the floor. His eyes caught sight of his alarm clock before it too crashed to the floor and broke apart. Ten minutes of five in the morning.

His first thought was that an earthquake had struck the capital. Devastating quakes happened all the time in Iran. But a moment later, when he heard the detonation of a bomb, he realized that it wasn't an earthquake at all. He suddenly became aware of the sirens wailing out an alert that had come too late as well as the sound of antiaircraft fire.

He was in a temporary U.S. military support station located on Talleghari Boulevard, less than a mile away from the U.S. Embassy, which had figured so prominently in the early days of the Iranian revolution. Given the luxury of time, Lisker might have reflected on the ironies of the current situation, with more American soldiers and advisers in Iran than were ever in the country in the heyday of the Shah.

But there was no time. Events were moving too fast, as was quite apparent from what was happening outside his window.

The one window of his room, situated on the tenth floor of the building requisitioned by the Joint Services Mission to Iran (JSMI), faced northwest toward the Hilton Inn, the Catholic Mission, and the Hyatt Crown Regency. In the grim gray sky above Teheran, Soviet bombers seemed to be operating with relative impunity.

With his practiced eye, Lisker could identify half a dozen Tu-22 bombers—most likely the Blinder-C model—along with several Bears with Kangaroo air-to-surface missiles under their fuselages, and another four Badger medium-range bombers.

Puffs of smoke from antiaircraft guns in and around the capital dotted the sky, but the bombers proceeded without being struck. Bombs were falling mostly on the perimeter of the city, from what Lisker could see.

The command center of the Joint Services Mission was installed on the third floor, and it was there that Lisker thought to go first. Throwing on some clothes, he ran down the stairs rather than wait for an elevator. His decision to do so was fortunate.

Halfway down the stairs the lights went out. He surmised that one of the bombs had just knocked out a generating station.

Emergency generators brought the power back to the Mission headquarters. Even so, the command center was in pandemonium. Personnel, some half dressed, were tearing about the one large room that made up the center, screaming orders, demands, and imprecations. It was like a bad day on the stock exchange. Men were trying to decipher telex cables that had been cut off in midsentence by the power failure, and no less than fifteen people were manning phone lines, shouting to make themselves heard.

Over the roar of voices and the repeated explosions from outside, Lisker could make out a few phrases—"The Kurosh-e-Kabir highway's hit!"—"Ten fighters destroyed at Doshen Toppeh"—"Mehrabad's taken several direct hits, the terminal's gone, at least forty dead there!"—"The electric station on the Vanak Highway's just gone out! They're working on getting the juice back from the station on Karaj."

Lisker discovered Sunderland in a corner, being briefed

by a liaison from Shastri's army. It was obvious from the expression on his face that Sunderland was becoming exasperated with the liaison, a dark, bearded man whose hands were in continuous motion.

Seeing Lisker approach, Sunderland turned away from the Iranian and said, "We gave them your warning last night and they goddamned ignored it. Shastri dismissed our intelligence, wouldn't believe the Soviets planned to attack."

Lisker was especially aggrieved, although not surprised, because it had been he who'd conveyed the warning to Sunderland as soon as he'd heard it from Drexell. (It was risky to communicate directly with Hahn and Zoccola, though they were only a hundred miles away, since messages might be intercepted or their position given away. Communication between Triad operatives thus had to be routed through Drexell on board the *Nimitz*.)

Sunderland had in turn gone directly to Shastri with the message. "First Shastri had me stew for an hour in his office before he would see me, then he told me that his agents had told him the Russians were bluffing, that they had no intention of opening another front to the north. Hell's bells, you see where that kind of thinking got them."

Redirecting his attention to the liaison, who seemed not to have understood a word of their exchange, he said, "I hope you're not counting on us to defend Teheran. Because if the Red Army decides to take it and absorb the losses, they can get here a hell of a lot more quickly than we can."

The liaison gave him a blank look.

"Did you hear what I said?"

"Yes, I heard. The Iranian army will defend the capital to the last man. We will preserve our honor."

Then he snapped to attention, gave a smart salute, and marched out of the command center.

"How do you like that?" Sunderland said, making no attempt to conceal his astonishment. "Honor, hell. I'm all for honor, but it's not going to help save Teheran."

All-clear signals were sounding now, but they could still hear the distant thud of more bombs as the Soviet bombers continued to target sites outside of Teheran.

Damage reports were arriving from all parts of the city now that it was safe to be outside. It appeared that the attack had been designed to knock out factories, airports, electric substations, arms depots, roads and other strategic installations rather than cause a catastrophic loss of life. The center of Teheran had been spared the worst though there were fires burning in many districts and hospitals were being flooded with casualties.

But it wasn't just the loss of strategic installations and jet fighters that was so disturbing. The predawn raid had wreaked such havoc and taken the residents of Teheran by such surprise that they stood in danger of becoming completely demoralized. Should Soviet tanks start moving up the Tarasht Highway, the inhabitants of Teheran might be tempted to turn out with red flags rather than Molotov cocktails.

Fifteen minutes after the raid had ended, reports began filtering in that Soviet ground forces had begun to move across the Shur River toward the city of Rey. If Rey, which was situated just south of Teheran, fell, then it would be only a matter of time before the capital fell too.

"Shit, I don't know what we're going to do," Sunderland muttered. Shouting to one of his aides, he said, "Would you get that son of a bitch Shastri on the phone. I don't want any excuses. I need to talk to him immediately."

As the aide was trying to comply, another aide, harried and unshaven, rushed up to him with a cable he'd just torn out of the telex machine.

Sunderland read it out loud: "A brigade-strength SPETSNAZ unit is moving on Karaj."

SPETSNAZ were diversionary troops, airborne forces used to carry out reconnaissance, assassination, and the sabotage of enemy headquarters and communications centers.

They were generally dropped at night preparatory to advancing subunits of the main force. That they should be sighted implied that a full tank army might be along imminently. Karaj lay just to the northwest of Teheran. The implications of its being a Soviet target were clear to both Sunderland and Lisker.

"My guess is that they're trying to encircle the city," said Lisker.

Sunderland concurred. "They realize that they'll incur

too many losses by trying to strike us directly. Instead they'll attempt a stranglehold of the city, I suppose, cut us off from food and any resupply lines, and force Shastri to capitulate."

To his aide he said, "Have you gotten hold of the colonel yet?"

"Wait a minute, sir, they're trying to find him."

"What the hell's that supposed to mean?"

"He's inspecting the damage to the presidential compound."

"Fuck the presidential compound. He blew it half apart when he seized it himself. What's he worried about?"

The aide held up his hand. "He's on the line now, sir."

Sunderland grabbed hold of the extension. His voice suddenly became polite; firm, but polite.

"Mr. President, I'd like to know how you intend to respond to today's attack."

Lisker had no way of hearing Shastri's reply until Sunderland hung up and told him, "He believes that we're going to come to his aid and says that he'll be able to hold out until we do."

"He's got a point," Lisker acknowledged. "Teheran goes down the tubes, it'll look very bad for the President."

"But you know as well as I, Jim, that we can't airlift enough troops and plunk them down here in time to save Shastri. Even if we had enough Galaxies to transport the thousands of boys we'd need, it wouldn't do us any good. Most likely we'd make them prisoners of an enormously difficult political and military situation. Who the hell expected that the Russians would try to take Teheran this soon in the war? Shit, we figured they'd wait until they were up to full strength."

"It might be a bluff," Lisker said, echoing Zoccola's assessment. "I can't believe that the Russians are prepared to operate on two fronts, here and in Khuzestan."

"You might have a point but, Jesus, it sure as hell looks like this is the place they've targeted. They have air support down in the Gulf, but their ground forces haven't gotten anywhere south of the Zagros yet."

"My bet's with Khuzestan."

Sunderland shrugged. "I suppose we'll have to wait and

see what develops. There's not much we can do now, not so long as our hands are tied." What he meant was that the Joint Mission still had no authorization to conduct combat against Soviet troops unless in self-defense. Besides which, it didn't have sufficient numbers or weapons at its disposal to assume a combat role.

"So what does Shastri intend to do now?" Lisker asked. "I can't imagine he's about to sit on his ass and let the Russians tighten the noose around him."

"He won't tell me. He just kept saying he plans a 'determined response.' That was his term for it."

"He still has some fighters, doesn't he?"

"The Russians didn't get them all."

"It wouldn't surprise me if he sends them over Qum and reciprocates."

"Wouldn't surprise me either," said Sunderland. "Now you're going to have to excuse me. I have a shitload of work that needs my attention."

A few minutes after Sunderland had left, a message arrived for Lisker.

It took him nearly an hour, in the privacy of his room, to decode it. When he'd done so, he read: "TRIAD: EYES ONLY. IF ALL ELSE FAILS, SHASTRI TO BE TERMINATED. SIGNAL WILL BE: BITTER FRUIT. DESTROY THIS. DREXELL."

Lisker held a match to both the original and his encoded copy and watched until they were in flames. When and if the signal came, he would be ready.

JOINT CHIEFS MEET AT WHITE HOUSE

WASHINGTON, April 25 (Reuters)—The Joint Chiefs of Staff were summoned to an urgent meeting at the White House today to discuss developments in Iran. Present at the meeting were President Creighton Turner, Defense Secretary Martin Rhiel, and National Security Advisor Thomas Kriendler. According to a White House senior official, the meeting, which lasted for three and a half hours, was held for the purpose of considering a response to recent Soviet attacks against

Teheran. "One of the options we're considering," the senior official said, "is to send Marines into Khuzestan Province." He added that the logistics were all in place and that the Marines could be put on shore "at a moment's notice." Pentagon sources say that the President has decided to delay at least for twenty-four hours any decision regarding the deployment of Marines in Iran.

PRESS PROTESTS NEW WAR REGULATIONS

NEW YORK, April 25—Morris Pennell, senior editor of the *St. Louis Post-Dispatch* and president of the American Society of Newspaper Editors, sent an open letter to the White House today protesting new government regulations regarding coverage of the war in Iran. Writing on behalf of the Society, he said, "It is inexcusable in a country that treasures the First Amendment as America does, that representatives of the press should be barred from covering the actions of U.S. forces in Iran and the Persian Gulf." Since the beginning of hostilities in Iran, no reporters or photographers have been allowed in that country. Six reporters who managed to slip in through Turkey were briefly detained by Iranian soldiers loyal to Colonel Shastri's provisional government and turned over to the Joint U.S. Mission in the country. The Mission promptly expelled them, citing personal safety as its reason. A spokesman for the White House said, in response to Mr. Pennell's letter, that "as soon as conditions in Iran are relatively stabilized, the media will be permitted in." Until this point, news of the war has come either from the Pentagon or from the few foreign press correspondents still functioning in Teheran.

24

10:00 P.M., APRIL 26
QUM

While the world waited for the United States to decide whether to send Marines into Khuzestan, further heightening the risk of an all-out confrontation between the two superpowers, Jerry Hahn and John Zoccola were preparing to free the one man who might be able to unify Iran, the Ayatollah Hadi Zayedi.

Muhammed Arif, who was being exceptionally well paid by Triad for his services, had made good on his promise and delivered five men armed with automatic weapons and grenade launchers, as well as an armored vehicle built to withstand a direct hit with an artillery shell. The vehicle was a four-wheel drive based on solid rubber tires, covered with a coat of paint that Arif said was computer-designed so that at night it would be virtually invisible. In daylight it appeared to be blue-gray.

Of the five men Arif had recruited, three were recognizable to Zoccola, who remembered them from the night they'd participated in the prison break-in in Teheran. They looked as disreputable as ever, capable of committing the most obscene crimes if they were sufficiently well compensated. They had an intriguing array of weapons with them, Bren guns, assault rifles, M-16's, and AK-47's. They neither knew nor cared what their mission was to be. In ordinary times they had been thieves, rapists, and murderers whom no society would tolerate beyond prison walls. But now they could operate freely; in contrast with the various regimes and factions that fought for control of the country, their crimes seemed trivial, undistinguished. When people were being regularly executed by the hundreds on orders from the government, the sort of murders they perpetrated seemed almost innocent. Their motives were base and petty; they killed because of greed or revenge or simply because they had the impulse to extinguish life, but they entertained no thoughts of killing off thousands because others did not believe in God or because they supported America or Russia. Such things made no difference to them. To their mind, the men who ran governments and prisons were equally deranged.

Hahn expressed his dismay about using these sociopaths for an operation so crucial to Triad's mission. But Zoccola reasoned that they were far better off with cold-blooded killers who went about their business in a reliable manner than with ideologues of one stripe or another. "Look," he said, "it's the best we could do under the circumstances. We were given twenty-four hours to work with. That's hardly enough time to smuggle a brigade of Rangers across the Shur River and into Qum."

Hahn conceded the point, but he remained uneasy. These men looked as if they were as ready to put a bullet into the Americans as into the Revolutionary Guards who surrounded the Ayatollah Zayedi.

At ten o'clock at night Zoccola gave the signal to move out. The truck, which Arif said had originally been used by a corrupt official in the Shah's time, was parked in an alley that ran in back of the safe house. Zoccola saw that what Arif claimed was true; from a distance the truck was submerged in the darkness. You knew that something was there; you just weren't sure what.

It was a clear night with a crescent moon as bright as a neon sign and lots of stars. Zoccola and Hahn would've preferred clouds; now they would be more exposed. But obviously the weather was not in their power to change.

It was eight and a half miles to their destination, a route

that took them through a narrow, twisted geometry of streets. A blackout was in effect, and to Hahn it felt as though they had gone back in time and were proceeding through a medieval city that would never see the dawn of the twentieth century.

Occasionally they would pass a patrol, and if their armored vehicle was spotted, it was assumed that it was a Russian personnel carrier of some sort. No attempt was made to discover who its occupants might be.

Twenty minutes after setting out, they reached their destination. Slits on the left side of the truck were suddenly filled with the barrels of a Bren, an AK-47, and a 50-caliber Browning machine gun.

Surprise was the key to the operation.

According to Farouk, who was at this moment obeying the curfew at home, there would be three guards in front of the ayatollah's house tonight.

And there were. They had the look of men who'd long grown bored with their assignment. One was drinking tea out of a mug. He was the first to see the truck. He seemed not to know what to make of the ghostly vehicle.

Before he could alert his friends, the Bren took him out with a burst of four rounds. As the other two were sighting their AK-47's, they too were struck. Since all three guns were fired simultaneously, no one could take credit for the kills.

Now the back of the truck swung open, the five commandos leaped out, still firing, with Zoccola and Hahn right behind. Zoccola was armed with his P-230, Hahn with the light .32.

A Revolutionary Guard who couldn't have been more than sixteen materialized at the front gate, which he drew open just an inch or so to see what had happened. A well-aimed round from Zoccola's gun hit him in the eye. Blood spurted out and, with a muffled scream, he fell back.

The gate was open.

Camouflaged by the sweeping leaves of a palm, a machine gun opened up on them from a pillbox mounted on top of the wall.

The attackers, however, were well acquainted with the

security arrangements of the house. One of the commandos was already training the pillbox in his sights, ready to demolish it with a grenade launcher, but he was felled in the gun's initial fusillade.

A second commando ran to retrieve the launcher, dropping to the ground to avoid his companion's fate. In the meantime, the others were pushing through the gate into the yard of the compound where the opposition was much more intense.

One of the most fearless of Arif's recruits was hit immediately. Despite the massive insult to his body, he staggered forward, loosing a barrage with the Bren that he'd balanced against his hip. He had the satisfaction of hearing a cry of agony come from a Revolutionary Guard, followed in an instant by the sight of him collapsing to the ground.

The Guard began to thrash, making a strenuous effort to get himself upright. Blood covered the whole front of him so that it was difficult to say just where he'd taken the hits. His beard was soaked through with blood and of his face very little was visible but the whites of his bulging eyes. At last he succeeded in picking himself off the ground. He was dazed, so traumatized that it was likely he couldn't register the pain. A burst from one of the automatics wielded by Arif struck him in the neck, releasing a torrent of blood and sending him down for good.

The Revolutionary Guards had staked out a position just in front of the house; with high brush and bougainvillea plants to conceal them, they held an advantage. Steady fire forced the attackers back toward the gate. One commando attempting to make his way back was cut down from behind, his head turned into a bloody pulp.

A few seconds later there was an enormous explosion as a grenade launched from outside the wall reached its destination and took out the machine gun nest. Fragments of the wall and the pillbox came raining down on them.

The grenade launcher was brought through the gate and aimed at the bougainvillea where the defenders were hunkered down.

More fire was being trained on them from the house.

Zoccola began to have the feeling that there were more

Revolutionary Guards here than Farouk had indicated. Had there been a leak or was it just by chance that the house had been reinforced on this particular night?

The commando inserted another grenade into the barrel of the launcher. Answering fire tore into the wall above his head. The grenade soared into the air, landing a foot from the bougainvillea. There was a flash of light and a concussive rumble. A body went flying into the air, looking like a marionette suddenly jerked up by its strings.

Fire still continued to come from the second-floor windows.

"We could be pinned down here for fucking ever," Zoccola said. Their problem was that they couldn't start blowing up the house for fear of jeopardizing the life of the man whom they'd come to save.

Another couple of minutes passed, with only an exchange of desultory fire. But they couldn't remain where they were for long; the defenders would have summoned reinforcements by now. The attackers had only a short time to get into the house, secure Zayedi, and get him out.

Zoccola and Hahn decided to go ahead with the contingency plan they'd agreed upon earlier. Leaving the three surviving commandos to cover them, they went back out the gate and returned to the truck. Arif was sitting at the wheel, and the motor was running.

What they intended to do was go around to the rear and clamber up the wall to the rooftop. According to Farouk, a door on the roof led into the house. It was exceedingly dangerous to use, though, because as soon as one opened the door he was likely to be exposed to murderous fire.

But to Zoccola it was worth taking the chance. And having gone this far, Hahn couldn't see that their situation could become very much more precarious than it already was. He seriously began to doubt whether he'd live to tell this particular tale.

The truck sped around to the rear; a blank white stone wall faced them. Neither Hahn nor Zoccola could see any Revolutionary Guards posted in the bulletproof windows, but they were certain that they must be there, anticipating an attack from this side.

Nonetheless, they slipped out of the truck and, propping a ladder against the wall, began the climb up. Arif, manning one of the Browning 50mm guns inside the truck, trained the weapon on the top of the wall in the event that one of the sentries should suddenly appear.

Zoccola was the first to reach the roof. Just as he was hoisting himself up, he spotted a Revolutionary Guard, his back turned to him, pacing restlessly from one end of the roof to the other. The crackle of gunfire in the front of the house had him distracted. Zoccola scanned the flat stone surface of the roof; there was a water tank in the middle, surrounded by a lake of water created by the bullets that had pierced the tank. Beyond that, in the glare of the floodlights that were set around the perimeter of the roof, he could see another four Revolutionary Guards crouched down as they fired on the attackers in the front.

Halfway down the ladder, Hahn was waiting impatiently for Zoccola to make his move. As quietly as he could, Zoccola pulled himself over the top and flattened himself on the roof. Hahn followed him up and, observing the Revolutionary Guard nearby, took the same precaution.

Now they became conscious of the drone of aircraft approaching from the north. The Guard also heard them, for he looked up toward the sky, shielding his eyes with his hand from the blinding brightness of the floodlights. Caught in the glow of the crescent moon were six B-52H bombers, each armed with twenty short-range attack missiles and conventional bombs.

Zoccola and Hahn were astounded. They'd been led to expect that Shastri might order a bombing raid on Qum, but they assumed that only Iranian army aircraft would be employed, mostly the F-4 Phantom II's which had seen service in the war against Iraq. But Iran had no B-52's in its depleted arsenal. The only conclusion they could draw was that the President had decided to authorize their use in retaliation for the predawn raid on Teheran that morning. Previously these planes, with a range of 12,500 miles and a maximum cruising speed of 595 miles, had only been employed in Iran against roads, rail lines, and bridges. Evidently that policy had undergone some change in the last eighteen hours.

As the planes banked and began unleashing their first

load of bombs, Zoccola motioned for Hahn to get himself in motion.

The sentry was standing only six yards away from them, his eyes fixed on the spectacle of the American bombers, their flight path punctuated by repeated bursts of antiaircraft fire.

All at once he heard the sound of footsteps behind him. He swiveled about, ready to discharge the AK-47 strapped over his shoulders, when Zoccola fired the P-230.

The Revolutionary Guard took the 9mm round in the chest and, with a muffled cry, staggered back, then toppled off the roof.

His companions toward the front of the roof were so preoccupied that they failed to see what had happened. Nor could they have heard much of anything with the furious noise erupting from bombs detonating to the north and west of the city. The whole sky seemed ablaze with light.

The door leading down into the house was situated a few feet from the ruptured water tank. Zoccola and Hahn ran to it. It wasn't locked, but there was now nearly half a foot of water swirling around it. As soon as they drew the door open, the water poured into the room below, making for a slippery descent down the narrow set of stairs.

They heard a man in an adjoining room shouting something in Farsi.

Then a Revolutionary Guard appeared, evidently expecting to see one of his comrades. Too late he realized that he was confronting two of the invaders. Before he could react, both Hahn and Zoccola opened fire. He grunted and fell. As water leaked in from the opening to the roof, it began to spread the blood emerging from the wound in his chest. He was barely alive, gurgling as the water gradually covered him over. And when he died, it was not from the wound but because he lacked the strength to lift his face above the rising level of water.

From the plans of the layout, the Triad operatives knew exactly where to find Zayedi. Unless he'd been transferred in the last twenty-four hours, they could expect to find him on the first floor, to the rear of the house, where he was confined to three small rooms.

A marble stairway led them to the first floor, past

what looked like funerary vases and Greek statues. The house had once been the home of an emissary of the Shah who had a penchant for collecting antiquities. A bust of Hera had recently lost a nose and developed a long ugly crack across both cheeks as the result of a stray round.

Glass lay strewn about the floors; the elegant arched windows were all shot out. A Revolutionary Guard was stretched out, motionless, among the glass, blood soaking through his camouflage jacket.

They moved into a narrow corridor, decorated with framed photographs of the Grand Ayatollahs, with the late Ayatollah Khomeini's portrait wreathed with black crepe occupying a special place. The corridor joined the front of the house to the quarters the imprisoned Zayedi had been placed in.

There was one Guard at Zayedi's door. Spotting Zoccola and Hahn rushing him, he fired, spraying the corridor with automatic fire that left the photographs of the mullahs riddled with bullets. Both Zoccola and Hahn threw themselves to the floor, returning fire at the same time.

Their aim was low, but one of Hahn's bullets, more by luck than anything else, struck the Revolutionary Guard in the ankle, just grazing it but causing him enough pain to make his weapon falter. In that instant Zoccola realigned his sight and fired twice. The Guard was spun around and, when he collapsed, his assailants could see where his brains, thrown out of a gaping hole in the back of his skull, now clung to the door in back of him.

They found the door locked. Zoccola applied a small quantity of plastique to the lock. The explosion that followed was practically soundless. The lock and bolt on the other side fell away. Zoccola kicked open the door.

Inside they discovered themselves in a small room. There was an elliptical basin set into a slab of black marble in the center of the chamber, and the only light came from candles set into niches in the walls. Near the basin, resting on his knees, was the man they had come for, the Ayatollah Hadi Zayedi.

Despite the bombs going off all around Qum, despite the unending clatter of automatic fire and the detonations of grenades, Zayedi was able to maintain an inhuman state of serenity as he continued his evening devotions. He didn't react to the sudden intrusion of Hahn and Zoccola. They might be ready to assassinate him, for all he knew, and yet he still did not turn around or show any sign that he realized they were there.

The Triad operatives stood immobilized for a moment, awed at the man's equanimity. In a night full of astonishing sights, neither Zoccola nor Hahn had witnessed any quite so astonishing as this.

"Excuse me . . ." Zoccola said.

At last the ayatollah turned his head and regarded them, still without altering his position on the floor.

For a man in his eighties, he appeared surpisingly strong, his eyes glimmering, his beard peppered with black and gray. Experience ran deep in his face, etching itself in lines and creases.

"We're here to free you," said Hahn a bit tentatively, for there was nothing about this man to suggest that he found his present situation undesirable. He looked as if he would be at home anywhere in the world.

Zoccola had heard Farouk talk of Zayedi as the savior of Iran, but he wondered how willingly he would actually assume such a role. But that was a question that would have to wait. Right now they had to get him out of this house.

Not sure whether he'd been understood, Hahn repeated his words in Farsi.

The ayatollah offered him a strange half-smile. "I know what you said. I understood."

He closed the copy of the Koran that he held in his lap and slowly rose. A flicker of pain passed across his face. His legs obviously troubled him. As he walked haltingly, Hahn went over to give him assistance.

From the front of the house there came a high-pitched scream, then the crash of glass and a concussive roar that sounded as if a grenade had just gone off. An intense exchange of automatic fire followed. Hahn shot a sidelong glance at Zayedi, but he still exhibited no apprehension.

They began back down the corridor, stepping over the body of the Guard killed minutes before. Zoccola ran ahead to see what had caused the disturbance. It was with relief that he saw one of Arif's men, bloodied but unbowed. The two others were right behind him. They'd obviously succeeded in overpowering the defenders and had now broken through.

The house was theirs. And so was the Ayatollah Zayedi.

25

APRIL 27
THE PERSIAN GULF OFF KHUZESTAN PROVINCE

In the Air Operations Center of the *Nimitz*, Admiral Jonas Brooks stood before the newly installed advanced-range computer screen, which measured over eight feet square. Glowing an electric blue in the darkness of the room, it depicted the location of all aircraft and ships within a 100-mile radius. Each plane on the screen appeared as a red line that would show where it had been for the last two minutes. Small green numbers above and below identified it and gave its current altitude. Blue designated American ships with the task force, orange designated neutral shipping in the area, and yellow designated suspected enemy naval vessels.

On shore the screen disclosed the presence of missile batteries that had been moved up to protect the Revolutionary Guards from further bombing and strafing attacks by American warplanes. Most of them were SA-5 missiles, known by the NATO code name Gammon. One of the largest antiaircraft missiles ever built, it was fifty-four feet long, with a four-foot diameter, and weighed 22,000 pounds. Propelled by a dual-stage solid-fuel rocket, it could reach a speed of Mach 3.5. As a fixed-site missile, it was vulnerable to strikes by low-level attack planes and so several additional SA-8 missiles had been installed to defend them.

White dots demarcated the SAM radar sites; as soon as their radar was turned on, a white line swept out from the site. When the beam located its target, it would lock on and white arrows would begin pulsing. In this manner the men in charge of the Air Operations Center could monitor the progress of the planes that took off from the decks of the *Nimitz* and *Independence* for the shoreline of Khuzestan.

At the moment there were only reconnaissance planes registering on the screen: E-3A's, which could provide surveillance and tracking of any airborne threat within a 250-mile range.

It was 0300 hours. Except for some sporadic fire from shore batteries early in the evening of April 25, there had been no fighting at all. The Black Sea Fleet was continuing to move closer to the American task force and was now at a distance of thirty miles from it. Russian reconnaissance planes continued making overflights, but there was no indication that the Soviets meant to engage the U.S. forces.

At 0310 hours William Drexell joined Brooks in the Air Operations Center. He looked as somber as the admiral had ever seen him in the three days he'd been on board the *Nimitz*.

"What's wrong?"

Drexell shook his head and mumbled something about being tired, but Brooks could sense that there was more to it than that.

And there was. Just two hours before, he'd received a message confirming that Zoccola and Hahn had rescued the Ayatollah Hadi Zayedi. Gratified that the mission had been successfully carried out, he'd promptly notified the White House.

But rather than agreeing to call off the invasion of Khuzestan by the Marines, the President had only acknowledged receipt of the message. Drexell surmised that his advisers, particularly Kriendler and Rhiel, had convinced him that Zayedi was not as important a factor in Iranian politics as Drexell had argued. No doubt they'd told him that American credibility in the world rested on the use of the military option. With Teheran in a Soviet stranglehold, they would've counseled a strong response. Since reinforcing the capital was not only logistically impractical, but also risked a catastrophic defeat, going into Khuzestan presented the only real military alternative.

So it did not surprise Drexell when at 0340 hours a top-secret telex was handed to Admiral Brooks. It contained only two words: Indigo Red.

Indigo Red. These code words gave Brooks the go-ahead he'd been hankering for. He gave Drexell a knowing smile.

Drexell did not need to have the message interpreted for him, Brooks saw. "I don't know whether you want to go and wake Phil up. I don't think he'll be particularly anxious to hear about this."

Drexell agreed that the presidential envoy would not be pleased that a decision had been reached to forgo diplomacy in favor of an invasion that might invite a full-scale clash between Soviet and U.S. forces.

"Anyway," Brooks continued, "I suspect he'll wake up as soon as he hears all the noise."

"And when might that be?"

Since preparations for an invasion had been under way ever since the task force left the Mediterranean for the Persian Gulf, all that were needed now were the orders to execute.

Brooks glanced up at the clock mounted above the computer screen. "We go at 0600 on the dot," he said.

He excused himself and left Drexell to watch the movement of blips on the computer screen. The latter could hear alarms ringing through the wards and corridors of the mammoth vessel, summoning the pilots up to the decks. All around him men were staring fixedly at computer consoles, depressing toggle switches, occasionally transmitting information to the pilots in the air.

By four in the morning, a score of fighters were in the air, speeding toward Khuzestan to try and soften up defense positions and knock out as many of the SAM missile emplacements as they could.

The computer screen in front of Drexell had become a confusion of lights and arrows as the American armada redeployed itself in the coastal waters and jets began on their missions of destruction. One after another, the SAM radars blinked white as they started to follow the progress of the approaching enemy craft.

Guns roared from the shore, creating enough noise to wake the dead of the last several days, let alone Phil Drummond.

Radios everywhere in the Air Operations Center, which had been mostly silent until now, suddenly came to life.

Drexell concentrated on just one exchange between the pilot of a Phantom II and the controller seated just a few feet away from him.

"F-4 on perch?" the pilot was saying through the static.

"Ready in one minute," the controller said, observing the Phantom's position, which the computer now put at ten miles offshore.

"Foco ready?"

"Roger that."

"Arm the gun."

"Gun armed."

"F-4 on perch."

The pilot sounded as if he were speaking from under water; his voice had a cold, almost disembodied quality to it.

"Go," the controller said.

The Phantom was now diving; the indicator above the blip representing it showed the loss of altitude. The computer screen Drexell had in view was exactly like the one that the pilot had in his cockpit.

It was a strange war, fought electronically. The pilot had only lights on a screen to guide him, and the voice of this controller, but otherwise had little idea as to what he was targeting.

A burst of blue lights, like a sparkler on the Fourth of July, indicated that the pilot was now firing his 40mm gun. The controller watched the screen without a flicker of emotion.

"Spectre launch," the pilot was saying.

"Roger."

A white arrow had begun to pulse toward the Phantom.

"You're locked on by target," the controller warned.

A moment later a blue streak sped across the screen and the white dot—and the white arrow—disappeared. One of the SAM emplacements had just been knocked out.

"Bull's-eye . . . bull's-eye," said the controller with undisguised glee.

"I'd like to have another go."

"Roger that."

Drexell didn't linger. Instead, he went out onto the captain's bridge to see the war with his own eyes.

The whole shoreline was ablaze, with black funnels of smoke rising into a gray-black sky. Planes repeatedly swooped over the beachhead, depositing bombs and loosing air-to-surface missiles. From time to time an SA-5 missile would soar into the air, find its target, and annihilate it in midair.

At the same time the *Iowa* and *New Jersey* were blasting the shore with sixteen-inch guns, the *Ticonderoga,* the *Tattnall,* the *Virginia* and the *Skipjack* were firing their smaller guns with such intensity that it seemed incredible that anyone would be left alive on shore.

With a little less than two hours to go until the landing, Marines were gathering on the decks of the various craft in the area, readying to put into amphibious launches.

Returning to the Air Operations Center, Drexell saw that the computer screen was now showing a number of black dots that hadn't been there a few minutes ago. They signified enemy aircraft approaching at a speed of approximately 1,500 miles an hour and at an altitude of 30,000 feet and descending.

One of the controllers hurriedly got in contact with the pilot of an E-3A surveying the battle area. "Do you have those incoming in view?"

"Roger, I see them," came the reply.

"What are they?"

"Tomcats. F-14A's, by the looks of them."

The controller registered surprise. He'd been expecting Soviet jets, just as Drexell was, but these were American planes manufactured by Grumman. One of the principal users had been Iran when the Shah was in control; eighty were bought just before he went into exile. But as far as

U.S. intelligence sources knew, the entire force had become nonoperational and was up for sale.

"Are you sure that's what they are?"

"Absolutely," the EA-3's pilot said. "Tomcats with camouflage markings, but Tomcats all the same."

The direction they were taking left no doubt that they were coming toward the task force. Six of them in all.

The controller now got on the phone with the *Nimitz*'s captain, who gave the order to intercept them before they could get to their destination.

Despite the best efforts of the American fighter jets, three of the Tomcats succeeded in getting through. They had now passed over the shoreline of Khuzestan and were coming in rapidly. Their altitude was down to 5,000 feet and they were still descending.

"What the hell?" the controller exclaimed.

For the first time that morning an expression of dismay flashed over his face.

Drexell hurried back out on the bridge, although he recognized that this was not the wisest course of action. It was obvious what the pilots of the three surviving Tomcats meant to do.

They were kamikaze fighters, fanatic Moslems who were seizing their chance to win a place in heaven by killing as many American imperialists as possible before they died. They'd probably cannibalized the parts of all eighty Tomcats to put a half-dozen of them in working condition. It didn't matter if they were barely functional; they only had to make a one-way trip.

The pilots had evidently determined their targets in advance; one was headed toward the *New Jersey*, one toward the *Iowa*, and the third toward the *Nimitz*.

The possibility had always existed that a $3.5 billion carrier like the *Nimitz* could be destroyed by a gunship worth a paltry million dollars. To protect itself the carrier had to rely on all its escort ships, which were now going into action, launching surface-to-air missiles at the attacker. The enemy plane was going into a dive when an SA missile from the *Belknap* caught it head-on. It exploded and fell in several flaming pieces into the Persian Gulf.

But the other two planes were somehow managing to avoid the missiles and antiaircraft fire directed at them.

Crewmen on board the forward deck of the *Nimitz* viewed the spectacle with disbelief. Everyone seemed to be holding his breath; it was as if time was suspended. The two remaining Tomcats appeared to hang in midair, so close to the decks of the *New Jersey* and the *Iowa* that someone on those ships might have reached up and touched them. Then both planes disappeared. There came what sounded like a scream, which was then followed by two furious explosions, one engulfing the other so that it was impossible to distinguish the two, and balls of flame in lurid hues of red, yellow, and blue shot up accompanied by thick clouds of brackish smoke. The *New Jersey* had taken the blow amidships. The armor on her was more than eighteen inches thick in places; nonetheless it was obvious that considerable damage had been inflicted. There was nothing to be seen of the conning tower and the bridge had disintegrated into a heap of mangled metal. Her sister ship, *Iowa,* had been struck on the bow and as the fire spread, setting off more explosions, she shuddered and began listing crazily.

There were Tomahawk and Harpoon cruise missiles capable of carrying nuclear weapons on board both vessels, but they were adequately protected so that even if the ships blew up entirely, the nuclear bombs would not be detonated. Still, the sight of two great American battleships in flames, their sirens blasting, was especially demoralizing to the Marines preparing for the landing on Khuzestan. Drexell imagined that the Iranian defenders watching from the shore would be buoyed, their determination to vanquish the Americans redoubled.

There was no way to tell how many of the 1,500 crewmen and officers on board each battleship were injured or killed, but Drexell suspected that the casualties would be heavy.

Admiral Brooks, having witnessed the kamikaze attack from the admiral's bridge, was giving orders to dispatch aid to the stricken craft. Already fireboats were racing toward the *Iowa* and *New Jersey* to assist in extinguishing the blazes.

Brooks was nonetheless resolved on proceeding with the invasion. He meant to adhere to his timetable because the enemy would otherwise have the opportunity to reinforce their positions.

The MAF (Marine Amphibious Force) going into Khuzestan consisted of an 18,000-Marine division made up of nine infantry battalions, thirty-two antitank guided missiles, eight 81mm mortars, thirty machine guns, a tank battalion of seventy tanks, four artillery battalions, an amphibious tractor battalion, and support units. There were, in addition, 110 aircraft attached to the MAF, including 21 UH-1N's for transport and 18 AH-1J's for attack.

The first Marine battalions were brought in by chopper while the others, including combat engineers, were put into LCU and LVT and LCM amphibious craft. The landing was to take place in four waves. The target area on shore was reckoned to be four kilometers wide and another four kilometers deep. This target area had been so softened up by the shelling and bombing that it was less like a beach than an enormous crater.

At 0530 hours, the first amphibious boats were launched. The admiral's timetable called for the initial landing to take half an hour.

Following the arrival of the assault units and combat engineers, the rifle and weapons companies would come in. They would be followed in turn by a tank company and the support units. Six destroyers and two cruisers were also participating in the operation, and up to 400 Navy and Marine aircraft were available to provide the necessary support in the skies.

By 0540, the helicopter-borne Marines put down in an area six kilometers inland. According to the first reports from their forward positions, two UH-IN choppers and one attack craft had been shot down, with all on board presumed dead. Even so, the operation, depending on a total of sixty-five helicopters, would have to be judged a success. Brooks had actually expected the losses to be much larger.

The first wave was on shore by 0555. At two-minute intervals, the next three waves put ashore until more than 3,000 men and 150 armored vehicles and artillery pieces were in Khuzestan Province. Thousands more men, with more weapons and equipment, would follow until the full complement of the Marine division was on the beach, establishing an airfield and supply dumps.

The combined forces of the Revolutionary Guards and Iranian army tried to maintain a steady fire against the invading force, but, overwhelmed by the intense firepower concentrated on them, they began falling back, retreating to higher ground.

"I think you can consider the landing on Khuzestan a success," Brooks remarked, observing the progress of the amphibious assault through binoculars. Enough smoke had cleared so that it was possible for him to have a fair view of what was happening in the target area.

Drexell stared morosely at the drama taking place before him. "It might be a success now, but this is only the beginning. Just wait until the Russians find out what's happening."

MARINES HIT THE BEACHES
AT KHUZESTAN
President Calls Assault "Successful"
Richard P. Grove
(Special to the New York Times)

WASHINGTON, April 27—American land and naval forces stormed ashore on the beaches of Khuzestan Province, the oil rich region of Iran, today at 6:00 A.M., local time. An initial force of 3,000 Marines secured a beachhead four to five miles wide and repelled a force of Revolutionary Guards and Iranian army and tank units defending the beach. Pentagon sources say that up to 500 Marines and sailors were killed and twice as many wounded in the first few hours of the strike. Kamikaze attacks by Revolutionary Guards manning F-14A's left another 140 dead and 326 wounded on board the battleships Iowa and New Jersey. Intelligence sources with the command on board the American task force in the Persian Gulf estimate that at least twice as many Iranian lives were lost. The assault came after two hours of intensive bombardment and air attacks intended to soften up the

Iranian defense positions. By the time the Marines came ashore, reports say, much of the beach resembled a desert wasteland, with gutted tanks and twisted wreckage lying in craters that American shells had created for miles up and down the coastline.

President Creighton Turner, in a fifteen-minute address to the nation last night, called the operation a "complete success." "Confronted with the prospect of a Soviet occupation of the oil fields and the imminent possibility that our access to oil in the whole Persian Gulf region would be denied, we had no alternative but to act as we did," he stated. He added that the United States had no intention of threatening the sovereignty of Iran and that all U.S. forces would be withdrawn as soon as "the Soviet Union comes to its senses and pulls all of its forces back behind its own borders."

REPORTS SAY U.S. MISSION TO LEAVE TEHERAN

ANKARA, April 27 (Reuters)—In a radio broadcast monitored here, Teheran radio reported that the 4,000-man American force composing the Joint U.S. Mission might soon be withdrawn because of the threat posed by Soviet forces now encircling the Iranian capital. According to the broadcast, American advisers to the provisional government of Colonel Ibrahim Shastri believe that the Red Army might decide to move on Teheran "at any moment" in response to the landing of U.S. Marines in Khuzestan Province.

MASSIVE SOVIET AIRLIFT TO KHUZESTAN UNDER WAY

DAMASCUS, April 27 (UPI)—The Syrian government newspaper Tichrin indicated today that the Soviet military command, now based in the Iranian holy city of Qum, was preparing a massive airlift to transport thousands of Soviet troops to embattled Khuzestan Province. A Marine assault force, launched from ships with the U.S. Sixth Fleet, is now occupying a beach head in Khuzestan. "It is expected that a sizable force is being assembled in Qum," the newspaper said, "sufficient to repel the invader." A longtime ally of the fundamentalist regime in Iran, Syria has taken the position that the principal threat to Iran stems from the United States. The Syrian government's ties with the Qum government are said to have grown closer since an army-led rebellion split Iran in two at the beginning of the month.

POLL FINDS AMERICANS SUPPORT IRAN EFFORT

NEW YORK, April 28 (AP)—The latest Gallup poll, taken just prior to the U.S. invasion of Khuzestan, shows that 56 percent of the American public favors immediate military action to prevent the Soviets from taking over Iranian oil fields and possibly shutting off the Persian Gulf to oil tankers bound for the U.S. and its allies. Thirty-eight percent of respondents were opposed to such intervention "under any circumstances," while 6 percent had no opinion.

26

APRIL 29
RIYADH, SAUDI ARABIA

Half a mile away from the Friday Mosque and just out of sight of the souk, the American and Russian met inside a mud-brick house that looked exactly like its neighbors. The only way to find this house was by means of a local guide, for there were no streets to speak of in this part of Riyadh, just a warren of paths that had originally been designed for men and mules.

"I had the devil of a time catching up with you," William Drexell was saying.

Maxim Kolnikov looked pleased; he delighted in being elusive. "For a time I thought I was in danger," he said. "When I saw you in Berlin it looked like the end. But then I am transferred, made a military attaché to the embassy here. The Saudis are beginning to like us very much."

"I don't blame them. They figure if you people win in Iran, they'll be looking to the Kremlin for protection, not us. I'd be currying favor with your ambassador too."

They were seated across a table on which a pot of tea had been placed. This particular safe house had been arranged by Kolnikov, not by Drexell, but then, it was the Russian who stood more to lose should it ever be found out that the two had met like this.

"So you believe your position is secure," Drexell said.

"It is as secure as it can ever be. Life in Russian military intelligence is a continual surprise. One is never sure when the good times will come to an abrupt end. Here I thought I was about to be disgraced and sent to the Gulag. And look what happens, I am sent to the middle of a desert. It is either too cold or too hot. No middle ground." He laughed mirthlessly.

"What interests me, Maxim, is how you managed to get hold of those documents you gave me in Berlin."

"Ah, a fascinating story. It will also explain why you only received the first half of the war plans and not the second. This is something I did not learn myself until recently. You see, in spite of all your propaganda, not every general and Politburo member is a warmonger. Many of the people surrounding the First Secretary live in constant fear of a clash with the U.S. Through certain channels, they decided to leak part of their plans to you, specifically the part that mentions we would employ nuclear weapons in the event of battlefield reverses. We wished you to understand this with utter certainty so that you would have no misconceptions. Your CIA director could not then falsely assure your President that we would not resort to such an extreme step. You would know it for certain." He shrugged. "But, you see, you went ahead with your provocative moves anyway."

"You're saying you were used when you leaked the documents?"

"Let's say that it was made easy for me. I find it intriguing to be found so useful to your people as well as to my own."

This admission made Drexell uneasy. Just how much trust could he put in this man? Probably not a great deal. And yet he had already proven his value to Triad. Moreover, at this critical juncture, his cooperation was absolutely vital. Drexell would have to trust him whether he wished to or not.

"What about the second half of the war plans you promised me in Berlin?"

"I'm afraid I have no access to them. But I don't think that it is important anymore. The situation has changed so many times that any plans that were drawn up have become obsolete."

Drexell could accept this. And, in any event, the war plans were not what interested him now. "All right, since you have an idea what lengths we'll go to, what does your government propose to do in response?"

Kolnikov gave him a long, sorrowful look. "I am afraid that your government has given our leaders no choice. It is impossible to let you control Khuzestan. We will have to fight you there. This is very regrettable and unnecessary. Your president is truly a dangerous man."

Drexell wasn't interested in his opinions of the American leadership even if he himself shared them at times. "And Teheran? Do you intend to blockade it or move on it?"

"Again we have been overtaken by events. Although there is no final decision, I imagine that the Red Army will go in and take it."

"That might result in huge casualties for you."

"I am aware of that. We'd hoped to use our military machine for political ends. We did not think that we would have to fight such a war against Iranians and Americans."

"What policy have your leaders reached governing the use of nuclear weapons?"

"I understand that they will be used only in the event that it looks as though we are about to be defeated in Khuzestan. Then that option will be seriously considered. In the end, who can say? It is such an unprecedented thing that I don't think anyone truly knows what he will do."

"There may be a way to put a stop to this before we get to that point," Drexell said.

Kolnikov looked at him with renewed interest. "Yes?"

"You might have heard that a couple of nights ago the Ayatollah Zayedi was freed from house arrest in Qum."

The Russian nodded slowly. "I heard something like this. What of it?"

"We have him."

"Yes, and what do you propose to do with him?"

"Put him in charge of Iran."

"Iran has one too many leaders already, I think."

"It might be possible to change all that. You take out

Ghafferi and we'll take out Shastri. Three minus two equals one."

"Simple arithmetic, complicated politics."

"Better that than blowing each other to kingdom come, don't you think?"

"It is an unusual proposition, I admit."

"Zayedi could rally the support of both the fundamentalists and the moderates. No one's ever going to get a hundred percent of the Iranians in back of him, but Zayedi has a shot at sixty or seventy percent. He's not identified with you, he's not identified with us. He's religious, but isn't fanatic."

"And he's eighty years old. How long do you think he will live?"

"Look, if he lives for a year or two, we've bought ourselves some time. Two years is long enough to establish a neutral Iran. At the same time our two sides agree to pull out. No one wins, no one loses."

"So you are suggesting we cut a deal, as you Americans are so fond of saying."

"Exactly."

"I will have to speak to some people, feel them out on this matter."

"What kind of response do you anticipate?"

"It is premature to speculate. But I think that there might be some interest. We will have to see. In the meantime, Mr. Drexell, perhaps you could bring me up to date on the condition of my account in Zurich."

"I was just getting to that," Drexell said as he unfolded the paper on which Maxim Kolnikov's fortunes were tallied.

27

MAY 1
KHUZESTAN PROVINCE

One of the principal problems confronting the Soviet force at the outset was establishing Ground Control Intercept headquarters for target acquisition, vectoring, and other necessary intercept capabilities. The only way that GCI could be brought into the lowlands south of the Zagros Mountains was by air, accompanied by fighter escort. However, in order for such an airlift to go off successfully, a GCI should already be in place.

The first attempt, on April 29, to bring in the GCI resulted in a dismal failure when low-altitude attack craft shot it down using forward-looking infrared technology.

It had long been common knowledge that U.S. pilots were better trained than their Soviet counterparts, that they had about twice as much time in the air and that they'd gained far more combat experience in Vietnam and Korea. Intelligence reaching the American troops on the shore in Khuzestan indicated that radars were being loaded onto Antonov-22's outside of Qum and that any day a new attempt to put down a GCI in Khuzestan would take place—most likely in daylight because it was apparent that at night U.S. pilots enjoyed the advantage.

Backfire bombers were reallocated from the Pacific Fleet

to the Black Sea Fleet to reinforce Soviet air power although this meant that the Vladivostok area, a strategically vital port, was left with much less of its usual defensive capability. Altogether sixty Backfires were deployed in Iran, almost the total inventory of Soviet naval aviation's force.

To get Soviet troops to the combat area was also a problem because the Antonov transport jets were big and sluggish and made for vulnerable targets. On the other hand, the Soviet command could not sacrifice the time that it would take to convey the troops overland, since that would allow the Americans to expand their control over Khuzestan and shore up their defenses.

Even so, the Soviets had to respond. Some Antonov-22's did make it through and by May 1 an airborne force consisting of a reconnaissance battalion, thirty-two airborne assault guns, an antitank battalion of eighteen 85mm guns, a howitzer battalion of eighteen 122mm guns, and a battalion of multiple rocket launchers along with other support battalions (communications, motor transport, chemical warfare, and an engineer company) were on the ground facing American troops. A SPETSNAZ company of diversionary troops was at work probing the forward positions of the American assault force, assisted by remnants of the Revolutionary Guards and Iranian army.

At the same time, Backfire bombers and MiG-25's began to conduct raids against the Marines, though American air defense was formidable enough to mitigate the impact these attacks would otherwise have had.

This then was the situation in the field that confronted General Clark Hammond, commander of the U.S. Marine force in Khuzestan, on May 1—hardly an auspicious day for the Russians to celebrate the revolution of the workers—when he went up in an EA-3 to survey the battle area.

The EA-3 was actually a Boeing 707 chock-full of electronic gear that could simultaneously track over 1,000 aircraft and control 100 friendly aircraft. It was also capable of tracking vehicles on land as well.

Hammond, a veteran of Vietnam, might have been mistaken for a gracefully aging Hollywood star, one who'd always been given the father-teacher roles. His benign aspect, however, was belied by his gruff manner and his impatience with subordinates and superiors alike who failed to act with appropriate dispatch.

Seated in the copilot's seat in the cockpit, he could better keep track of developments on the battlefield on the computer screen in front of him than by looking out the window. But there was one visual feature that did not require the intervention of electronics for him to remark on.

All across the oil fields, blown by a wind coming off the Gulf, was a haze of smoke. "What the hell is going on there?" Hammond asked the pilot, but he already knew the answer.

Although the oil fields had yet to be captured by the American expeditionary force, the Iranians, acting on the assumption that they would sooner or later, had decided to sabotage their own wells. Scores of them, perhaps hundreds, were now burning out of control. From horizon to horizon, almost to the foot of the Zagros Mountains, smoke rising from the blazing wells hung in the air.

Hammond directed the pilot to turn when he reached the Zagros, and they were soon over the battlefield again. The U.S. forces were now in Attack of Position Day 2+, which was regarded as attrition fighting, the slow, steady hammering away at the defense until all of Khuzestan was taken.

As the EA-3 approached the beachhead that had now been extended so that Marines occupied Khuzestan to a depth of thirteen kilometers and a width of twenty-two, the sounds of battle greeted them. Artillery exchanges, on the east between American and Iranian gunners, and on the west between American and Soviet gunners, were going on all across the battle lines. But though there were repeated clashes between advancing Marines and Revolutionary Guards, there were no reports of hand-to-hand combat between American and Soviet forces.

Hammond didn't think this was because of any political decision on the part of the Kremlin; rather, he believed that, until the Red Army could bring their forces here up to full strength, they were not anxious to risk a direct confrontation with the Americans unless they had no choice. Better to let the Iranians do the fighting for them for the time being.

The closest the Russians were to American lines, according to the EA-3's sensors, which were capable of picking up sounds, magnetic presences, and changes in shape and color, was a long-range reconnaissance patrol of twenty-seven men, six of whom were officers. What the sensors could not show, though, was whether they were on intelligence duty or a sabotage operation.

One way or another, Hammond saw no reason why they shouldn't be taken out. He radioed back to base, called Khuzestan One, with directions that the reconnaissance company should be interdicted. "If possible," he said, "try and capture some of their officers. We'd like to ask them a few questions."

Within fifteen minutes a company of Marines, armed with grenades, light machine guns, and M-16's, moved out in personnel carriers. Hammond could observe them and the Russian force on one of several video map consoles in the cockpit. To the right of the console there was a panel reading: "1 MAY: 10:12:09: LINK UP." Underneath this were the words "HYDRO/CITIES/ROADS/RR." This was followed by another series of codes and the words "CONTOURS" and "GRIDS."

The map was in full color, although it was mostly a blur of greens and browns, with minute blue lines trickling through to indicate water. The American contingents were designated with blue triangles and a code representing the relevant grid coordinates; the Soviets were designated with red triangles, the Iranians with green.

Whenever Hammond wished, he could zoom in on any part of the map and enlarge it for a better view. What would seem a maelstrom of gunfire, grenade detonations, smoke, and death from the ground, on the video console seemed a perfectly plotted, almost elegant affair. He watched the console as from the north and east the Marines moved on the reconnaissance patrol, striking them on their left and at their rear. Blue arrows swept out into the red triangle, showing where the Soviets had taken direct hits.

Hammond instinctively sought to see if he could view the battle directly, but all that was visible below was a cloud of smoke shrouding most of a dried-out ravine. The only way to tell what was happening was by looking at the map console which was processing information being fed into it by both active and passive sensors. While the active sensors like radar and sonar bounced signals off objects, the passive ones simply listened.

In less than fifteen minutes, while the EA-3 circled the battle area, Khuzestan One on the Marine beachhead radioed that the Russian company had been captured, with five Russians dead and eight wounded, against a loss of two Marines killed and four wounded.

"I expect you got a few of their officers," Hammond said.

"Yes, sir, including their commander," the dispatcher confirmed.

By the time Hammond had landed back at Khuzestan One, intelligence officers had already begun the interrogation of the prisoners.

The Russian commanding officer was in his twenties. Although unharmed, he looked shaken and apprehensive. He sat inside the tent with his hands folded in his lap, his eyes downcast, like a penitent waiting to be punished.

Hammond conferred with Major Richard Brett, an intelligence officer on loan from Langley. Brett was not only fluent in Russian, he was also a student of Soviet military strategy, and as a result knew what kind of questions to ask and, just as importantly, he knew how to frame those questions and what tone of voice to use.

"Well, Major, what does he have to say for himself?" Hammond asked.

"His name's Vaseli Orlov, comes from Tashkent. He's a captain, been in recon for six years now. My feeling is he's SPETSNAZ. He seems to have a good feel for topography too.

"But the most important thing," he went on, "is what he said about his mission. He was trying to locate our airfields and command centers."

"That doesn't strike me as anything out of the ordinary."

"No, but that's only half the story. It was what he was trying to locate them *for*. He isn't absolutely certain, but he feels he was collecting information so that the Soviets could target our installations for air strikes—"

"Still, I don't see . . ."

"Wait, let me finish, General, please. He wasn't talking about air strikes with conventional bombs."

Hammond's mouth fell open. "You mean to say that they're thinking of nuking them?"

"I'm afraid so, sir."

28

MAY 2
WASHINGTON, D.C.

At seven o'clock in the morning, May 2, the National Security Council was summoned into urgent session by the President to consider the crisis in Iran.

Present at this meeting were Jeffrey Schelling, Marty Rhiel, Thomas Kriendler, Morse Peckum, Stanley Burns of CIA, and William Drexell.

The President opened the meeting, saying, "We've just received some disturbing news from Khuzestan that indicates the Soviets are thinking about a nuclear option. Marty, how much credence do you give these reports?"

"I think we might have to give them a lot of credence. From all indications, the logistical difficulties of establishing a Soviet force in the area south of the Zagros are only getting worse. A second attempt to install Ground Control Intercept has failed. One of our F-16's shot a Condor—that's an Antonov 400—out of the sky last night. And we also managed to down two of their Blackjacks, I might add. So they really haven't the ability to consolidate their air power, and they're experiencing a hell of a lot of trouble moving their ground forces into the area."

"I think that that goes far to confirm my assessment that the Red Army never meant to move on Khuzestan in the first place, Mr. President," Drexell said, the control in his voice failing to conceal his anger.

The President chose to ignore him. "Go on," he said to Rhiel.

"So it appears that the Soviets lack the ability at this time to prevent us from taking Khuzestan. I think your judgment on this was correct, Mr. President. We went in and took them by surprise. If we'd waited longer, they would've had time to deploy their forces there. Now they have to content themselves with a rearguard action."

"The implication, then, is that because they know damn well they'll lose, they feel they have no choice but to use nuclear weapons, is that it?" Kriendler asked.

"That's more or less the situation," Rhiel replied.

"You think we're getting into a blackmail thing here?" the President's chief of staff, Morse Peckum, asked.

"It could be that," Rhiel agreed. "But I don't know whether they'll go through with it once they threaten us. I imagine the Kremlin will announce that either we pull out of Khuzestan forthwith or they'll go ahead and use nuclear weapons on our forces there."

"What do we do?" Schelling asked. "Call their bluff, threaten to use our nuclear weapons against their forces?"

"When it comes right down to it, I don't believe that they'll risk it," Kriendler said. "For what? To save the mullahs? They know just as we do that it could escalate into a nuclear war that no one would win."

Now Drexell spoke. "I think you're getting out of hand, if you'll pardon me for saying so. We have no way of knowing what the Kremlin will finally do."

The President shot a look at CIA director Stanley Burns.

Burns understood what he wanted to know and said, "He's right, Mr. President. We can't gauge Soviet intentions on Afghanistan or SALT talks; how can we predict something like this?"

"And what about your sources?" the President addressed Drexell.

"My sources are good, but even they can't tell me for certain what would happen if we decide to stay in Iran and not back down. The Russians may feel compelled to go ahead and make good on their threat even if they don't want to. That's what you can expect when you back them into a corner like that."

"Hell, they backed us into a corner," Rhiel said. "What would you have us do, apologize and go home? We do that, the Red Army will be all over Khuzestan the next day. Maybe they didn't want the oil fields in the first place, but they'll take them if we withdraw, mark my words."

"No, they won't—not necessarily," Drexell said.

"What do you mean?" the Defense Secretary said, an incredulous expression on his face.

"I mean that there's a political solution to this mess. The one I mentioned to you gentlemen back at our last meeting. But now we're in a better position than we were at that time. I have Zayedi in hand."

"Who the hell is Zayedi?" Peckum asked, annoyed at the mention of one more foreign name.

Patiently Drexell explained to the gathering who the Ayatollah Zayedi was and described what an important role he would play in the future of Iran. Then he outlined his plan for installing Zayedi in power and eliminating Colonel Shastri as well as the fundamentalist leader Ghafferi.

"What you're saying is that you want us to kill our own ally, Colonel Shastri!" Kriendler shouted. "That's madness. Look at what kind of shit we got into when we overthrew Diem."

"What's madness, Mr. Kriendler, is allowing a nuclear confrontation because neither side will give over a few thousand oil wells that are burning out anyway."

"But you don't know whether the Russians will buy this scheme of yours and reciprocate by getting rid of their own man, do you?" the President said.

At that moment the discussion was interrupted by an aide who entered the room and approached the President. The aide leaned down and whispered into his ear, then handed him what looked like a cable.

The President's face went ashen. He dismissed the aide, then gazed down the length of the long, polished table and said, "Gentlemen, it appears as if our worst fears have been realized. I have just received a wire from First Secretary

Kadiyev which reads as follows: 'Mr. President, I regret to inform you that unless all military forces of the United States are removed from Khuzestan, beginning within twenty-four hours and ending not later than the fourth of May, the Soviet Union is prepared to use all forces and weapons at its command to bring this illegal and unprovoked aggression to an end. Let there be no mistake about it, Mr. President. If a catastrophic nuclear war does break out, the blame will be on your head. I appeal to you, for the sake of all peace-loving peoples, to abandon your aggressive activities in Iran and withdraw your forces.'"

The President raised his eyes, expecting a reaction, but for the first time there was silence. No one knew what to say.

CONGRESSIONAL LEADERS PROMISE
BIPARTISAN SUPPORT

WASHINGTON, May 2—Leaders of both parties today promised "unconditional support for the President's policy in Iran" at a news conference held today at the Capitol. John Van Halan, the Democratic speaker of the House, read the bipartisan statement, which began, "At this difficult and solemn time in our nation's history, it is vital that we come together as one. As a people, we have always united whenever a threat menaced us from the outside. We have prevailed before. We will prevail again."

—the Washington *Post*

SENATOR BIDS PRESIDENT HOLD FIRM
ON IRAN

WASHINGTON, May 2—Senator Russell Beach, the influential head of the Foreign Relations Committee, saying that the Soviet threat to use nuclear weapons against U.S. troops in Iran was "nothing but a bluff, sheer and simple," condemned critics of the President's position regarding involvement in that country. "To pull out now because Kadiyev is blustering and fulminating about dropping H-bombs on us is the height of idiocy," he declared at a hastily called press conference. "It would be ridiculous to take our boys out of Iran now that they're winning. Almost a thousand Marines have died taking Khuzestan. Are we going to let their sacrifice be in vain?" Pointing out that the United States had already, in his words, "lost Iran once when we abandoned the Shah," he asked, "Are we going to lose Iran a second time because we're running scared? I think not."

—the *Chicago Tribune*

HALF A MILLION TURN OUT AGAINST WAR

NEW YORK, May 2—At least a half-million people demonstrated today in Central Park against the U.S. war effort in Iran. Police say that the mild spring weather made for a larger attendance than expected. With signs declaring "U.S. Out Now!" and "Better No Oil Than A Billion Dead!", the demonstrators listened patiently as critics of the administration denounced U.S. involvement in Iran and demanded an immediate pullback before the Soviet deadline of May 4. The police arrested half a dozen people for disorderly conduct, but said the demonstration, which lasted until early evening, was by and large peaceful.

—the *New York Daily News*

29

2:15 P.M., MAY 3
TEHERAN

As soon as Drexell deplaned at Doshen Toppeh military air base, he was greeted by James Lisker. Strewn over the air base was evidence of the bombing raid of April 26. Three Phantoms and two Intruders lay in charred ruins, wings and fuselage separated, gaping holes where tails used to be. It was a sorry sight.

The two men shook hands and went immediately to where a car, specially armor-plated for insecure road journeys, was waiting for them at the edge of the airstrip.

They did not speak until their driver had deposited them at the Hyatt Crown Regency where rooms were waiting for them. He and Lisker were among the few guests. Ever since the Joint Mission had been evacuated and the Soviets had ringed Teheran with tanks and soldiers, the number of Americans in the capital had shrunk drastically.

"Have you heard what's happening in Khuzestan?" Lisker asked. Depending as he did on the rumor mill of the capital for information, he'd heard nothing but conflicting reports.

"As far as I know, the fighting has subsided," Drexell said. "Everybody—the Russians, the Iranians, and our boys too—seems to be waiting to see what happens tomorrow.

Certainly there's been no move to pull any of our troops out. I talked to the President last night just before I left, but all he'd tell me is that he's holding consultations with the British and Germans and French, and then he'll make up his mind."

Lisker, noting that it was already midafternoon, pointed out that he had little time to spare. "Do you think the Russians are going to extend their deadline?"

"I wouldn't hold my breath on it," Drexell said. "If they do extend it, the President will be convinced his strategy is working and that they're backing down. Who knows, maybe they will. But I wouldn't want to see us chance it. That long-range bomber fleet the Soviets have deployed in Qum is ready to go at a moment's notice. We know for a fact that there are nuclear weapons on board those planes."

"I assume we'd respond in kind if they approach Khuzestan."

"Harpoon and Tomahawk cruise missiles were loaded on our bombers yesterday. The only question now is do we wait for the Russians to be the first to drop a nuclear bomb and then retaliate or do we preempt them? In the first case, it means deliberately sacrificing thousands of men. In the second, it means we've become the first to start a nuclear war. I'd hate to have the responsibility for deciding that."

Lisker, like Drexell, supported a political solution. And the political solution hinged on one man, the Ayatollah Zayedi. "Have you been in contact with Zoccola and Hahn?" he asked.

Drexell nodded. "They have Zayedi secured in a safe house in Qum. It's too dangerous to try and smuggle him out of the city. Once they hear that Ghafferi and Shastri are out of the picture, they'll be ready to present him to the public."

"Has Zayedi made any comment about all of this?" Lisker wondered whether anyone had bothered to ask him. As a symbol he was vital; as a person, he seemed almost irrelevant.

"From what John tells me, he's looking forward to running the country. He believes he's on a rescue mission and thinks of John and Jerry as emissaries of God."

Lisker laughed; he liked that one.

"The only thing I'm waiting for now is for that damned Russian, Kolnikov, to get back to me and let me know if the Soviets are willing to bite."

"When did he say he'd call?"

"Yesterday," Drexell muttered. "Yesterday."

"And you can't get hold of him yourself?"

"He wouldn't hear of it. Says it'll screw up everything if I do. So that leaves me no alternative but to wait. He did this to me in Berlin, he's doing it again. I could kill the son of a bitch."

Kolnikov was in possession of a telephone number that, once dialed, would instantly be routed to wherever Drexell was staying.

The call came at 5:20 in the afternoon, while he was in his room at the Hyatt.

Drexell assumed the Russian was calling from Riyadh, but there was no way to be sure.

"Are you having a good day, Mr. Drexell?"

"I don't know. It depends on what you've got to say to me."

"It was a complicated procedure to get to the proper authorities, but I succeeded. I have the pleasure of informing you that Kadiyev will deal."

Drexell was so gratified that for a moment he couldn't speak a word.

"Are you there, Mr. Drexell?"

"I'm here. What are the conditions?"

There were always conditions, often enough of them to make the original agreement unpalatable.

"The conditions are these: that Shastri is to be ousted first. If that is done, Ghafferi will go."

Drexell sensed that he wasn't finished. "Go on."

"I'm afraid you're not going to like the second condition any better than the first. American troops must pull out first and apologize for infringing on Iranian sovereignty. If that is done, all Soviet forces will withdraw."

Drexell had to presume that this was a maximalist position and that it would be possible to negotiate a compromise. Otherwise there was no question that it was completely unacceptable. He made this clear to Kolnikov.

The Russian was not surprised. He said, "I will talk to my people and I will call you back."

"When? Tomorrow, the day after?" Drexell shouted angrily.

"Mr. Drexell, I am as aware of the urgency of the situation as you are and am as anxious to settle this as soon as possible. Please wait by the phone."

Drexell hated to, but he waited.

In an hour's time the call came. "There is a possibility of compromise," Kolnikov said. "The withdrawal of troops can be worked out in such a way that it takes place at the same time. But on one condition they will not give. As a sign of your good faith, you must dispense with Shastri first. The Soviet Union must be satisfied that he is no longer in power in Teheran."

Drexell believed he could live with that. "If that's done," he said, "you will deliver Ghafferi."

"As soon as we have confirmation that Shastri is out, then we will deliver Ghafferi. Perhaps in a couple of hours. It should not take long. We have agents among even the Grand Ayatollahs. He cannot take a shit without us knowing about it."

"How long do we have?"

"The long-range aircraft will be in the air at seven o'clock tomorrow morning bound for Khuzestan unless you put an end to Shastri. That should give you some idea as to how long you have."

With that, Kolnikov hung up.

That left Drexell with thirteen hours to act. He first phoned Lisker, who occupied room 216, and told him to wait there until he called. "I'm going to see Shastri now and see if I can't persuade him to step down in the interest of national unity. If he refuses, I'll have to threaten him."

"And if that doesn't convince him?"

"Wait for my call," Drexell said again, replacing the receiver.

His driver was waiting in the empty lobby of the hotel. The sight of Drexell caused him to brighten; he'd been under the impression he faced a long and idle night.

The streets were dark and so were most of the buildings they passed. The government maintained that a blackout was necessary in the event that the Soviets decided to stage another bombing raid, but it was also likely that the authorities were anxious to save on electricity, of which there was an increasingly diminished supply.

They arrived at the presidential compound a little before dark, and Drexell was obliged to undergo a rigorous search by the guards before he was allowed in. He noticed that the damage done by the bombs had yet to be fully cleared away.

Half an hour was exhausted while Drexell was kept waiting to see President Shastri. There was every indication that Shastri was in his office, though the aide that welcomed Drexell and insisted on offering him a cup of Turkish coffee every five minutes said that he was away and was expected back at any moment. There were still people, most of them high-ranking officers, going in and out of the inner office.

At last Drexell ran out of patience and, ignoring the fervent protests of guards and aids alike, strode across the reception room and threw open the door to Shastri's office.

He found Shastri, a commanding presence, sitting at his desk. Two heavily decorated army officers conferred with him. They looked little short of horrified to see Drexell walk in.

A sentry, catching up with the intruder, thrust an M-16 against his chest. Drexell managed to ignore it.

Shastri gave the sentry an order to lower his gun and return to his post. "You are Mr. Drexell?" he said, smiling. "I am sorry to have inconvenienced you. I did not realize you were waiting outside. My aides are neglectful."

Drexell very much doubted that his unnecessary wait was the fault of any aide, but refrained from saying so. "I have a matter I must speak to you about in private, Mr. President," he said, fixing his eyes first on one officer, then the other.

"These are my good friends and advisers. They can be privy to anything you have to say."

Not wishing to waste any further time in useless argument, Drexell took a seat and began, mincing no words. Without explaining any of the details that would compromise such a delicate operation, he stated that the United States government could no longer support him and that he was standing in the way of a possible settlement with the Soviet Union.

"I do not care about the Russians," Shastri said, his face livid with fury. "What about the mullahs? My war has always been with them. You and the Russians have your own fight."

Without saying that Ghafferi would be overthrown if he cooperated, Drexell hinted that even the civil war could be negotiated to an end. "I assure you, Mr. President, that I would not come to you with such a request if there were any other choice. I know how difficult it must be for you. But if you step aside now, you will not only have the gratitude of the nation, you will also be left in a very influential position. I'm sure your advice will be much sought after by whatever government comes in after you."

Shastri scoffed at this. "I know what will happen. I will be executed if I stay here after resigning. I would have to go into exile. My country will fall again under the mullahs and you will have had a hand in allowing that to happen." He rose now from his desk. "There is nothing more that I have to say to you. But please know that tomorrow I wish you to leave Teheran. You are persona non grata here."

The colonel was trembling with anger, and it was obvious that the interview was at an end. Drexell wished Shastri a good night and hastened out of the office. It had been as unpleasant a meeting as he had expected.

He was not surprised by the results. He knew Shastri to be a stubborn and belligerent individual seldom given to compromise. He clearly regarded himself as the savior of his country and was not about to permit anyone to usurp that role from him.

Drexell stopped at the desk of a secretary and asked him if he might use his phone.

The secretary picked it up and listened to see whether it was still functioning, which was not always the case in Teheran these days. Then he handed it to Drexell, who dialed the number of the Hyatt Crown Regency and asked for room 216.

Lisker picked up immediately.

Drexell spoke two words, "Bitter fruit," and then hung up.

In the Hyatt Lisker began to go to work.

30

10:15 P.M., MAY 3
TEHERAN

Osman Khalif lingered late in his office at the presidential compound. He had a great deal of paperwork to do, but could not concentrate on it; he was too uneasy, too anxious.

Opposing the rule of the mullahs, he'd supported Shastri. Now it seemed that it was time to betray Shastri in the same way he'd betrayed his previous masters. For weeks Triad had paid him a sum of money that flabbergasted him; it was more than sufficient to provide for his extended family and keep his wife and children happy. All he'd had to do was to supply information about Shastri, information not just about policymaking and strategy, but about his movements, his routine, when he showed up at work and when he left at night, who his friends were, who his mistresses were and where they lived. All this he fed to Triad, never once considering what the Americans would do with it. But earlier tonight the debt had been called in.

He was instructed to call a certain phone number as soon as Shastri left his office. Because Shastri feared for his life—and he had good reason to—he would leave the compound at different times, occasionally sending doubles ahead of him, men of his build, wearing his uniform, whose appearance was meant to lure any assassin out of hiding. Like a Byzantine emperor, he had someone taste his food for him before he touched it; better the taster drop dead of poisoning than him. He slept in different quarters every night, sometimes in the presidential compound but more often in various barracks outside of the capital. The only people he really trusted were the soldiers, especially the other officers who'd conspired with him to launch the coup.

Khalif recognized that Shastri was almost completely isolated from the people, that with the Russians encircling Teheran, his power was concentrated entirely in the capital, and even there it had become shaky. Yet he would not for one second contemplate stepping down. He, whom Khalif had once seen as the savior of Iran, now seemed to be nothing more than another power-hungry officer overtaken by events he couldn't control.

Nonetheless, he did not like to think that he would be the one to precipitate his downfall. He did not know to what use the intelligence he provided tonight would be put, but he feared the worst. Moreover, what was to stop Triad from jettisoning him, leaving him to the wolves? Nothing. And yet he knew that should he fail to deliver the promised information, he would only be inviting retaliation from Triad.

It is so simple sometimes, he thought, to put oneself in an absolutely impossible situation.

At almost exactly 10:30 the door to Shastri's office came open and the colonel, accompanied by six bodyguards, appeared.

Seeing Khalif, he bid him good night.

Khalif watched him proceed down the stairs toward the door that would lead him out of the presidential office building.

He made the call.

That was all he was obligated to do. But still it might have been too much.

Lisker took the call in a house located two blocks away from the presidential compound. The building had long since been vacated for security reasons on order from the last government. In theory, it should have been guarded, but in fact it was looked at only every couple of hours by a passing patrol.

The phone had been installed months before by spies working for Shastri. However, Lisker was not someone who took much stock in ironies like this.

Putting down the receiver, he buried the PPKS Walther in his waistband, concealing it with his windbreaker. His mouth was covered by a kefiyah that he'd thrown over his head; only his eyes and nose could be seen.

For this particular mission, he was using a motorcycle, a Harley-Davidson.

By the time Lisker reached the corner opposite the heavily guarded gates of the presidential compound, Shastri had already gotten into a car, not the usual sleek Lincoln with the tinted windows, but the more modest Ford Torino behind it. There was a third car, a two-door Chrysler, up ahead of the Lincoln. Accompanying the convoy were four policemen on motorcycles. Exactly what Khalif had led him to expect.

The three cars pulled out and roared off into the darkness of Teheran. Khalif had said that tonight Shastri would be sleeping in the barracks at Doshen Toppeh.

Following from a distance of more than a block, Lisker maintained a speed of fifty miles an hour all the way up Talleghari, past the U.S. Embassy and the military garrison. They were now heading toward the Karaj Road. It was a circuitous route to Doshen Toppeh, but one that Shastri's security favored, presumably to throw off any tail.

At the junction of the Karaj Road, the convoy split up. Two of the cars, the Chrysler and the limo, went north. Accompanied by two motorized police, the Torino continued straight.

Lisker, accelerating, followed the Torino. It was only now, on this empty stretch of road, that Lisker felt conspicuous. One of the policemen glanced back and spotted him.

Lisker increased his speed and started to come abreast of them. Both policemen were aware of him and they began to maneuver to cut him off.

Lisker ignored them. Suddenly slowing, he moved to a position directly behind the Torino. The distance separating him from the car was less than twelve feet.

With the graceful motion of a major league pitcher, he gathered hold of a cassette player small enough to be cupped in his hand that had been resting in the pocket of his windbreaker, and flung it toward the Torino.

It was a good throw and it landed on the trunk. Being magnetized, it stuck.

Seeing this, the police escort was confused. They understood that danger threatened, but they couldn't figure out just how to respond to it.

The cassette player contained a bomb that was nicely engineered for Triad's use. Long a staple in the arsenal of world terrorists, this type of bomb could be set off with a long-range radio-controlled timing switch. The timing switch was built into Lisker's digital watch.

The Torino was pulling ahead, as if this would take it out of danger, and Lisker slowed up. One of the policemen had managed to get out an automatic gun and train it on him while still heading his motorcycle forward.

Lisker stopped the second hand of his watch at 12, then released it again.

The bomb went off.

The whole rear end of the Torino exploded in flames with enough force to pitch the policeman on the right off his cycle. The one on the left somehow succeeded in remaining seated.

Shastri's car veered off the side of the road and plunged into a ditch. The rear left door swung open and a man—not Shastri—came tumbling out, obviously badly hurt.

A second man, again not Shastri, emerged, holding his hands to his eyes; they'd been injured or temporarily blinded by the flash of the explosion.

The still-mounted policeman stopped and began to get off his cycle just as Lisker pulled by him and shot him in the face. He was killed instantly.

A third man piled out of the Torino, firing his pistol at Lisker. Out of the corner of his eye Lisker saw that it was Colonel Shastri.

Two rounds tore into the back of the Harley. The colonel wasn't such a bad shot, Lisker thought as he slowed the Harley to avoid the fire, then drew in front of the Torino.

Leaping off, he returned the fire, forcing Shastri to take cover. Somebody was yelling—one of the injured.

Lisker crawled alongside the Torino. The smell of acrid smoke was leaking from it, and gas and blood. It was a wonder the whole thing hadn't gone up.

He had to assume it was Shastri on the other side. The blinded man was making his way toward Lisker, stumbling against the wreckage that the car had become. He was crying out something in Farsi that Lisker couldn't understand.

All at once he spied Shastri, who'd raised his head above the roof of the car to see what had happened to his antagonist.

Lisker fired. The round came within a hair of striking the colonel. He dropped back.

Sirens were coming from somewhere down the Karaj Road. Lisker took a risk and threw himself across the length of the hood, which was still more or less intact.

Shastri was hunkered down. The colonel did not expect to see Lisker where he was. He sighted him with his pistol, but by that time Lisker had fired the Walther twice in succession.

The colonel let out an astonished gasp, clutched his chest, then began to stagger away from the car. His pistol dropped from his hand. Lisker shot him a third time. The colonel collapsed and lay still.

31

MAY 4
TEHERAN

Punctually at seven in the morning, three Backfire jets and three Tu-95 bombers, all armed with air-launched ASX-15 cruise missiles, took off from air bases in the Caucasus and outside of Qum, and headed for Khuzestan. The cruise missiles were intended for launch against selected targets on the beachhead U.S. Marines held in Khuzestan.

Ten minutes later, eight F-16's were sent into the air from Khuzestan with the object of intercepting the Backfires. Several additional bombers, B-14's, were also dispatched toward Qum, armed with nuclear cruise missiles similar to the ASX-15; their mission was to destroy Soviet military installations and command centers.

At 7:18 Teheran radio confirmed the assassination of Colonel Ibrahim Shastri along the Karaj Road the previous night. Fundamentalist Shiites acting on orders from the Grand Ayatollahs were accused by the radio of perpetrating the deed.

At the same time the official broadcast announced that the Ayatollah Zayedi was at liberty and that he would be welcome in Teheran whenever he wished to come. "The Ayatollah is a great patriot and the provisional government announces that it is ready to cooperate with him in establishing peace throughout our country," the broadcast concluded.

While the Soviets had learned of Shastri's death only half an hour after it had occurred, they wanted to wait to hear how the government in Teheran would respond. It was possible that the men who'd supported Shastri would want to pursue the war; if that were the case, then Shastri's death would have been meaningless. The announcement that Zayedi was accepted by Shastri's colleagues as a compromise candidate indicated that the settlement would be observed by all parties concerned.

A minute later the Southern Military Command of the U.S.S.R. rescinded the order to bomb Khuzestan and instructed the six warplanes to return to base. The F-16's however, continued on. After buzzing Qum, the American fighter jets disengaged and flew home to Khuzestan.

Two hours later the four principal members of Triad gathered together in Drexell's room at the Crown Hyatt Regency. A bottle of Piper-Heidsieck was ordered up from room service. The bellboy who brought it allowed that it might be the last bottle of bubbly left in the capital.

"Has there been any word on Ghafferi?" Drexell asked Zoccola and Hahn, seeing that they'd arrived from Qum only that morning.

It was Zoccola who answered. "Whereabouts unknown: that's the official word. He seems to have cleared out."

"I think somebody did the clearing out for him," put in Hahn. "My friend Farouk says that he's been spirited behind the Iron Curtain and may be in Lubyanka."

"It's possible that the Russians figure they might have to use him later on," Zoccola added, "so they didn't want to terminate him."

"In any event," Drexell said, "the Russians kept their side of the bargain—at least in regard to Ghafferi. And what's happening with Zayedi?" He addressed the question to Zoccola and Hahn who, after all, were the ones who'd extricated the ayatollah from his imprisonment.

"He's presenting himself this morning to the Sources of Inspiration. It's a fait accompli. The ayatollahs are already prepared to accept him as their leader."

"I heard on the radio that Shastri's colleagues—his surviving colleagues—are also ready to accept Zayedi as a provisional leader," said Lisker.

Drexell had the most important news: "I spoke to the President just before you came. Even while our bombers were in the air, and he informed me that he had no intention of using them, that it was just a show of force."

"I wonder," Zoccola said.

"I'm not in a position to speculate on the President's motives," Drexell explained, "but he did promise me that, as early as the end of this week, he'll send Schelling to Geneva to negotiate a draft treaty calling for a mutually timed withdrawal of all forces from Iran and a joint U.S.-Soviet recognition of a neutral government under the direction of the Ayatollah Zayedi." Noting Hahn's empty glass, he said, "Have some more champagne. I insist."

Hahn complied.

"But I see there's no cease-fire on the ground right now," Zoccola said.

"I know," Drexell said resignedly. "That's one thing the President won't budge on until Geneva. He says that he'll try to arrange a tacit understanding with the Russians to avoid shooting at each other, but there are still a lot of fanatics running around, so he isn't ready to agree to a cease-fire."

In spite of the ever-present risk that full-scale war could even now break out between the Soviets and Americans, the Triad operatives were united in their relief. Nuclear weapons had not been used; that was the most important consideration. Because, for all the game plans and contingencies that the Pentagon—and presumably the Defense Department's counterparts in Moscow—had come up with, no one had any idea what would occur following even a limited nuclear exchange. Would the Americans and Soviets agree to stop, accept the loss of thousands, possibly hundreds of thousands of lives? Or would they feel no choice but to escalate further, increasing the risk of a global conflagration? It was not a question that neither Drexell nor any of the men under his command ever wished to have answered.

At least now they could take satisfaction in knowing that partly through their efforts, the day of man's judgment on his fellow man had once again been postponed.

"The weird thing is that if there hadn't been any Shastri, if there hadn't been any coup by supposedly pro-Western elements, we would never have gotten involved in this in the first place," Zoccola said. "And the mullahs wouldn't have felt they'd been pushed into a corner and invited in the Russians. At times you wonder who the hell's really pulling the strings."

Drexell refilled their glasses, but he didn't want to hazard a reply. Neither did anyone else.

About the Author

W.X. Davies is the pseudonym of a well-known writer. He took on this new series both to entertain and to argue for a more sophisticated espionage capability for the U.S.

The Strategic Operations Group is an informal advisory council whose military, intelligence and security experience provides much of the background for the series.